Must Fit the List

ALLIE ABLE
BECCA TAYLOR

Cover design: Pink Ink Designs
Formatting: Champagne Formats
Editing: Editing4Indies

Dedication

This is dedicated to all the boys who showed me exactly what I didn't want and to all the women who moved on to real men.

Part One

The dating struggle is real

Oh. Dear. God. Please tell me you can't be serious with this one.

As I'm sitting across from my date, I'm starting to wonder why I agreed in the first place.

I'll tell you why. Last night at the bar, he seemed nice. I was talking to my friends, and he bought me a drink. Score one point. He looked in my eyes when he talked, asked great "get to know you" questions, and the way he asked for my number was sweet. I had him up to a plus ten when he called, not text, to ask me on a date. He actually picked up the phone, dialed my number, and said, "I'd be the luckiest guy in the world if you'd go out with me this weekend. So how about it, Cass?"

As I watch him now, he's dropping to a minus five, possibly even lower than that. Seriously, Universe, are you fucking with me? Because I am ready to pound my head on the table at the way he is eating his food. Do you think I'm being un-fair? Maybe you even think I sound like a bitch, but I'm really not. I'm a nice person who is at the end of her rope when it comes to men and dating.

First, he showed up at my apartment and honked his horn. Not just one beep either; he laid on the fucking thing until I came outside. I'm guessing it was because he figured it was easier than walking up all those stairs. He didn't both-er to get out of the car or open the door for me, either. That deducted at least ten points right there between those two. When we get to the restaurant . . . no, not a restaurant; it's a barbecue pit with peanut shells covering the floor, the smell of stale beer filling the air, and the table is still sticky from the couples who sat here before us. I was not impressed at all.

When the waitress came to the table, he ordered for him-self first—not just drinks but his dinner too. What man does that? Dustin—that's his name, by the way—ordered the rack of ribs and garlic mashed potatoes. Not exactly first kiss food, but with the way I feel at the moment, he won't even get a handshake good night. I ordered a burger with no onions or ketchup because it's the safest way to ensure my new dress stays clean.

That's right; I bought a new, slinky, off-the-shoulder dress from a high-end store for this date. It may have been on the clearance rack, but at least I look good. Unlike Dustin, who seems to think ripped jeans and a t-shirt that says "I Like to fuck on the first date" look good. The hoodie he's wearing covered it at first, but he took it off when the food came.

Now, as I watch Dustin, he looks like he's bathed his face in rib sauce; it's coating his beard like he plans to save some for later. I'm guessing this is the reason he took off his jacket;

God forbid that might get dirty.

When I saw his beard last night, my friends told me beards on guys are the new thing, and it gives you an extra thrill ride when they go downstairs on you, or something like that. I don't think they pictured a beard quite like this.

When he licks the bright orange sauce from his fingers, I want to pick up the napkin, shove it at him, and tell him to use it. At this point, I'm about to pick up my purse and get the hell out, but instead, I sit here, pretending like I can't hear him over the obnoxiously loud music, finish my burger, and come up with a plan.

I excuse myself to the restroom after I finish eating and call my bestie, Emma. Maybe I should be happy that Dustin actually stands when I get up, but then I see that he is just adjusting himself in front of the whole restaurant. The Emma date night rescue just went from emergency to dire, and the bitch had better answer on the first ring.

Lucky for her, she answers before the second ring completes.

"Hello," Emma says in a tired voice.

I move the phone away from my face to look at the screen. It's only eight o'clock. Why in the hell is she asleep?

Focus, Cass. It doesn't matter if she's been asleep since five; you need her to get you out of here ASAP. There is no time for questions.

"Em, call me back in three minutes and fake a death in the family."

"Why are we faking a death?" She yawns loudly.

"Because he's a minus . . . something. I can't keep track. Just be my bestie and get me the hell out of here."

"Gotcha. I'm on it." She sounds more alert, and this is

why she's my best bitch. I press the red end button before exiting the bathroom then head back to three more minutes of hell.

When I sit down at the table, my date starts rambling on about how good his dinner is, and then he mentions something about coming here again. I pretend to listen to Dickhead Dustin—that's his new name—but the sauce on his face starts sliding down his mouth, past his beard, and hangs there in a dripping strand. I think I just gagged out loud. After seeing that, I don't even care enough to try to listen to him anymore. Instead, I avoid looking directly at him while counting down the seconds until I can leave.

Right on time, my phone rings.

After a short conversation and some fake tears, a must for every girl to learn, I ditch Dickhead and walk out of the restaurant like my ass is on fire.

"Do you want me to take you?" The dickhead asks. At this point, the sauce has made it onto his shirt, which helps make my face pale more, only adding to my great acting job.

"No, stay. Enjoy the rest of your dinner."

"I'll call you later," he says and smiles. I'm sure I see some meat stuck in his teeth.

Please don't. I wave while I run in my five-inch heels, which is almost impossible.

When I make it out the door, I take a deep breath as I hail a taxi. This shit is getting old.

As soon as I walk into my apartment, my heels come off. I go into my bedroom to take my dress off and don't even care that it lands somewhere on my closet floor. I know I'll never wear it again. From the dresser, I grab my favorite pair of wool socks, and I throw on an old football jersey from college. The next stop is crucial. My kitchen. Tonight calls for a bottle of wine. I don't even bother with a glass; I simply pop the cork and go to town. I'm a woman on a mission.

When I get back to my room and settle on my bed, I take a big swig right out of the bottle before picking up a pen and a new journal.

Let me give you a quick rundown. My name is Cassandra Quinn, but my friends call me Cass. I'm twenty-seven years old but quickly approaching twenty-eight. I have long blond hair, big brown eyes, and curves that I inherited from my Nana, but I work double to keep them under control because I love to eat . . . well, everything.

I was raised in New Jersey, I use the word like more often than I don't, but after I had graduated college, I moved to New York City to work with the best of the best in marketing and advertising. As a little girl, I thought I'd become a personal shopper simply because I love to shop. I can devour a book in a single night, which means I rarely watch television, but on occasion, I will watch a movie. Last but not least, I have the worst luck when it comes to dating. Too short, too tall, too egotistical, or too dumb. You name it, and I've dated it. Like the guy I was with tonight . . . Tonight was the straw that broke the camel's back. Dickhead Dustin is the last in a long string of men who aren't right for me. I'm done. I'm starting a list—a list of all the qualities I want in a man. If it's on the list and you can't do it, you're out. No exceptions, no excuses. This has to work. This is totally going to work. This had better fucking work.

I take another drink of wine before I put my pen to paper.

My mind wanders back to all the dates gone wrong and exactly what had made them so terrible. A slew of memories returns to me. It's as if the floodgate opens and I can't stop. One after another after another—the bad dates or awkward moments become more vivid. And it's like I'm writing a montage of my life. But it feels so good to purge these moments because it's a lesson in what Cass shouldn't do again or put up with anymore.

I look at my bottle of wine on the nightstand, thinking one may not be enough to complete this journey down memory lane.

1. The "L" word

I've learned my lesson. Don't expect me to say I love you first. It's not happening. But when you say it, and the feeling is mutual, be prepared because I'm going to love you back . . . fiercely.

When I was a little girl, I loved fairy tales. My parents read me a different book each night that made me wish I were a princess too. And I knew that as I grew older, I would find my prince, and we would live happily ever after. My first love didn't turn out quite as I'd expected.

Each day, I would wake up excited to go to school, even at the age of six. Then again, at that age, school was more about socializing than learning all day.

I loved everything: waking up in the morning, eating the pancakes that Mom made to look like smiley faces, and riding the school bus. Every day, I wore the same sparkly pink shoes that matched my pink notepad and pencil. Mrs. Callan, my kindergarten teacher, allowed the class to decorate their desks for the school year, and my mother got me both pink and green streamers to wind around the legs of the desk.

"Cool idea," a little boy told me.

"Thanks. I got to practice on the kitchen chairs," I said back as I wound the two colors together and wrapped them up and over my desk. When I looked up at the little boy with big blue eyes and messy, dirty blond hair, I fell in love for the first time.

"I'm Jason."

"Cassie."

"Do you have any extra of the green?" he asked me.

I handed him the whole roll.

"Cool. Thanks, Cassie. You're pretty cool for a girl."

My heart skipped a beat.

Every morning, on my desk, I would find a note on green paper. Sometimes, it would just say, "Hi." Other times, it would be a hand drawn picture. At that age, we couldn't exactly write big words.

Jason was my first boyfriend, as much as he could be at the age of six. We were inseparable. During recess, the two of us always played together; he'd push me on the swings, or I'd watch him climb to the top of the monkey bars.

One day while we were playing in the sandbox, he built me the biggest sandcastle. It made me feel like a princess, and to thank him, I gave him a kiss on the cheek.

"I love you, Jason." I honestly believed he was the one. We would grow up together, and I knew one day, I would become Mrs. Cassandra Carter. We would get married in a backyard filled with flowers. My dress would be big and poofy like a Disney princess. When I twirled around, I would look like a ballerina. After we said, "I do," instead of releasing birds, we would have fireworks. Lots of fireworks, especially the ones that filled the sky and looked like a waterfall. Those were my favorite.

Then it went terribly wrong.

"Eewww. Gross. Girl cooties," Jason screamed as he stomped the sandcastle. My princess castle was crushed, and at the same time, it felt like he stomped on my heart.

That wasn't enough for Jason, though. Sand hit my face; sand that he picked up and threw right at me. I tried to cover myself as best as I could, but some managed to get in my eye. I ran to Mrs. Callan crying because it hurt so much—not just my eye but my heart too. The teacher's aide brought me to the nurse, who washed out my eyes then called my mom to come pick me up. I had to go to the eye doctor where he checked to see if any sand remained. He told me the nurse got it all out, but I had a scratch on my eye. My mom would have to put drops in my eyes, and I didn't like the sound of that. When he told me I had to wear an eye patch for the week, I cursed Jason's name. At least, I got to pick the color I wanted—pink.

Two days later, a new note was on my desk. I could read it, but I knew he didn't write it. Jason had been ignoring me.

Roses are red
Violets are blue
Cass has cooties
And looks like a pirate.

It didn't rhyme at all. It was a terrible poem, but the joke was on him, though.

"I cursed you, Jason. Just wait and see what happens." I did too. I picked up a Ken doll I had stopped playing with and pretended to curse him with my princess fairy wand.

He laughed as if it was a joke, but at recess, when he was trying to impress another girl by climbing to the top of the monkey bars, he slipped. He fell, straddling the bar, and hurt his little boy penis. Jason had to go to the doctor too but didn't get a cool eye patch. Everyone called him monkey man for a week.

The next month, Jason moved away. Mrs. Callan told us his mother got transferred with her job. That made getting over my first heartbreak a little easier. Add in the fact that I walked away with a new best friend, and I was winning, for sure, because Emma and I were the ones who were inseparable after that. Even our moms became best friends. A best friend was way better than having a boyfriend.

This is why I will never say I love you first. I will even wait until long after you say it before the words come out of my mouth. In fact, I won't say it until I'm one hundred percent positive you're the one.

I swore off boys for a long time. Well, more like I went through puberty late and boys didn't really notice me. It didn't matter, though, since boys didn't really impress me either. In middle school, they were obnoxious and immature. Until I was in high school.

2. Pick me up in a clean car

The way a man treats a car is how I picture his apartment. If you have to move garbage in order for me to sit down, I won't be setting foot in that car. Along with that, your clothing belongs in the closet. I don't mean the extra business suit you keep for emergencies. But when I see ten shirts in the backseat, it sends the wrong message—one that says you don't spend the night at your house as much as you should.

If you had a car, you took care of it; this was the way I was brought up. My father told me when I was old enough to help him wash his truck, "A vehicle is never clean until you clean it twice. I don't mean just the outside either, Cassandra. You need to take care of the inside too and don't forget that the engine needs the same treatment. It only takes a few minutes to hose it down and scrub the under part of the hood. A clean car is a happy car."

He didn't just say this once; he said it every time we washed that truck in our driveway for more than a decade. No joke, he told this to me at three years old, when I barely understood him. Now that I thought about his advice, I think it was his way of getting me to wash the truck. Slave labor. But those words were embedded in my brain.

It was my first date. I was seventeen, and it took a lot of convincing to get my parents to let me ride in my date's car. Ryder was one of the most popular boys at school with a devilish grin and a car to go with it. It was black, sleek, and vintage. I think my dad referred to it as a muscle car, which didn't make him happy. The large backseat made him even more nervous.

Dad gripped Ryder's shoulder, walked him into his office, and stopped directly in front of his gun collection. "Let's have a talk before you take my princess out, shall we?" I was mortified. There was more than one eye roll from me directed at Mom that night. I begged her to get him to stop.

When they finally emerged from the room, Ryder kept his distance until we got in the car. As my dad watched from the front porch, Ryder opened the door for me like a gentleman. When we pulled away from the house, he checked the visor mirror to make sure my dad was gone before he pulled me under his arm. The front bench seat gave me the ability to get close. Really close.

Then I saw it, staring me back in the reflection of the rearview mirror. It was like a scene from that hoarding show. Coats, shirts, a backpack, books, discarded water bottles, and soda cans littered the backseat. I tried not to look again, but it was like someone was egging me on. *Look, Cass, look. This is the nightmare your father taught you to avoid.* My eyes kept glancing up, thinking maybe I didn't see right.

I was relieved when the pizza place came into sight. The two of us were going to the Friday night hangout spot, and I would be doing it under the arm of my date. The boy who all the girls talked about in the locker room. The boy who would lift his head in the hallway in that acknowledging way as he said "'Sup?" and you would hear the collaborative sigh from the other end. The boy who usually dated the head cheerleader and not the girl from the bottom of the pyramid. The boy whose car was starting to smell like dirty gym socks.

When he leaned over me and opened the car door, I didn't know if I was more thrilled at the fact that his body brushed against mine or the fact that I would now be getting some fresh air. Air, glorious air won that round.

The minute his hand took mine as we walked through the parking lot, all thoughts of the car catastrophe were gone. He even held the pizzeria door open for me without releasing my hand. I felt like I won the lottery of dates, as long as I didn't think about the car. Girls looked at me like I was the luckiest person in the world. I was.

Even though we sat with a group of people, I didn't care. I was there with Ryder fucking Dean the fourth. He was that cool that his name had a number in it. It made him sound like he was royalty or a god. Maybe not a god, but at seventeen, he was the high school equivalent to one.

We ordered four pizzas and a few pitchers of fountain soda, and Ryder kept his arm around the back of my chair except when he was eating, of course. When it came to dividing the bill, he paid for me. No boy had ever paid for me before. I may have swooned a bit.

Ryder's best friend mentioned taking a ride to the abandoned drive-in that had turned into the local teenage makeout spot. I was thrilled about going but not the car ride. Just thinking about it had a horror movie theme song playing in my head. Before we left, though, he cleaned out the backseat. He tossed everything in the trunk of the car. Out of sight, out of mind. At least, I told myself that. Since it was a cool night, we opened the windows as we drove side by side with the other cars from our group. The fresh air never smelled so . . . fresh. Music was blasting from all the cars, playing the same hit radio station and song. Everyone was dancing and singing along as we cruised the strip. I finally felt like I'd made it with the in crowd.

Nerves struck me as we rounded the turn into what we called "The point." I let out a puff of air when everyone started to get out of their cars. I mean I'd kissed a boy before but not the real kind of kiss. The kind that involved tongues. There was only one guy I wanted that with, and I was sitting right next to him. A log had fallen at some point and formed a spot for us to hang out and have a small bonfire. Someone had left their car windows down so we could listen to music while we talked and drank . . . soda, of course.

Slowly, people started heading to their cars for "alone time." The squeeze on my hand was Ryder's way of a silent invitation. I swallowed and nodded. At the same time that he stood, he offered me his hand to help me up then led the way to his car.

This was it. I was about to have my first French kiss.

The back door of the car opened, and there was no turning back. As I slid inside, I kept my eyes focused on Ryder. I was waiting for a cue from him as to where he wanted me. He pulled me close, and when his leg touched mine, a shiver ran through my body at the contact.

"Hi," he said as he eyed me up like I was some prize.

The lump in my throat made it hard for me to talk, but I managed to get out one word. "Hi."

"Do you want to listen to some music?"

"That would be nice."

Ryder leaned over to the front seat and turned on the radio. He sat back down, turning toward me. Then he leaned in. The kiss was soft, but as the minutes went by, he demanded more. His tongue slid across my lips, and I did nothing to fight him. It was good. So deliciously good.

Slowly, my body began to lean back. He gave me every indication that he wanted me to lay down. My heart was beating out of my chest. What if he tried to touch my boob? I mean second base was expected when you were in the backseat of a car the size of a bed. But then it happened. My head touched the bag of leftover pizza. Only, we had no pizza left from dinner.

Oh, god. It was greasy too. I could feel it touching my hair, and it was nothing like the coconut oil treatment I gave myself once a week.

Casually, I pulled the bag out from under my head.

"Oh, shit. Sorry, Cass. I didn't have time to clean out my car after football practice today because Coach kept me late."

He stepped out of the car, heading for the nearest trash can to dump the offending bag. The mood was broken, though. I climbed out of the backseat, slightly disappointed that my lips weren't quite numb and my boobs were still untouched.

On our next date, he got to second base. We took my car instead since his broke down. We even dated for the rest of the year, but he was a grade level ahead of me. By mutual agreement, we decided to break things off when he went to college.

To this day, if I see a greasy paper bag leftover pizza in the trash, I get nauseated.

That's why I want a clean car. You'd better pick me up

with your vehicle reeking of that new car smell, or you are guaranteed not to touch the girls . . . and my boobs are pretty fucking amazing.

3. Must have cock and know how to use it

You see, just because you have a big, average, or even small dick doesn't always mean you know what you are doing. The art of making love, or just to become amazing at fucking, takes time. Learn the craft because when it's good for me, you can bet I'll make it equally as fantastic for you.

Maybe I read too many books. I couldn't help it. They were one of my passions. I started reading books, even the sexy kind, at the age of sixteen. Back then, they weren't as graphic as the ones I read now, but I still got the idea. Hot man instantly fell for girl, they had many passion-filled nights, it was beautiful and romantic, and then the two of them got married and had a happily-ever-after life.

Possibly that made me, in turn, romanticize the first time I would "make love." When you were a teenager and thought you were "in love," or in my case, "in like," that was what you called it.

Making love, making *love*, or *making love*. No matter where you put the emphasis, it sounded so amazing. The reality was if you were a teenager, and I was, there was no lovemaking. It was all hormones and lust and thoughts that did not come from your heart. It was all driven by a different part of your body.

I thought my first time would be all bed of roses, candles, and dim lighting. That was not the case. It was supposed to be the most spectacular night of my life. My prom. The night my boyfriend and I would seal the deal. It was memorable, all right . . .

Ryder was not my first, unfortunately. We did plenty leading up to, and there were close calls, but he never slid into home.

Randy was not quite the most popular, but he was the nice guy in school. He was a chip off the old block. I wasn't sure who said that to him, but I was sure glad Chip stuck as his nickname because even though Randy was always randy, his name was lacking. What caught my eye about him was the way he talked to every crowd in school. He fit in everywhere.

Emma and I both splurged at a high-priced salon and got the works: mani, pedi, makeup, and updo. The grand total was almost six months of my babysitting money. My parents helped me pay for my dress, so I didn't spend my entire year's salary. I loved my dress; it was elegant and made me feel like a queen. I didn't win that title, but I was a member of the court. Back to the dress . . . It was long, flowy, pale teal, strapless, and had a sweetheart neckline filled with bling.

Our dates arrived an hour early, along with everyone else, for the required picture time. Chip looked handsome in his tux. The one he chose was different from the traditional black; the jacket was white with a black lapel. I loved it, and it fit his personality. He was slim, fit, and tall with long hair that had that messy yet tamed look. He had this hipster look about him—cool and relaxed. Leather ropelike bracelets were always on his wrist; the first time I saw them, I thought it was strange, but it was like dressing for his hands, and boy, did he have nice hands. Really, really great hands.

"Cass, you look gorgeous," he said as he gave me my corsage. It was beautiful. Dendrobium orchids with teal accents filled a silver cuff bracelet—not an elastic band—that had teal butterflies.

"You do too. I mean you look handsome."

After one too many pictures, everyone piled into their cars and headed to the hotel where our prom was being held. We decided against taking a limo; it was pointless since everyone was getting a room at the Chateau Vander Shaw. The building looked like a castle on the outside but was very modern inside. On the main level, different types of seating areas filled the rooms. The actual prom was on the second level. On one side was the dining hall, and on the other was the dance area. The remaining levels were the guest rooms. Whoever decided that allowing teenagers to rent a hotel room was a smart idea was indeed the dumbest person alive. Especially here at a fancy place. There was a fight between a female server and a girl in our class because, apparently, the girl's boyfriend and the server were having a thing behind her back. It resulted in security escorting my classmate out, and the server being fired. I think twenty people from one room were also arrested for smoking, and they weren't passing cigarettes around the room. Another group decided to sneak alcohol in, and from what I heard, many girls were sick that night.

The people I came with were drama free. We did everything and anything you are supposed to do at a prom. We ate, we drank sparkling juice, and we danced our asses off. The DJ was awesome. He played the right amount of line dance songs, jump up and stupid dance songs, and my favorite, slow songs. Chip held me close to his body and made me feel like I was the only girl in the room. He danced a slow and simple Texas two-step when he pulled me close, oh so close. We each wrapped one arm around the other's bodies while my other hand was in his where he guided me expertly. It was all so romantic.

After the last song played, dubbed our class song, everyone slowly made their way to their rooms for the night. Eight of us, which included me, Chip, Emma, and her date, ate late-night snacks and drank sugary drinks until well after one in the morning. There were lots of lingering kisses and touches going on between every couple and even though Emma and I were supposed to be sharing a room, I had no doubt in my mind that we were both ditching our V-card tonight.

When we made our way to have some alone time, I thought I would be nervous. Instead, I was just ready to jump into it. Chip, on the other hand, didn't seem to want to rush. At all. By this time, I had shed my dress and was wearing the typical high school girl's nightwear—a tank top and pair of men's boxers. He was also wearing a pair of boxers and a t-shirt. It was almost thirty minutes before Chip even attempted to reach under my shirt. In fact, I gave up, took my shirt off myself, and put his hands on my boobs to help him out.

His hands were incredible. So big and strong. He was skilled with his fingers too. Although he had never let me touch him below the belt until now, so I was beginning to wonder if he was even turned on by what we were doing. I didn't feel much until he said, "I'm so hard right now."

I figured that maybe he would keep growing. After all, he was tall and had big feet too. But whoever said that lied; big feet did not mean big boy parts.

I stopped thinking about it when Chip started touching me between my legs. Let's face it; it doesn't take much for a teenage girl to get off. When a boy touched you, it was instantly hot.

"Let's do it," I said to Chip.

His eyes went wide. Really wide. Like saucers. "Are you sure?"

"I'm more than sure." I got up and grabbed the condom I had in my overnight bag. Emma and I bought a four-pack box at the drugstore and split it. To prove I was ready, I took my boxers off and stood before him naked. Was I scared? Suddenly, I was and started shaking. Was I terrified of him seeing me completely naked? Absolutely. Did I want him to treat me like one of the girls from the books I read, sweep me off my feet, and lay me on the bed? Oh, my god, yes, yes, yes.

That didn't happen, though. Chip quickly jumped off the bed, only to climb under the covers. He wiggled around a bit then his boxers were in his hand. I made my way to the bed, faking that I was confident. I had no clue, but after reading what I had, I knew enough that a man loved a woman who was not ashamed of herself. So I held my head up and put an extra sway in my hips. Which I still needed some work on that sexy sway. Emma and I tried it out, but we were still awkward teenagers.

I handed Chip the condom, figuring he knew what he was doing, but he didn't, so I told him how to put it on since I had practiced on a banana.

"It's a little loose," he said.

"Like how loose?"

"The top is," he said with his head under the covers. I tried to look too, but it was dark under there. I couldn't see shit.

"It's supposed to be," I told him.

"Oh. Okay then. Are you ready?"

I was.

He kissed me a little and started touching me everywhere, but when I went to touch him, he pushed my hand away.

"Why can't I touch you?" I asked as Chip kissed my neck.

"I'm afraid I'll come too soon. No girl has ever touched me there, and I want this to last."

I thought his honesty was sweet. He kissed me until I was ready to scream. Well, not scream, but until I semi begged, "Put it in me."

Chip climbed on top of me and between my legs.

It was going to happen. I was about to lose my virginity. I was excitedly nervous. My hormones were raging. I thought the minute he put it inside me, I would have my first penis orgasm.

"Oh, god, Cass that feels so good."

I thought I missed something. Chip was rocking like a bunny rabbit, but I didn't feel anything more than that. "Are you in?"

"God, yes."

"Are you sure?"

I thought I was supposed to feel pain. Or at least something.

"It feels amazing, doesn't it?" he asked me.

Umm . . . I didn't feel much of anything. Okay, maybe I felt something if I turned a little to the left . . . nope, nothing. Leaning right was even worse. If I pushed my hips up, I felt like the tip was touching, but that wasn't going to get me off, so I needed to do something. I reached between us and touched. He was there all right. I skimmed the latex with my fingers. When he started moving faster, it was the first time I felt it. It felt okay but not like the amazing fireworks I was expecting.

"Are you going to come soon? Because I'm going to and I don't think I can wait."

I thought about what I had read in books, and really, I shouldn't have been thinking about that at all. I was supposed to be having my mind blown. "Touch me with your hand. You know that spot I like."

He touched that magic button, and finally, I forgot. Thank God for hands. He rubbed and rubbed while he thrust and thrust. He came first. Loudly.

"Oh my god, oh my god, oh my god." Over and over, he said it.

He pulled out of me and started to pull his hand away. I wasn't having that, though. With my hand on his, I held him in place until I got mine.

The next morning, he asked if we could do it again. I let him. We even continued to do it until we graduated. But Chip was not a grower. Poor Chip had a teeny weenie peenie, but I liked him. He treated me well, and if I think about it, he taught me a lot about different ways I could get mine and how I liked to be touched. We broke up just before we went to college and after time we lost touch.

After high school, my focus changed. I wanted to do well

in school and really wasn't looking for a man per se. I was over the whole first sexual experience and didn't want to become the dorm hookup girl. That wasn't my thing but give me a good make-out session with some heavy petting, and I was golden.

4. Must be a good kisser

I'm not talking about just the first time. Every time we kiss, I need to feel it from my lips all the way down to the tips of my toes. If I don't get that "oh god" feeling, I just can't.

It was my sophomore year of college when I finally started to come out of my shell again. I wasn't always the curvy, confident woman I am today. The word awkward was put in the dictionary for me. I was sure my picture was in there too as the photo description. Not only that, but I was also a late bloomer. My boobs were small in comparison to the rest of me, and my body really had no definite shape, but let me tell you, when I finally grew into my body, it was noticed. That didn't mean the rest of me still wasn't a little awkward.

I was in the library studying when Jordan Riley approached me.

Now, let me pause right here and tell you a little bit about Jordan. He was fine with a capital F. He was a senior; he was tall, muscular, had short blond hair, and bright blue eyes. The dimples he sported on both cheeks made my belly do flips every time he flashed them. Unpause.

I knew of Jordan but had never really spoken to him.

We had mutual friends, and I would occasionally see him around, but this was a big college; it wasn't like we bumped into each other every day, and he certainly never sought me out. Imagine my surprise when he waved in my direction. I swear I physically had to turn around to see if anyone was behind me. The only options were the librarian or me. And while Mrs. Florence was hot for her age, I think there was a forty-year age difference, which meant his attention was all on me. As he moved closer to my table, I squirmed in my seat. That beautiful smile and those dimples were damn distracting, especially when he aimed them right at me. I could feel the sweat start and the pink glow warm my face. I just prayed that I didn't hit tomato red because when I was nervous, sweat and a red face could become an issue.

"Hey, Cass."

I remembered trying to recall a time when I had introduced myself to him and came up empty, but I decided to be cool and just roll with it.

"Hey, Jordan," I said with a wave. Yes, I fucking waved, and it was not a cute wave either, but one of those raise your hand in the air and motion like crazy waves. Don't judge me. He was hot, and I was off my game. Only, I didn't have game. I'd never had game, but I could fake it like a champ.

He smiled at me again before running his hand through his hair. I might have sighed.

"I was wondering if you wanted to go out Friday night?"

I was stunned speechless but quickly got my act together and agreed. He told me he would pick me up from my dorm at seven o'clock and said to wear something nice. I blushed and agreed with a simple, "Okay," or "Yes," or "Good god, yes." I can't say for sure because, in my head, I was doing a happy dance from the thrill of an upperclassman asking me out.

When Friday night finally rolled around, I was waiting outside my dorm wearing my favorite Free People dress and a killer set of heels. I was so damn excited I could hardly sit still. He pulled up in a brand new Lexus, which at the time I thought was super clean and classy. But looking back, I realize that should have been my first sign we weren't right for each other. Nothing against a Lexus, but come on, we were in college.

He greeted me with a smile and held the door open, before whisking us away to the fancy restaurant downtown. I had never been to a place like that before; sure, my parents took me out somewhere special on my birthday every year, but a man in a tuxedo was serving me dinner. As a twenty-year-old, I was thoroughly impressed. The beef wellington we ordered was overpriced and beyond delicious. Throughout dinner, Jordan was very charming, attentive, and an all-around sweet guy. We talked until well after dessert about our hatred for the school meatloaf and soda but found that we both had a love for the library. In fact, he said that he'd seen me there every day but was afraid to talk me. *He was afraid to approach me.* When he said that, my nerves had finally started to disappear, so when he asked me to come back to his place to watch a movie, I agreed. I know what you're thinking, but I was young, in need of a good make-out session, and very distracted by those dimples.

It turned out that his parents had bought him a condo off campus. Lucky bastard. The drive to his place was filled with small talk and me quietly freaking out in the passenger seat of his fancy car. The leather kept sticking to the back of my legs, and I kept moving around. Then it happened, the noise.

No, I didn't let one rip—it was my leg against the leather. He flashed me a concerned look, but I just smiled like this was all normal. It was far from normal for me. Most of my hookups, which I could probably count on one hand at that point, were in a car or at my parents' house when they weren't home. It wasn't every day I went back to a guy's house, and this was Jordan Riley.

I felt like I was on cloud nine walking into that beautiful condo. I mean here was a hot guy who was nice, seemed into me, and had his own place. Those were hard to come by in college. When he went into the kitchen and popped the top off a beer, he offered it to me first, but I declined. While he drank the beer, I fiddled with the strap of my purse, not really knowing what to do. For a second, I regretted my decision to come here until he took my hand and led me to the couch. He put on a movie, but to this day, I still couldn't tell you what it was because I kept watching him out of the corner of my eye the entire time, trying to decide when he was finally going to put the moves on me. You know the moves—the one where he reaches his arm around my shoulder or casually brushes his leg against mine. I was more than ready for his moves. Finally, he wrapped his arm around me and pulled me closer.

He smelled good, like some expensive cologne, until he leaned closer and I could smell the beef he'd eaten earlier in the night. In fact, he started smelling like a combination of meat and beer, which might taste good, but not after it was already been digested and I could still smell it on your funky breath. The guy needed some gum, badly.

I ignored it, though, because this was Jordan, and he finally had his arm around me. In my young mind, that was awesome. His fingers played with my hair as we continued to watch the movie. He would laugh occasionally, and just so he would think I was watching it too, I would giggle with him. It was all very romantic.

I will never forget the moment he turned to me, and I knew he was going to kiss me. A million butterflies took flight in my belly as I watched his face dip down to mine. This was going to happen. Jordan was going to kiss me. I closed my eyes and waited for the moment when his perfect lips met mine. I held my breath, but I wasn't sure if it was in anticipation or because the beer and meat smell was really starting to get to me. I'm going to have to say it was probably the second. His hand came to rest on my cheek, and I sighed as I felt him finally against my mouth. It was incredible for about two seconds. That was when he started doing the stabby thing with his tongue. It was literally bumping against my teeth to get in there. I was a little confused as to what was happening, so I opened my mouth. Jeez, the guy really wanted in there.

To my utter horror, it got worse. It was wet and sloppy, and the damn stabby tongue thing never stopped. I couldn't even try to figure out his rhythm. The meat and beer smell intensified as I could feel the spit from his mouth dripping down my chin. I opened my eyes and looked at him. His were lightly closed, and he seemed really into it, so I tried again. I closed my eyes and did the stabby tongue thing back. Maybe I had been kissing wrong all these years. This wasn't one of my finer moments. It was all-out chaos after that. I sat there politely for what felt like hours, and I let that gorgeous man who was a fucking terrible kisser suck my face.

When I finally pulled myself away and excused myself to the bathroom, I felt like I had swallowed a gallon of beer and meat-flavored saliva, to be exact. As I looked in the mirror at myself, drool had dripped onto my beautiful Free People dress. I washed my face and searched his medicine cabinet for mouthwash to use before walking back into the living room and telling Jordan I needed to get home. When he drove me back to my dorm room, he leaned across the seat and puckered his lips. I, however, unbuckled my seat belt and ran. I spent the next year avoiding the stabby tongue, drooling face sucker.

Jordan wasn't the only bad kisser I've encountered. He just happened to be one of the most traumatic. That is why if you are going to date me, then you'd better make me tingle. Your kisses need to be hot and make my panties melt because if I ever have to experience another tongue stabber, I may bite him. And another thing—I don't mind being wined and dined, but overindulging is a big no-no with me.

5. Must know how to hold your liquor

It doesn't matter to me if you like to drink socially or if you have a little something with dinner. But we will have a problem if you are one of the following: a sloppy drunk, an angry drunk, or just plain fall down stupid drunk. When your emotions are a combination of all three, I'm never going out with you again.

I had just turned twenty-one and was working while going to school. It wasn't anything special, just a few hours here and there at a local pharmacy, but it gave me some spending money.

Across the street, an apartment building was being renovated, and the workers would come over throughout the day to grab drinks and snacks, but one guy, in particular, Bates, would chat with me for a while before going back to his job.

During my lunch breaks, I would sit outside on the bench out front. When he would see me eating alone, Bates would stop and join me for a few minutes. Then he started having lunch with me. For a month, we sat and talked for the half hour about all the things we have in common.

He was cute but not over-the-top good looking. The

paint flecks that covered his clothes and his body told me he was hard working. On more than one occasion, he asked me on a date, but something held me back.

I talked to Emma about him, and her suggestion was to invite him to the party we were having at the townhouse we had just snagged off campus. It sounded like a good plan. *Sounded* was the key word. It ended up being the worst plan ever in the history of plans.

The day of the party came around, and it was getting late, so I figured Bates was not going to show up, but unlucky for me, he did. With his face and clothing free of his hard day's work, he looked like a completely different man, which wasn't a good thing. Apparently, the paint covered the lines around his face and eyes so well that I thought he was younger than he appeared. Without it, he looked to be about thirty. Later, I found I was wrong. He was, in fact, thirty-six. Not cool, dude. He probably thought he hit the jackpot with a twenty-one-year-old.

In his hand was a giant bottle of whiskey, and maybe that would have been nice if he'd shared. But, no, Bates drank the entire bottle himself. He was literally drooling anytime he attempted to talk. Anytime a man came near me, he'd pull me close. I kept doing the duck and run move because I didn't feel anything for this guy. No attraction whatsoever.

Emma and I tried to come up with an idea as to how we could get him to go home, even when the party died down. Thankfully, we had friends staying with us, two of which were men, Emma's cousin Jack and his roommate from college, Bill. Yes, we gave them the nickname Jack and Jill. They weren't happy, at all. Even though they weren't happy with us, they stepped up when we needed them most.

You would think the pawing, drunken old man would be the worst of it. Not quite.

Basically, I told him it was time to say good night and not to bother with lunch again. The guys ushered him to the front door. Emma and I hid next to the kitchen window, listening and watching as they attempted to get him to leave.

"It's time for you to go home, bud," Jack said.

"I can sleep on the couch," Bates slurred back.

"I don't think so. The lady made it clear she's not interested. We can call you a cab, and you can get your car in the morning," Jill stressed.

"I don't have a car."

"How did you get here?" Jack asked.

"My mom. I lost my license three years ago."

Em and I just looked at each other with wide eyes then started cracking up.

"Fuck, dude. I'll call you a cab. Just do me a favor, lose Cass's number and forget her address." Jack was also laughing as he pulled out his phone.

When the guys came inside, Bates banged on the front door begging to come inside to wait. There was no way we were letting him, though. The cab came, and everyone assumed he left.

We thought wrong.

Emma and I were settling in bed together since I gave up my bed to her cousin. It seemed like the nice thing to do, but apparently, we chose the wrong room. The lights were out, and we'd just said our good nights. I rolled over to sleep on my left side, which faced the window, when I heard a sound.

"Em."

"I'm sleeping, Cass."

"Well, wake up because I think I heard something at the window." I said it through clenched teeth. I was trying to remain calm, but it wasn't working.

"You're hearing things. There's no one there. We're on the second floor."

"Go look," I told her as I pulled the sheet up to just below my eyes.

She got up, stomped to the window, and opened the curtain. There he was with his face plastered against the glass.

I had my first, "Stella!" moment.

Bates—his name should have told me from the get-go that he would be a little off—was screaming, "Cassie. Take me back. I need you."

"Oh, shit."

We both screamed like the girls we were and ran into my room where Jack was.

He went over and tried to shoo Bates away like a fly. He literally said, "Shoo, go away."

But the fly looked like it had a horrible accident and hit the glass at full speed.

Jack called 911. Within ten minutes, the cops were peeling him from the window and were hauling the fly away.

We slept in the bed with Jack and Jill that night. The next morning, when we came back from breakfast, we found evidence of the previous night. Apparently, when the cops found the fly, he was naked. All his clothes were still on the roof. Jack grabbed the broom and tossed everything in the trash. Along with the broom.

I would never touch that sucker again.

Lessons of the day—don't ever take a guy home who is covered in paint chips. And don't drink and drive.

After that, I continued to focus on my finals for school and not boys. The real world was fast approaching, and I had to stay on track if I wanted to get that dream apartment with Emma in New York City.

6. Must know how to have fun

I'm definitely not a little girl anymore, but sometimes going back to the basics in dating is needed. For example, take me bowling, to play mini golf, or to a carnival and win me one of those god-awful stuffed animals by dunking a basketball. I will love it, cuddle it, and sleep with it.

Fresh out of college, I went into the workforce. Finding a great job was next to impossible when you didn't have much experience. Working in marketing and advertising . . . let's just say, it was a rise to the top field. I started as a switchboard operator, and if I had to say, "Thank you for calling Hype; you name it, we spread it," one more time, I was going to staple my mouth shut. Yes, that was their actual slogan. I could just hear the childish comments roll off people's tongues. It was the only job I could get after graduating; it paid the bills and got me one step closer to that city apartment.

My boss was an ass. A complete and utter ass. Most days, I wanted to throw the same stapler at him, but if I did, I wouldn't be able to use it on my mouth. Mr. Hinee (told you he's an ass) would walk in the front door and start in on me. "Do this, don't do that, wear something more hip, not that hip, get me a coffee, the coffee is too hot, there's not enough milk in the coffee, now there's too much." I just smiled that fake smile Monday through Friday, praying I would find a better job.

Then there was Scott. He was about eight years older than I was. He was the McDreamy of the advertising world. He would come in the front door and say things like, "Chin up, Cass. You're doing great. I love your dress. Don't worry about him." His compliments made my hellish days better. When he asked me out on a date, I literally fell off my rolling chair.

His actual words. "Would you want to go out and have some good clean fun tonight?"

I really needed fun. Maybe not the good clean kind, but after a month of working for this company, having a good time with a hot guy was in order.

But instead of me being able to answer him right away, the wheel on my chair went rogue, and down I went. "Dammit. I didn't stick the landing that time. And my answer is yes, by the way."

He laughed while helping me up, but I got the impression he wasn't laughing *at* me; he was laughing at my witty comment. I was just trying to cover my occasional pop-up awkwardness. The bitch showed up every once in a while just to keep me on my toes.

There was a state fair in town, and I was secretly hoping that Scott would take me there. I dressed in my tightest pair of jeans and a shirt that revealed just the right amount of cleavage since he told me comfortable and casual. The jeans weren't exactly comfortable. Especially when I needed a hanger to pull up the zipper, but once they were on, my ass looked ah-ma-zing. Scott showed up in jeans and a button up sweater. Not a Mr. Rogers sweater but more like out of the pages of an expensive magazine.

His sports car told me he was successful at his job, but I already knew that. Part of my job was to put paycheck stubs in envelopes. I saw what he made; it was impressive. His check could buy a whole lot of the sale only pasta that I currently lived off of. One check would feed me for the year.

Much to my disappointment, we drove past the state fair. Okay, so maybe he had something better in mind. I was game. Pool hall, a baseball game, go-carts, even bowling came to mind. Apparently, his version of fun and mine were different. By different, I mean taking that same stapler to my head would have been more fun than this.

We pulled into the local library and headed down the stairs where they hosted special events. Now, you know I love books. And well, the library was quite awesome here, but not this time. It was the monthly bug-collecting club. I didn't remember what their actual name was because the minute I saw the tarantula tank, I hightailed it out of there. Nope, couldn't do it.

I didn't even say anything, but Scott saw the look on my face. While his was full of excitement, mine was full of terror. *Fear Factor* terror. Horror movie terror. And every other kind of "I'm-about-to-run-out-of-this-room-screaming-my-head-off-in-fear" terror you could think of was showing on my face.

And that was exactly what I did. I ran. I screamed. And felt like bugs were crawling all over me for the next hour.

Once again, Emma came to the rescue. She picked me up and drove us straight to that fair. My best friend and I rode every questionably safe ride, ate everything that wasn't fit for my current diet, and wasted the paycheck I just got on too many prize booths and stale beer. That was more fun than I'd had with any other date.

On Monday at work, Scott came up to the desk. "I take it you don't like animals?"

"Puppies, yes. Kittens are adorable. I hate to break it to you, but those things were not animals. They are the creatures that keep me up at night."

"Did you know the average person swallows eight insects a year while sleeping?"

Did he not just listen to me? "How would they even find that information out? Is there a study group on this? Wait, don't tell me. I really don't want to know."

"Do you want to go out again? I promise there won't be any animals involved."

I thought about it. He sounded like he wanted to try, so I gave him the benefit of the doubt. Scott really had no concept of fun, though. The following weekend was his stamp collectors monthly get-together.

As I look up from my notebook, I notice a tiny spider as it crawls up my wall. I pick up the nearest object, a tissue box, and throw it. It doesn't accomplish much, and I'm pretty sure I only angered the little bugger. I just really don't like bugs or snakes or anything with a million legs that can eat me alive.

7. Must slay all insects without hesitation

My fear of spiders should overrule whatever else you have going on. You must come to my rescue and handle any insect that comes within a five-foot radius of me, and you must do this without screaming like a little bitch. Man up.

I was really starting to doubt my man finding skills. I kind of gave up for a while again and decided I was just going to have male friends. Ones with clean cars and great hygiene, who I could just hang out and have good clean fun with.

Jeff, aka Wookie, and I bonded over our love of *Star Wars* movies. Don't get me wrong, I'm a lover of chick flicks, but movies that reminded me of Sunday movie day with my family were a runner-up. Both Jeff and I even went to a Halloween party as Hans Solo and Chewbacca. FYI, I wasn't the furry one.

The party was amazing. Even though there was a cover charge, the drinks were included in the price. They flowed all night. The owners of the Victorian house modified it into a three-level nightclub. Each floor was dedicated to a genre; the rock, club, and dance levels each played a different era of music each night. The story was that in one room, a family was murdered, and occasionally, they liked to get down and boogie with the guests. I didn't believe it, but the actual story was true. I looked it up before we came.

At midnight, they turned the backyard into a haunted walk. Another thing you should know about me—I hated being scared, but Wookie loved this kind of stuff, so I was willing to give it a try.

"Come on, Cass Solo. I'll protect you from the brain eating zombies," he said while he held out his elbow for me to take.

"If anything jumps at me, you'd better take cover. My inner Jedi will take over, and I can't be held responsible for what might happen," I joked back.

"You're not a Jedi."

"Shit. Why didn't I come as Luke?"

He laughed back. "Next year, you can be Luke."

"And you can be Leia."

"No," he said adamantly.

"But you'd look really cute in the Slave costume."

"Fuck, no. And you're stalling." He'd figured me out. The next thing I knew, I was walking through a curtain; it was too dark for my liking until we turned the corner. The light blinked on and off, giving a strobe effect as zombies jumped out at us. I buried my face in my Wookie and prayed for it to be over fast. Every time someone jumped out at me, I said through clenched teeth, "I'm going to kill you for this."

Jeff was enjoying it, though. He walked as slow as possible because he didn't want to miss a thing. One of the rooms was set up to look like an old attic, and it was creepy. Old furniture filled the room; it even had that musty smell and was full of spider webs. We ducked around the sticky web-like strands, but some were unavoidable. We were both trying to shake them off as we came to a mirror. To exit the room, you had to look in the mirror and recite the words written on it. They were dripping and looked like they were written in blood.

"You say it," I told Jeff.

"You read it," he told me back.

"I'm not doing it. This was your idea. You're the one who likes this shit."

"Fine," he said right before he read the words, "Bloody Mary," three times.

The ghost of a woman appeared and screamed, scaring the shit out of me. I grabbed Jeff's hand and ran to the next room, not even caring we were going directly through the spider webs. It was the exit, and that was what I wanted—out of this place. We both had a case of the heebie-jeebies, pulling a million strands from our bodies. The stuff felt so real.

When we had finally made it outside, I saw something on my Wookie.

"Um, Jeff."

"Yeah?"

"There's something on you."

"More webs," he said while he spun, looking like a dog chasing his tail.

"No, it's right there." I pointed at his shoulder where the spider was. It was big and hairy and terrifying.

Then I heard this high-pitched scream. I thought it was someone who had just suffered the same torture as we had moments ago, but nope. It was Jeff.

"Get it off me. Get it off me, Cass."

I didn't know a man's usually deep voice could screech like that. It had to be ten octaves higher than normal. He swatted, and it fell to the ground. His body was doing this wiggle, jump movement until he hid behind me.

"Kill it," he ordered me.

"Hell, no. It's a spider, and it could eat me. You're the man. You kill it."

"No way. It tried to bite my face."

Remember what I said before—bugs were not my friends. I wasn't going to touch that thing, but it was blocking me from getting through the door and ordering a drink. Only, I noticed the thing hadn't moved. For sure, it would have scurried off. I was ninety-nine-point-nine percent positive it was a prop. Fake, I could handle.

Just to toy with my cowering Wookie, I picked the thing up and started walking toward him again. "It's so cute."

"Cass," he warned with each step I took.

When I threw it on him, his own Jedi moves took over. It looked like an epic battle, and the Wookie was about to go down. I decided to put him out of his misery.

"It's fake."

Jeff stopped at my words. "What?"

"The spider isn't real."

He looked at the spot where the rubber spider had landed, but he still wasn't satisfied with just knowing. His size twelve shoe came up and stomped on the defenseless toy. The gel that filled it squirted everywhere. If you've ever accidentally stepped on a ketchup packet, the effect was much the same.

"Do you feel better now that you slayed him?" I asked

while I laughed.

"Fuck, yeah. I hate spiders."

"I couldn't tell. So if a spider were to attack me . . .?"

"You're on your own."

"Really?"

"Really."

As if to mock me, the spider in my room stopped back to say hi. The first thought that entered my mind was I need a man who will take care of that thing for me. If it's not rubber, I'm not going near it. And if it's moving, you'd better slay it like the Wookie did or you are guaranteed no nookie. Ever. Again.

I take another little break to apply my face mask. It is part of my nightly routine, but secretly, I'm just trying to ignore the pest on my wall. After I washed the remnants away, I apply my night eye cream, reminding me of another requirement.

8. Learn the color of my eyes

Eyes up here, bucko. One of the first things I notice about a man is his eyes. A close second is his lips. Tell me the color of the shirt I'm wearing makes my eyes pop. And don't tell me how you love how blue or green they are because they are brown, by the way. I want to hear things like they look like melted chocolate or remind you of the topping on your favorite dessert.

After the disaster with Bates, I was still more than a little reluctant to spend time with a man. I knew not every man was certifiably insane, but after that incident, who could blame me for being a little cautious. When Emma came bursting into my room one Saturday afternoon to tell me that we were going out, I knew there was little chance of me getting out of it this time. She was loaded down with shopping bags and had a determined look on her face. The kind that told me she was going to drag me out of this room if that was what it took.

"Cass, it's like the last party of the year. You have to go," she whined.

"Technically, I don't have to go. There's nothing stating

'Cass has to go or the party is not happening.'"

She stared me down for a solid two minutes without saying a word until I finally relented.

"Fine. Where is this party of the year?"

"In Thompson Square. A friend of a friend told me about it. Can you believe it?"

Emma and I managed to snag an apartment in New York City; it was cozy and rent controlled. Thompson Square was the high-class part of town, and by high class, I mean the houses were like mansions. I had never been to one of the parties over there, but I had heard about them, and that really wasn't my scene. I wrinkled my nose in disgust.

"I have nothing to wear to that. Also, a friend of a friend? Who are these friends of friends?"

Maybe I was a little suspicious.

I watched as Emma laid the bags down and started digging through them.

"I found these at the antique shop." She sounded so excited about the fact she had found clothes at an antique shop, and I was trying to hold back my laughter. That was until she pulled the dress out of the bag.

"Look at it. And I know it's going to fit you perfectly. It was a sign."

With my mouth hanging agape, I stood from my bed and reached for the most beautiful dress I had ever laid eyes on. The gorgeous cream-colored vintage dress looked like it had stepped out of the pages of a 1920s magazine. The detailed silver beading over the entire dress made it look feminine and delicate, the deep plunging neckline gave it sex appeal, and the long cream-colored tassels would move as I danced around the room. She was right; this dress looked like it had been made for me. Just by looking at it, I knew it was going to hug my curves perfectly. I needed somewhere to wear this dress, and if that meant I was going to that damn party, then so be it.

"What time?" I asked, glancing back over at her.

She squealed and clapped her hands. "We need to leave here by nine."

It was only a little after five, which gave us plenty of time to get ready. That also meant we had plenty of time to research hairstyles to match the era of the dress.

We had a pre-party drink or two while we did our makeup and hair. By the time I stepped into that dress, I was on cloud nine.

"Holy shit, Cass. Your boobs look fantastic," Emma said as she walked into the room. I had to admit the girls did look fantastic; the neckline cut in a way that came down way past where my bra should have been, which meant I was free boobing it tonight. It was tastefully done, and I had to give props to the decade when this dress was created. They just didn't make clothing like this anymore.

I gave myself one last look in the mirror and was pleased with what I saw. I had the smoky eye look going on, Emma had spent an hour pulling my hair up into a complicated bun type style, and my lips were painted red.

I felt sexier than I think I'd ever had.

"We look hot," I said as I turned to look at Emma.

And I wasn't lying. Emma was a knockout any day of the week, but her dress was a short little number that showed off her long legs and the color made her olive skin glow.

The two of us made our way downstairs where the cab was waiting and hopped inside. Thompson Square was across town, and I knew the cab fare was going to kill my budget this month, but I was willing to splurge tonight. Neither of us wanted to drive anyway.

About thirty minutes later, we finally pulled into the circular driveway. The house was stunning, and cars were parked everywhere. Some even on the perfectly manicured lawn. I took it all in as we walked up the cobblestone drive-way to the front door. It was wide open, and I could hear the music before we ever stepped inside. This might have been a party in a rich neighborhood, filled with extremely wealthy people, but we were still in our early twenties, so I wasn't ex-pecting caviar and classical music. Emma grabbed my hand as we stepped inside and weaved us in and out of the people. She seemed to know where she was going, and I was praying that it would lead directly to the alcohol.

We walked through several rooms filled with people dressed much like us before Emma finally led us outside where not one but two bars were set up. Want to know the best thing about parties in that neighborhood? Free alcohol. When you were in your twenties and on a strict budget of noodles and tap water, free booze was pretty much the best thing ever.

As we both slid onto a barstool and ordered our usual vodka and cranberry, heavy on the vodka, I glanced at our surroundings while Emma chatted with the bartender. We had just been served our drinks when I felt someone sit down beside me.

I glanced over and smiled at him. After all, I didn't want to be rude. It *was* a party, and he was all up in my personal space.

"I'm Steve," he told my boobs.

I bent my head down a bit until I could catch his eyes.

"Hi, Steve. I'm Cassandra."

He glanced up briefly to look at my face before going back to the boobs. I wanted to roll my eyes but refrained. Instead, I turned on my stool toward Emma. Sure, he was a good-looking guy, but he wasn't really having a conversation with me anyway, just my boobs.

The message I sent came across loud and clear, and I heard his stool slide back before he walked away. Emma and I had two drinks at the bar before we decided to mingle. I just really wanted to check out this house and the view. While she carried on conversations with total strangers, like only Emma could do, I studied the art on the walls. It really was like a museum in there. I was looking at a beautiful abstract by Jinlu when Steve came back over.

"Beautiful, isn't it?"

I turned to make sure he was talking to me. This time, he was looking at the painting, and I took a moment to study him. He was about my age and very well dressed. His clothes practically screamed wealth and privilege. His hair was perfectly fixed, and I wondered if he was wearing hairspray with how it never moved, but it looked good, so I let that minor detail slide.

He turned to look at me, and this time, he met my eyes. His were light green and very pretty, and when I saw his long eyelashes, I was actually a little jealous of them.

"It is beautiful," I said, referring to the painting. I could have been referring to him too, but luckily, he thought I was still discussing the artwork.

"Thank you. My parents bought this just a few months ago."

"This is your parents' house?" I asked.

He nodded his head, and his eyes briefly dropped to my cleavage again, but I forgave him since they did quickly come back to my face.

"Yeah, they are in France right now."

I wasn't a materialistic woman, but that house was absolutely stunning, and the handsome man who lived in said house was making an effort, so you couldn't blame me for instantly forgetting all about our first meeting earlier in the night.

"Want to go get another drink?" he asked, while lightly touching my elbow.

I looked around for Emma and saw that she was still talking to the group of people. She caught my eye, and I gave her the signal. Ladies, this is important. If you are out with your girlfriend, always have a signal—either a look or a gesture—that tells your friend you are about to go off with a man and she may or may not be seeing you again that night. The signal could also be an escape plan. In exactly thirty minutes, Emma would call my phone. If all was well, I would tell her I'd see her for lunch tomorrow. If I needed rescuing, I would fake an emergency.

I looked back over at Steve and smiled. "Sure."

He led us back outside and ordered us both another drink before finding a quiet corner so we could talk. And by talk, I mean he went right back to staring at my boobs. Sure, he carried on a decent conversation; he was highly intelligent and well spoken, but I think he looked at my face twice since we had sat down.

When Emma called, I dug my phone out of my purse and answered it.

"How is it going?" she asked.

"Hold on."

I pulled the phone away from my ear and addressed Steve.

"Hey, Steve. What color are my eyes?"

"They're blue and stunning, Cassandra."

I sighed and put the phone back to my ear. "I'll meet you out front in five."

I put my phone back in my purse and stood. I wasn't even going to play it off as an emergency.

"Where are you going?" Steve, the idiot, looked so adorably perplexed as to why I was leaving.

I patted him on the head as I passed by. It was meant to be a condescending move, but my bracelet got stuck amongst the gel and the hairspray. Well, at least I figured out that mystery. It was a combination of the two, and I was really stuck. To make matters worse, in order to dislodge from him, his face practically smothered in my chest. I was pulling with all my might to break free, during which I'm pretty sure I felt his tongue give me a lick or two and I heard him moan. Apparently, he liked a good hair pull while attempting to motorboat my breasts.

When I finally was free, I wiped my hand on his shirt and shook my head.

"My eyes are brown, and that's the last feel you'll cop of me, jackass."

I didn't give him a chance to respond before walking inside and toward the front door. I met up with Emma, and we hopped in our cab.

She looked over at me, and her eyes dropped to my boobs.

"Jesus! Not you too," I grunted.

She laughed and looked back at me. "Peaches and Rose do look fantastic in that dress."

Yes, my boobs had names, but that didn't mean I wanted you to carry on a conversation with them more than you did with me.

I laid my head on Emma's shoulder and said sadly, "He thought my eyes were blue."

She snorted but otherwise didn't comment as she patted the side of my face.

I decided right then and there that if someone wanted to date me, they had to maintain eye contact while I was talking, and they had to compliment my eyes before they complimented my body. I didn't mind men checking me out occasionally—it was a boost to my confidence—but at least know the difference between blue and dark brown.

9. I am not your mother

Let's get a few things straight. I am your girlfriend. AKA partner. If we are going to share a dwelling together, we will share ALL responsibilities. Cooking, cleaning, and laundry are both our responsibilities. I'll even make a little chore chart if it's difficult for you to figure out what should be done. I can color code it—pink for me, blue for you.

It was a while before I gave my all in a relationship. I dated, but nothing monumental came from it. Then I decided to give it a try and moved in with a man. I should have stayed in my cozy apartment with Emma, though; it would have saved me the trouble of moving twice in the same year.

I had just gotten an amazing job. I suffered at Hype for a year before I decided to move to another company, VYBE . . . Visualize Your Business Expanding. They won points for having a much better slogan. My boss, Phoebe, rocked too. Every project she worked on—from car wax to an ear hair removal device—was exciting because she made it that way. Instead of having me make coffee, which I did anyway because I liked her, she asked my opinion. The first project she had me help with was for a solar cell phone charger. We worked day and night to perfect the ad campaign for Because Vitamin D. It was brilliant, direct, and to the point. At the end of every day, I was mentally exhausted. I just wanted to go home, relax, and read a good book.

His name was Derrick, and he was a model, with golden highlights in his hair and wardrobe beyond compare. The man could mix drinks and could dance hip-hop. He tried to be a rock star, but he ended up tending bar.

I should have known our relationship was doomed if it could be summed up to the tune of a disco song.

Anyway, the short and long of it was we met, we liked each other a lot, and then we took the leap and got an apartment together.

I warned him beforehand that I had a slight case of OCD. I didn't like clutter or mess of any kind. He said he was the same way, and his old apartment was, for the most part, clean. Plus, you would think a man who only worked weekends could maintain a clean apartment or throw a load of laundry in the washer, especially when that man changed outfits more than a woman reapplied her lipstick. That wasn't the case, though. The apartment we shared was a mess. The sink was always full of his dishes. Our bedroom had clothes laying right the fuck next to the laundry basket. Was it that much of an effort to drop them two inches to the left? Apparently, it was.

Not only that, all those dishes in the sink weren't from food he cooked for me.

"What's for dinner?" the jerk asked me.

"Umm . . ." That was the only sound I could form.

"I'm starving," he whined. Full-on childlike whine.

"Buttered noodles." That was quick and easy; plus, I

didn't have it in me to argue. I could make that. Then he did it again.

"You know I can't eat carbs. What if they call me tomorrow for a photo shoot?" Whine, whine, whine.

He hadn't done a modeling job in two months. "I'm sorry. How silly of me to forget."

Did you hear my sarcasm? That sentence was full of it.

"I worked hard all day." He said it with such a straight face that all I wanted to do was laugh.

Instead, I looked around the living room. The mud on the floor was probably from his running shoes. His workout equipment was all over the place. Along with sweaty towels. Oh, I got it . . . He worked *out* all day, not worked.

"Right. Well, I had a cup of coffee and a granola bar at work today. So I'm good."

"But I'm hungry. My mom—"

I stopped him right there.

"First of all, I'm not your mom. Girlfriend," I said as I made a circle around my face with my finger to prove my point.

"She would—"

"Girlfriend. Got it? Second, you were here all day. Not stuck in an office. Third, fourth, and fifth, dishes meet dishwasher. Towels meet washing machine. Mop meet bucket." Luckily, they were all side by side by side in our tiny, affordable apartment.

"I hate doing those things. That's woman's work."

I think the look on my face was enough to make him snap his mouth shut. I'm sure smoke was coming out of my ears and fire was about to shoot from my mouth. He saw it too. Inch by inch, he backed away when he realized his mistake. It was a big one.

I stormed to the bedroom. *If the goddamn motherfucker thinks I am going to clean up after his ass, he has another thing coming. Who in the hell does he think he is? What's for dinner? I'll show you what's for dinner.*

Then it hit me. Those words running through my head—I just became my mother. He pulled that out of me.

I packed an overnight bag, but before I left for Emma's, I had to make myself clear. "If this place is not cleaned by to-morrow, I'm out."

Was that a bit extreme? Nope, not one bit.

When I came home the next day, his mom was there wearing rubber gloves and dinner was in the oven. As for me, I packed my belongings and didn't look back. Not before I ate dinner, though. She made tacos. Who would turn down Taco Tuesday? Not me.

10. Must put the toilet seat down

If my ass falls into the toilet bowl at 3:00 in the morning, you will be kicked out of my bed at 3:02. That is gross and unacceptable. It takes two seconds to lower the lid. Do it. Enough said.

I told you I left for Emma's place. Right after I moved in with Derrick, her grandmother told her she was getting too old to live in the city and that her apartment needed someone young and lively, not a woman who likes to crochet and watch reality television. Grandma took over Emma's old bedroom at her parents' house and gave her an amazing three-bedroom apartment. One room was supposed to be mine B.D. (*before Derrick*), so I quickly reclaimed my room. We rented out the third bedroom, but we were particular about who we allowed to live with us. Insert Colin.

Colin paid his rent on time. He even did all the things that Derrick didn't do. We had a chart on the fridge dividing all the weekly house duties. He was great . . . until that night.

When three people shared one bathroom, things got tricky. Showers were scheduled according to what time we had to leave for work. Emma and I took care of the counters, and Colin's job was to clean the bottom of the toilet. There was no way in hell I'd be cleaning his piss off there.

I just didn't get how a man could miss so much. He tried to explain it to me, but when I heard the words morning and wood, I shut down. Not that he was a bad looking guy, he just wasn't my or Emma's type. In fact, we weren't his type either. He preferred male company. That was why we allowed him to live with us. He was a brother type to us, and a sister never wanted to know about her brother's morning erectile issues. Gross.

One night, Colin brought us to a drag strip joint, and we had the best time. I was never so jealous of anyone in my life. The three of us drank a smidge too much. Hell, let's be honest, we were sloppy by the time we got home.

In the middle of the night, I stumbled into the bathroom, desperate to pee. I sat, and that was when things went south. It was one of those slow motion "oh, shit" moments. I tried to grab the sink counter, but I was still seeing triple. The buzzer went off in my head. Beep, you chose wrong. My ass was wet, and I got stuck. I couldn't get out. Arms and legs were flailing as I tried to grab anything to help me out of the wet situation.

Emma heard the commotion and came to the rescue. She was still drunk too and kept reaching for the wrong hand.

"It's the one in the middle," I screamed.

"I'm trying, but there are arms and legs everywhere."

Good Lord.

"Just get me out of here."

"When in the hell did you grow an extra set of limbs?" She was laughing. I was drowning in the toilet, and my best friend was laughing.

This is why you'd better make sure you always put the seat down for me. I can't be humiliated like that again. And because it took both Emma and Colin to lift me out of the toilet, I came up with my next rule.

11. Must be able to carry me

I'm not talking about lifting me. I'm talking about full-on pick me up, toss me over your shoulder, spank my ass, and carry me up the stairs to my bed. This is not optional. It's a requirement.

Literally, I wanted someone to sweep me off my feet. I told Brad about my romantic fantasies. One of which was to be carried into the bedroom, laid on a bed of roses, and "made love" to by candlelight. I was twenty-five and had never been treated to such a date.

It was our first Valentine's Day together.

Brad tried, he really did. He picked me up for what I thought was going to be a romantic dinner. Much to my surprise, we headed back to his apartment. He was a terrible cook but was great at calling takeout from one of our favorite local Chinese restaurants.

While having dinner, we attempted to eat with wooden chopsticks. Unfortunately, neither of us were good at it. From a local bakery, he picked up a cheesecake that was absolutely divine. He tried so hard to make our night unforgettable, and it was.

The memory of what happened next stuck out more than dinner. It took Brad three attempts to pick me up. I kept my eyes shut tight because I feared he would drop me. When we got the bedroom door, it was closed.

"I guess I didn't think this through. Would you mind opening the door for me?" Brad asked with a slightly embarrassed look on his face.

I opened the door, and that was when everything went wrong. What Brad should have done was turn sideways, but he failed to realize my body would not fit through the door. Not once, but twice, he tried to walk straight through the door. My head hit the doorjamb with a thud on the second try.

"Oh, shit. Sorry, Cass."

The third time, he turned his body. My head was pounding from the abuse it just took until I saw the roses on the bed.

That wasn't the end of it, though. I'd love to say we laid on the bed and made sweet love.

The true story—I couldn't make this shit up—was a slow motion *nooooo* moment.

Brad tossed me on the bed, but it was only because he tripped and dropped me. He wasn't the alpha at all, tossing me like I envisioned. He was too clumsy for that. My back hit the roses. But I didn't land on rose petals; actual thorns stabbed me. When I jumped, I knocked over the candle and not just one either. It was like a domino effect. One after another, they fell.

The *nooooo* turned to *fuuuuuuuck*.

Flames hit the nearest object, the curtains.

In a panic, Brad grabbed the two full glasses on the other

nightstand and tossed the liquid at the burning curtain. I was partially in the way, and red wine soaked my body. Wait, did he toss alcohol? Yep, he did.

That made the fire very unhappy. It was like one of those circus people who spit fire, or even better, a dragon. The flames shot out at me and singed my hair.

Lucky for us, his roommate came to the rescue. He took care of my hair first before the charred curtains. With a yank, he pulled them down—rod and all—and the fire was out. The curtain rod struck Brad on the head, knocking him out cold before the fire department showed up.

Both of us were taken to the hospital. Other than having slightly shorter hair on one side, I was fine. Brad, however, suffered a concussion and had to stay the night.

So if you are going to pick me up, you'd better be able to hold up to my expectations. And no open flames by the bed. Or thorns.

12. Needs to know how to run a good bubble bath

Some days you need a night to relax. As an intuitive guy, you need to be able to look at me and know when I need that. You need to take the initiative and walk your ass to the bathroom, get the temperature just right, and know where the bath salts are.

Also, refer to the list item above because it would be super if you could carry me there and not light me on fire.

After the Valentine's Day disaster, which I chalked up to a day just gone wrong, Brad tried to make it up to me. He sent me flowers, minus the thorns, and so many boxes of chocolates that my ass was starting to show the effects. I begged him to stop.

After a particularly long week at work, I asked Brad if we could stay at my place and watch a movie. He came to my apartment with a bag in his hand. As he had told me to, I waited on the couch while he did whatever he was doing in the kitchen, and when he came out, he was holding my favorite movie *The Notebook* and a glass of my favorite wine.

"Don't start the movie yet. I have something else planned first. How does a nice bath sound?"

It sounded perfect.

I heard the water start up, but it seemed like an unnaturally long time for him to be gone. Brad came back looking rather proud of himself.

"I promise no candles or thorns. I got battery-operated lights and fake flowers this time. But I want to try something again."

He walked over to me, and I didn't know if I should be nervous. This time, he picked me up with ease.

"You've been working out, haven't you?"

He winked at me, and my heart sped up at the thought of what would happen next.

It wasn't far to the bathroom since it was located right off the living room. As we got closer, I heard the trickling sound.

"Brad, was the water running this whole time? You were in there for a while."

"Don't worry, Cass. I got this covered. All you need to do is relax. I even picked up this new organic bubble bath. The girl at the store said they can't keep it on the shelf."

I trusted him. He was trying so hard to be sweet, and I really wanted to take a nice bath. He even kissed me the rest of the way to the bathroom, which only excited me more. Brad could kiss; it was one of the qualities I liked most about him.

We made it safely through the bathroom doorway until he stepped on the tile floor. Brad slipped and bit my tongue. Hard. A copper taste filled my mouth.

I didn't even have time to react since the sudden sensation that we were ice-skating across the floor hit me.

"Oh, shit," Brad yelped.

Not again.

Brad had overfilled the bathtub, and it was spilling over the edge. To make things worse, soapsuds were everywhere.

We stopped when his feet hit the ceramic tub and in I went. Clothes and all. I swallowed a mouthful of bathwater and soap.

When I finally got my bearings, I stood—a dripping, soapy mess.

"What the fuck, Brad? I told you the water was on too long. And how much soap did you use anyway?"

"Umm, Cass."

"What?" I said impatiently.

"I think I need to go to the hospital."

I wiped the soap from my eyes so I could see what was wrong with him when I was the one who just went head over ass into the tub. When my eyes finally focused, I noticed he was covered in splotches.

"What the hell happened?" I ask him.

"I think I'm allergic to the soap. My throat is closing."

Shit. I slipped across the floor to get to him, not even caring that I was wet. I grabbed the bottle of bubble bath and threw it in my purse so I could look at the ingredients.

When we got to the hospital, the nurse wheeled him into the room and quickly gave him an epinephrine shot in his leg. When he calmed down, the doctor asked him what he was allergic to.

"Nuts."

I looked at the bottle. Organic almond bubble bath made from the oils in almonds.

"Did you even read this?" I asked him.

"Yes."

"It's made from nuts."

"I know," he said, totally not getting it.

"And you used the whole bottle when it clearly says to just use a capful."

"Well, I thought you'd like the extra bubbles."

Right then and there, I decided two awkward people don't make a right. Plus, I feared for both of our lives. At that point, I had to get home and take care of the flood in my apartment, but since I wasn't a complete bitch, I did pick him up from the hospital the next day and gave him a week before I ended it. Brad's comment to being dumped, "Thank God. I think if I had to try one more of your fantasies, I might end up in a body cast."

After that, my dog became the only male to share my bed for a while. My trusty sidekick likes to cuddle, too, even though he does have this tendency to whine. At least he's loyal and doesn't back talk . . . much.

13. Must love dogs

You see, I have this loyal friend. Did I mention that he's a little insane? He pisses on my date's shirts, he barks when I leave the house, he sleeps next to me, and he loves me unconditionally. Are you willing to share me?

I had just started my new job a few months earlier, and while I absolutely loved where I worked, my busy schedule didn't allow me to have much of a personal life. And by that, I mean that it had been a while since I'd had sexy time, and let me tell you, I was really getting desperate for it. When a friend of mine wanted to set me up on a date, I was all for it. This poor guy didn't know it yet, but he was going to get lucky on the first night. Don't judge me; a woman has needs too.

I decided to meet Emerson at the new Italian restaurant a few blocks from my house. As badly as I needed to get some booty, I still wanted to make sure he wasn't a serial killer.

When I walked into the dimly lit restaurant, I searched the room for someone who looked like the picture my friend had shown me. At the same time as I saw him, he saw me. As I made my way to the table, I smiled. He stood, smiling in return. I took a second to really look at him.

He towered over me. And with his built frame, he looked like he could pick me up with no problem. I felt absolutely giddy when I saw the tattoos peeking out from under the sleeve of his t-shirt. He certainly passed the inspection. I looked up at his face and extended my hand.

"Hi, you must be Emerson."

"I am, and you must be Cassandra." He smiled at me, and I think I actually sighed at how handsome his face was. Yes, this one would work perfectly for making sure to take care of me.

We both sat down, and when the waiter came, we ordered our drinks. While I had wine, Emerson declined and had water.

Throughout dinner, we made small talk while exchanging flirty glances. When the waiter delivered our check, I took a large gulp of my wine and did what had to be done. I threw all caution to the wind, and I gave him the opening.

"Would you like to come to my apartment for a nightcap?"

He quirked one sexy eyebrow at me and smirked. Oh yeah, he knew what was up.

Without another word, he paid the check, and we walked out of the restaurant together.

The walk to my tiny apartment was quick, and I was feeling damn good about myself. Emerson's hand rested on my lower back the entire time. Did I mention his hands were big and strong too? It only added to my excitement.

When we reached my apartment door, I was surprised when he spun me around and pinned me against it. His mouth was on mine before I could even blink, and damn, he was good with it.

I made a mental note to send my friend some flowers and wine for setting me up with this man.

His hands were on my ass as he lifted me up and settled himself between my legs. I could practically hear my vagina thanking me. It had been so long, and she was primed and ready.

"Inside," I mumbled against his lips. I mean this was great and all, but I lived here. There was no sense in my neighbors seeing the whole show, and if we weren't in my apartment in five seconds, I couldn't be held accountable for my actions.

I wiggled in his arms, and he set me down. I pushed the key in the lock and led us inside where Razor immediately started barking.

Now let me tell you a little about my precious dog. Razor was a micro teacup poodle. He was so tiny that he often got lost in my covers at night. I had to check the couch before I sat down because one time, my ass almost squashed the little ball of fur. It was traumatic for the both of us. I loved this dog, but Razor liked to bark . . . a lot. He was also very possessive of me, and he didn't like men.

Anyway, when Razor saw Emerson walk in behind me, he went bat shit crazy. His little body was bouncing up and down as he barked his head off. I turned to look at Emerson, but his eyes remained on my dog.

"Just ignore him," I mumbled as I stepped toward him.

Before he focused on me again, he gave Razor one last look. I used his shirt to pull him toward my bed. I wanted more of those kisses, but I was also ready to see how good his mouth actually was.

I looked up into his eyes, and they became heated as he focused on me this time. Silently, I was doing a little cheer because damn, he was so sexy. Even more so, I was freaking ecstatic that my dry spell was about to be over, but it seemed Razor wasn't as excited as I was that his mommy was about to get laid. As soon as Emerson laid me down on the bed, Razor jumped up and started pacing above my head. His barks were getting louder, and he growled like he was a goddamn pit bull. I reached my hand up and tried to push him away, but he just took that as me needing help. He latched onto Emerson's shirt and started shaking his head back and forth. I think he actually foamed at the mouth at that point. Emerson tried to push him away, but Razor got his name for a reason. Those razor-sharp teeth of his sank right into Emerson's hand.

"Fuck!" He looked at my dog like he couldn't believe that just happened. It did. All I could do was sigh.

"Ignore him," I said again.

"He bit me."

I almost rolled my eyes. The dog weighed no more than four pounds. How much damage could he do?

I pulled Emerson's mouth back to mine and tried to take his mind off my dog. Even though I could still hear him, I chose to pretend I didn't. I had a singular focus. Nothing was going to stop me until I had an orgasm that didn't come from my own hand.

We were really getting into it. Hands were wandering, our lower bodies were grinding against each other, and then it happened. My precious little doggy took his hatred of men to a whole new level.

"What is that?" Emerson asked as he lifted his mouth from mine.

"What is what?" I was a little dazed or intoxicated from making out. He was going to have to clue me in.

"Where's the dog?" He looked to the left and the right.

I shook off the drug-like state his kiss had me under, and everything came back into focus. The room was quiet, and Razor had stopped barking, which should be a good thing, but when I looked up, I saw him standing on Emerson's back. I swear to Christ, the dog was smiling at me like he just did me a favor, and I knew without even having to ask, but I did anyway.

"What happened? Why did you stop kissing me?" I asked in a cautious but resigned voice.

His eyes came back to mine with a confused look. "I felt something wet on my back."

"I'm pretty sure my dog just pissed on you."

He looked stunned at first before a look of disgust passed over his face. Luckily, Razor picked that moment to jump off him. He wasn't done yet, either, because lifted his leg one last time. Nothing came out; it was just a show. The act got bigger as he scratched his back legs as if he was dismissing Emerson then continued on to sit on my pillow. As he snuggled there, he looked very fucking proud of himself.

Emerson jumped up off me and squealed like a little girl as he spun in circles trying to see his back. I sighed and propped myself up on my elbows, watching as he ran around my small apartment. Emerson, not Razor.

Eventually, he turned and looked at me. "He pissed on me. Your fucking dog pissed on me."

I blinked a few times because what else could I do? "I don't think he likes you."

"Yeah, well, I don't like him," he said while pointing a finger at my sweet Razor.

I sat up on the bed and folded my arms over my chest.

"Hey! You don't even know him."

"He pissed on me!"

"When are you going to let that go? It happened like five minutes ago. Let's move on."

"Move on. You want to move on? What the hell, Cass? I have dog piss on me."

I could see his point, but dammit, I was looking forward to sexy time. Resigned to the fact that I wasn't going to see any action, I stood from the bed and walked past him, where he was still pacing the floor. I opened the front door and motioned for him to walk through it.

"I had fun. I'll make sure to send you a new shirt. You're a little upset, and I'm guessing this isn't going to happen now so good night."

He shook his head and glanced at Razor one more time before walking through the door without saying a word.

I never saw or heard from Emerson again after that night, but I guess it was for the best. I did get his address from my friend, and I sent him a new t-shirt, but it was returned to sender. Apparently, he just didn't have a sense of humor, or maybe he had a problem with the color yellow.

So this is why you must love dogs because Razor "little shit" Quinn is my BFF, and if you aren't down with him, then you can't get down with me. (Yes, that is his full name.)

Since my sexual needs weren't going to be met that night, I needed some kind of outlet. I turned up my stereo and got to it. Moving around my apartment wearing my underwear and tank top seemed like the perfect way to get over Emerson and his hatred for my dog.

14. Must know how to dance

A little fun fact about me, I love to dance. Everywhere. I dance in my living room when I've had a bad day. If a good song comes on the radio while I'm driving, I've been known to bust a groove. But the truth is if you know how to move your body, that tells me a little about how you are behind closed doors. You've seen Magic Mike. I'm almost one hundred percent positive their partners are sa-tis-fied.

Emma and I went to one of those sex charged vibe clubs one weekend. Strobe lights and smoke filled the dance floor while both female and male dancers were hanging in cages overhead. The music was so loud, tomorrow you would be sure to have ringing ears.

Two reasons you went to this place—to dance and hook up. Maybe three, if you added the ladies' night drinking specials.

We were getting one of the bar's signature drinks that was pure alcohol when someone bumped my arm. Luckily, everything stayed in the glass.

"Watch it," I yelled over the deafening music as I turned to the arm bumper. My jaw hit the floor when I caught the dark-eyed hottie next to me.

"Sorry," he screamed back.

This club was not made for small talk. Instead, he pointed at my drink, silently asking if I wanted another. I quickly downed it and then nodded my head.

"The name's Thad." Or at least I thought that was what he said.

"Sandra." It wasn't a total lie. Technically, it was part of my name. When Emma and I went out looking for "fun," giving our real name or number was not happening. She used Leigh, short for Emmaleigh, and you already knew mine.

After the first drink with hottie, Emma found her fun for the night. They were out on the dance floor shaking it. Well, grinding against each other was a more accurate description. As Thad and I finished our drinks, he pulled me between his legs. The more the alcohol I sipped, the more my hips swayed to the music. His hands were quite nice. The way he touched my hips and thighs as I moved; I thought for sure he was a good choice.

By the time we finished our second drink, I was ready to hit the floor.

I turned around and pulled Thad from his chair. He took the last sip of his beer then followed along. The way he walked, I could tell he was going to rock my world tonight.

His whole body exuded confidence and screamed male.

The song changed, and it was just the right kind of music to get a little sexy to. I figured he'd pull me close to do a little bump and grind like Emma and her guy were doing, but what happened next was straight out of an episode of *Seinfeld*.

His thumbs went up and started thrusting outward while his legs were kicking in these odd movements. For a moment, I was stunned; I didn't know what to do. How the hell was I supposed to match those "moves"?

Then the train wreck got worse.

It was like my legs gained seventy pounds, and I couldn't move as Thad's dance moves went from worse to I feel sorry for him, but I couldn't stop staring.

He started sliding his feet across the floor while pretending to dig a hole. As he screamed, "The shovel."

Again, his thumbs went up, and he kept motioning backward. I thought maybe he was done with dancing, but apparently, no . . .

"Reverse. Reverse."

Yes, he said the word with each step he took.

"Trimming the bushes," was yelled while he moved his arms like he was using hedge clippers. Or at least that was my guess. What was going through my head was . . . hell to the no, you are not getting anywhere near my bushes.

The final straw was when he walked up behind me. He was trying to be sexy, I think, and he rolled his body against mine. It was more of a gyrate meets the funky chicken move, though. While he was doing it, he tried to whisper, "Rolling the log."

I was in hell, absolute hell, and there definitely was no log in there. Calling it stick was being generous. You know that little stem where leaves grow? That was what it felt like.

Emma must have seen all of this going down because she came to my rescue and got my feet working. She politely told Thad that she needed me. When I finally came to, I noticed a crowd had gathered around him, clapping along. It took two strong drinks and a friend of the guy Emma was with to get "Thad the Terrible" out of my head.

I had it after that and decided to give the clubs a break. I needed some good quality reading time with one of my amazing book boyfriends.

15. Must enjoy reading

I'm not talking about reading Facebook posts. Don't tell me, "I'll wait for the movie," either because that is just wrong on so many levels. I'm an avid reader, and I want to see you pick up an actual book. My book of choice is anything romance. I want to lay in bed across your chest while you read to me. This is non-negotiable.

Right before I went to bed, my boyfriend at the time was playing on his phone while I picked up the current book I was reading. Lately, Corey had been staying more and more at my apartment. It was a natural progression in our "relationship." We'd grown close after only one month of dating. He was sweet, had surfer good looks, and that lean muscle look going on. But that night, it started bothering me that he was constantly playing games on his phone.

"Don't you get tired of playing that?" I asked him as I placed my book on my lap.

He gave me a look then simply said, "No."

"Do you like to read?" I'd never seen him read anything besides his social media pages. Don't get me wrong; I was all about Facebook, Instagram, and Twitter, but that was not reading. That was a distraction.

"I haven't read a book since I was forced to in high school."

Corey ran his own landscaping business. He told me he didn't go to college. Everything he learned about plants and trees was self-taught or from someone at the local nursery.

"Really?" The thought of not reading a book in so many years disturbed me.

"Yes, really. I've learned all that I'm going to at this point in life. So why do I need to read?"

I was shocked at his ignorance. "There is no way you've learned everything, and a book isn't just about that. A phenomenal book can take you on a journey to somewhere, help you meet new friends, and make you feel every emotion in the world."

He picked up my book and read the title out loud. *Coming Undone* by Allie Taylor. This book is going to do that, huh?"

"Yes."

"What's it about?" he asked. While he held my book, he thumbed through the pages as I talked.

"It's about a woman who was wronged by a man. She moved from the city to a ranching town to forget the past and discover herself again."

"And you relate to this shit?"

"Very much."

He started looking at the chapter I was reading, which happened to be an intimate scene. The main female character went out to a local farm for some produce and met a cowboy a few chapters earlier. Every weekend, she went to that farmer's market they had at the ranch, and the two had become close. Very close.

Corey started reading aloud.

The way Wyatt looked shirtless had Anna feeling things she never had before. His back glistened with sweat while his strong back muscles flexed each time he bent to pick up the bale of hay. She studied him as he lifted each one from his pickup truck and stacked them in a neat pile in the barn.

I took the opportunity to get comfortable. Corey had a great voice for reading.

"That's the end of the chapter. You really like this book?" he asked.

"Yes, keep reading. I like your voice." I laid on his chest with my arm and one leg draped over him.

Before he turned the page, Corey put his arm around me. "It changed to his point of view."

"Yes."

"I didn't know books could do that."

He really had no clue. It was cute the way he sounded so surprised.

"Authors can write whatever they feel like. Now, keep reading."

He cleared his throat and finally continued.

I knew Anna was watching me because I kept stealing the same glances at her whenever I walked by. We'd been doing this dance for too long; the one where she would come here right before closing time, gather her favorite jams, talk to my family about what she was going to bake that week, and smile in that beautiful way she did when she looked my way. We had been dating for the past month, and I was at my breaking point. Today, I wanted to give her a reason to smile.

She was pretending to study the labels on the jars, but I saw her licking her lips when I took off my shirt. When I winked at her, her face turned this adorable shade of pink. Mom asked me to take Anna to the cellar where we kept the extra canning jars; she wanted to give her some of the secret stash of her famous rhubarb preserves. I was more than happy to take Anna there. She followed me through the barn, just beyond the fresh stack of hay.

Corey stopped again. "Are you joking? This is crap."

"Keep going, and it's not crap."

He sighed but kept reading.

When Anna and I were out of sight and earshot of everyone, I turned to face her. She looked at my body, taking notice that she affected me too. Her eyes went wide when I pulled her to me.

"I can't wait much longer for you. I'm going insane not being able to touch you out there," I told her just before I brought my lips to hers. Anna's body melted against mine. It fit against me like no other woman had before. Our tongues dueled in a way that left me hard and aching, but I couldn't keep her here forever. I knew someone would come looking for us any minute. Reluctantly, I pulled away.

"Meet me here at nine," I demanded.

"Okay."

"This is when it gets good," I told Corey.

"You've read this before?"

"Yes, a few times."

"That's weird."

"No, it's not. You'll see why if you keep going."

He read a few more pages, which were the buildup to the sexy scene. When he read the next part, it was hot as hell.

Anna showed up. I was having doubts that she would. But

when she walked through the barn door, I couldn't help myself. I had wanted her from the first time I saw her.

Everyone was fast asleep inside the house. The life of running a farm has most of us in bed early and waking well before the sun was up. My house was just up the road, but I had this fantasy of being with her here, in my barn, far too many times. It was time to make that fantasy a reality.

"Do you want me, Anna? Because I want you."

"Yes. Desperately," she whispered.

I laid her down on the blanket that I placed on top of the hay. She was wearing the perfect outfit for me to peel her layers off. Which I planned to do, slowly.

"Kiss me, Wyatt."

I put everything I had in that kiss. My lips and tongue moved over hers, hoping that I would show her how badly I wanted her. When she started moaning beneath me, I knew she wanted me just as much.

I kissed my way down her neck around to the sensitive part of her ear until her nails started digging into my back. That's when I sucked the flesh until my mark was left on her skin. I wanted everyone to know she was mine. No man around town would touch her again when they saw it.

Her button up flannel shirt tied up and bared her flat, tanned stomach. It was tight against her body, showing me every curve, but I needed to see more. I worked the buttons and knot open all while continuing to kiss her. What she had underneath that shirt would bring any man to his knees. She wore absolutely nothing, and I was the luckiest son of a bitch in the world. Anna's breasts were full with the perfect teardrop shape. Immediately, I needed to touch them. As I ran my thumbs over her hardened nipples, her back arched off the ground. The rougher my touch became, the more she moved beneath me.

"Please, Wyatt. I need you to touch me."

"Where, Anna?"

"Everywhere."

She reached for the hem of my shirt and ripped it over my head. We took turns removing each other's clothes until we both were completely naked. In front of me, Anna sat with me kneeling between her legs while we studied each other's bodies. She was the sexiest woman I'd ever seen.

Her hands raked down my chest, over my abs until she was gripping me. The way her tiny hand twisted as she ran her fingers up and down my length had me on edge. As much as I wanted to stop her, I couldn't. It felt too fucking good. When her thumb traced over the tip of my hardness, gathering the pre-come that was there, a groan erupted from deep inside me, and something primal snapped to life. I gripped her hair in my hands and laid her down again. My mouth devoured every fucking inch of hers. I couldn't get deep enough.

Corey sounded hot reading the words to me. He stopped more than once to clear his throat or to adjust himself. Yep, he got just as turned on as I did.

Her long leg wrapped around my hip to pull me against her body. As much as I wanted to sink into her, I wanted to continue exploring at the same time. I reached my hand between us and ran my fingers between her lips. She was warm, inviting, and dripping with arousal, which turned me on even more.

"Wyatt, I want to feel you in me."

That was my undoing. Hearing Anna say that and the look in her eyes, I couldn't hold back any longer. Inch by fucking inch, I slid inside her until I couldn't get any deeper. As I began to rock in and out of her, she moved her hips in circles. It felt . . .

The book fell from Corey's hands, and he pounced on me. It was the hottest sex we ever had. The problem that followed that night was he seemed to develop a need to read one of my books in order to get aroused. Literally, Corey needed to read word porn just to get it up. It became an issue when he went through every book in my room. At the time, I only had a few. I was living in an apartment with little storage, and my book collection was at my parents' house, so I kept only a few of my favorites on hand. Thankfully, he never figured out about the three hundred plus books on my tablet.

"Come on, Cass. Don't you have any new books to read?" He started whining every night. I gave him a twenty-five-dollar gift card to a bookstore and sent him packing.

As much as I want you to read to me, I don't want my books to become your "porn." I need to be your fantasy, not my paperbacks.

16. Don't be afraid to show me the real you

Just as I want you to learn about me, I want to learn about you. I want to know what sports you like, how crazy your family is, and what turns you on. Also, it's okay to show your softer side. Even the strongest of men cry. I want to know the parts of you that you don't show to the world, to a certain extent . . .

I had been going to this wine bar for years located directly between my work and my house. It was convenient to pop in on my way home when I'd had a bad day or really any day for that matter, but what made it even more appealing was the new bartender they'd hired a couple of weeks prior. This guy was smoking hot and well worth the overpriced wine that didn't really fit into my tight budget.

Literally, I had been prancing my ass around this bar for a solid week trying to snag his attention. It was time to finally get him to take notice because honestly, I was one more Pinot Grigio away from going into some major debt.

I had shortened my pencil skirt by rolling it a few times,

unbuttoned the two top buttons on my shirt, stuffed my hands down my bra to perk the girls up in a coffee shop window next door, and then gave my hair a good fluff. I got a few funny looks, but I was a girl on a mission, and the guy sitting by the window, drinking his coffee and looking at me like I was deranged, wasn't going to stop me from doing that. Seriously, did he not have a phone to look at or something?

I walked into the winery past the beautiful, high-class sitting area where I would normally sit and made a beeline for the bar area instead. The hostess tried to stop me, but I waved her off. I saw Jackson serving another couple at the far end, so I hopped up onto the chair and settled in. While he chatted with the older couple, I took a long moment to study him like I had been doing every other night. He was classically tall, dark, and handsome. It was his linebacker build, and the natural swagger of a man you just knew was good in bed that had me drooling. He screamed confidence and sex, and I was determined to make him mine.

Finally, he finished serving the drinks to the last two girls at the bar and turned my way. They looked unhappy when he flashed me a smile and grabbed my preferred bottle of wine before he made his way over to me.

"Cassie, good to see you, darling."

Oh, did I forget to mention the accent? Yeah, he had an accent to beat all accents, and it practically melted my panties every time he said "darling" in that Southern drawl of his.

"Hi, Jackson." I practically purred his name, and I leaned in a little closer as he set my glass on the bar and began to pour. I casually sniffed him. As casual as one could be when smelling someone.

"Enjoy," he said as he slid my drink over to me and

turned to walk away.

I slumped back in my seat and took a huge drink of wine as I watched his retreating form. Well, shit. It looked like it was going to be a long night of wooing for me, so I pulled out my phone and started googling random things to talk about to a bartender. Before I knew it, I had a whole list of conversation starters at my fingertips. I just had to wait.

By the end of the night, Jackson was still ignoring me, and I was more than a little tipsy on the bottle of wine I had consumed. Not to mention, I had spent almost a half a day's pay for nothing. He didn't seem interested in any of the topics I chose, and I was really beginning to doubt this sexy ass man was even straight. I mean my assets were pretty much hanging out of my shirt, and he barely even glanced down at them all night.

I was about to grab my wallet, pay my tab, and go home to sulk when he suddenly appeared in front of me.

"So, Cassie, tell me if I'm off base or if I'm being inappropriate, but would you like to have dinner with me sometime?"

In my drunken state, I almost stood up and did a little happy dance, but luckily for everyone in my proximity, I refrained.

I managed to play it cool as we exchanged numbers and made plans to meet at the new Thai place on Saturday. As I made the walk—or should I say stumble—home, I'm practically vibrating with happiness.

During the rest of the week, we exchanged a few texts, and when Saturday rolled around, I shaved, plucked, and scrubbed myself within an inch of my life. I took a taxi to the Thai restaurant so I didn't risk breaking a sweat in the summer heat. The last thing I wanted, after finally scoring a date

with Jackson, was to show up with pit stains. He was standing outside the building when I pulled up. With a wiggle of
my fingers, I waved and added an extra sway to my hips as I
made my way over to him.

After a friendly kiss on my cheek, he led us into the spicy
smelling place.

So here's the thing. I loved spicy foods, but Thai food really wasn't my favorite. It messed with my stomach big time,
but he seemed so excited when he told me about it that I just
couldn't say no. I just hoped to God that my stomach would
hold up until later in the night. Much later.

When we sat down, he looked over the menu and helped
me choose what to order. In my mind, that just made him
even more attractive.

All through dinner, we talked and laughed. He told me
funny stories about the worst pick-up lines he'd heard while
bartending, and I told him about the worst advertising slogans people had come up with. It seemed like we had so
much in common, and have I mentioned how hot he was? He
was really fun to look at.

When the check came, I had already made up my mind
that I was either going back to his place or he was coming
back to mine. It had been so long, and I'd had way too many
failed attempts. I needed to get some loving, and I needed it
badly. I really couldn't have picked a better guy than Jax. I
even gave him his own cute nickname; that was how well this
date was going.

He paid our check and gave me the look. You know the
look, ladies, the "are you or are you not down to fuck" look. I
was down, I was so down, so I gave him the look right back.
Which was probably me looking like I had something in my

eye, but that was just a minor detail. We made our way outside, and he directed me to the parking garage, where he'd parked his beautiful Mercedes. Honestly, how much do they pay at that fucking wine bar? Maybe I should get a part-time job there and get a discount.

I glided onto the smooth leather seats and breathed in that new car smell. He was getting more handsome by the second, and I wanted to jump his bones. My eyes followed him as he walked with that sexy swagger over to the driver's side and got in.

"My place or yours, darling?"

Oh, that darling got me every time.

"Yours," I said, leaning across the console to give his cheek a little kiss. I would prefer mine, but I couldn't chance Razor "little shit" Quinn screwing this up for me again.

I sat back in my seat and buckled my belt as he pulled out of the garage. I watched the downtown lights and reveled in the thought of how lucky I was to have had such an amazing date that was finally going to land me in bed with this hot specimen of a man.

That was until it all went to hell in a handbasket. I thought I heard a little noise, and I peeked over at Jackson. It must have been the seat—remember that squeaky noise leather made when I was with Jordan? Yeah, it was like that. He showed no reaction, so I chalked it up to my imagination, but then to my horror, he leaned over toward the door, lifted his leg, and let it rip. I'm sure I didn't have to explain further, but in case I did, he farted. It wasn't just a little one either; oh, hell no, this was the fart to end all farts. It was loud, and it was powerful.

Much to my dismay, he turned and smiled at me as he

settled back into his seat.

"Damn Thai food does it to me every time."

I might have forgiven a little slip-up, but this guy actually seemed proud of the gigantic amount of gas that came out of him.

As if this situation couldn't get any worse, the smell hit me. I turned in my seat and put my shirt over my nose. I wasn't sure what to do. Every few seconds, a new noise came from him. It sounded like a flute and tuba were stuck up his ass, and my eyes were seriously starting to water. I frantically reached for the button to roll the window down, except it wasn't there. Come to find out, in this fancy ass car, all the controls were hidden, and I had no clue where to even start looking. My eyes were beginning to burn, and Sir Farts-a-lot just kept on playing his tune.

"For the love of God, roll my fucking window down!" I screamed as I kept searching for the damn button.

I guess having my shirt pulled over my nose garbled my words because he gave me a questioning look. I'd had enough; I started fumbling with the car door. If I had to, I was going to dive out of this gas chamber. He looked concerned as he guided the car to a stop on the side of the road.

"What are you doing, darling?"

His accent was no longer cute. I was dying at the hands of his flatulence. I didn't care anymore if he had the best dick on the planet and knew how to use it. There was no way in hell I was spending one more second in his car. I pulled the door handle and jumped out, taking in a huge lungful of air as I did so.

It took me a few seconds of pacing the sidewalk to finally feel like I couldn't smell him as badly anymore. I was sure it was going to take much longer to get the mental pictures out of my head.

I made my way back to his car, grabbed my purse, and called a cab. He looked upset and offered to wait with me, but he was leaning over to let another one rip as he asked the question, so I declined.

When I finally made it home that night, I had to take an extra-long bubble bath and light ten scented candles to try to get the smell out of my nose. I thought about sniffing Lysol, but when I called Emma, she suggested against shoving disinfectant up my nose.

Needless to say, I want to know all of the little things about the man I'm seeing, but we can skip the part about knowing that your gas doesn't smell like roses.

It took me a few days alone to get over the Thai food incident.

17. Must understand that some days I need to be a recluse

You need to be able to handle the fact that some days, I simply just need to be alone with only my blanket and ice cream as company. There is no need for you to send me a hundred text messages on my phone or come over unannounced to check up on me. You need to be secure enough to know that even if I don't answer those messages, or calls, or in some cases, the door, it doesn't mean I don't like you. I just need a break from life.

A few weeks after the incident with Jackson, I was on my way home from work. It was a Friday, and I'd had a hell of a week. Usually, I would have stopped at the wine bar to have a few drinks and unwind, but I was trying to avoid that place at all cost. Sure, I still received a few text messages and calls from Jackson. I even responded a few times. He was hotter than sin, but I was still trying to get the gas chamber incident out of my head. I hadn't had any luck yet, but I was trying to keep an open mind. Since the bar wasn't an option, I decided to stop at the store and stock up for a weekend full of doing absolutely nothing.

I grabbed my shopping cart and took off for the frozen food aisle. I tossed in some frozen meals before making my way to the adult beverage section. It only took me ten minutes of shopping before I was fully prepared for my weekend of either being a recluse or for an impending apocalypse, it was hard to tell which. In my cart, I had tossed five bottles of wine, three frozen fettuccine meals, two cartons of ice cream, popcorn, and those vegetable potato chips—because I needed something healthy in there. I also stocked up on a few of my favorite magazines that I hadn't had time to read in a while.

The lady at the counter gave me a concerned look, but I didn't give one shit. She just didn't know the therapeutic powers of hiding under the covers all weekend and basically becoming a sloth. It really was good for your soul.

Instead of having to walk six blocks with all of my necessities, I decided to splurge and hail a cab. I was home in under five minutes and ready to commence sloth mode, but first, I had to walk Little Shit. I set my bags down on the kitchen counter and grabbed Razor's leash.

We were almost to the dog park, and as my luck would have it, I ran into Jackson on the street. Of all the people in this city for me to happen to run into, I ran into him. I looked up at the sky and cursed my luck as I watched him approach.

"Cassie? Is that you?"

For a split-second, I thought about pretending I was someone else, but I didn't think he would fall for it.

"Hi, Jackson."

At that point, Razor had stopped sniffing the bush and was barking his head off. I gave his leash a tug, but that didn't deter the little shit.

"It's so good to see you. What are you up to tonight, darling?"

"Just walking my dog," I said, gesturing toward Razor.

He glanced down and watched as Razor jumped around like an angry piranha out of the water.

"Cute dog, but I meant what are you doing later? I was thinking about calling you."

I wasn't about to tell him that my plans involved only wine, ice cream, and trashy magazines. Instead, I told a teensy weensy white lie.

"Probably getting together with a few friends."

"Oh, yeah? Where are you going?"

Well, fuck. That was why I didn't like to lie. One turned into another and before you knew it, it had escalated so much that I didn't even know what the truth was.

I looked down at Razor and pulled on his leash again. It was impossible for me to have a conversation when he was practically foaming at the mouth. Seriously, he looked like a rabid dog. Guard up, fur sticking on end, paws grounded, and he was making these little growly sounds. "I'm not sure yet. I really should be going."

"I'll walk you home," he said with a charming smile and those dimples. Fucking dimples.

"That's not necessary."

"It's dark out, Cassie."

I felt like the conversation could've gone on forever, so I finally just conceded.

We didn't say much as we walked side by side back to my apartment. When we reach my building, I turned and thanked him before he got any ideas that he may be invited up. Nope, that was not happening. Even if he wasn't Sir

Farts-a-lot, I had plans, and those plans didn't include any type of socializing.

He frowned a little at my dismissal but gave me a brief kiss on my cheek before stepping back.

I let myself into my building and took the four flights up to my door. I was huffing and puffing and cursing Razor all to hell by the time I got inside. They really should get an elevator in this building.

Finally ready to collapse on my couch, I shed all of my clothes and pulled on an old t-shirt. I grabbed my favorite fluffy blanket, a carton of vanilla ice cream, and a bottle of red wine as I made my way to my couch. I'd already spread my magazines out on my coffee table, which really was just an old trunk that I had converted. It was great for storage.

I sank into my couch cushions and twisted off the cap on the wine bottle. Whoever invented twist-off caps needed to be hugged. No glass was required, and I didn't have to worry about spilling it.

I grabbed a magazine and started flipping through the pages while I shoved a spoon of ice cream into my mouth.

As I was reading about the latest Kardashian drama, my phone started ringing. I glanced over at my kitchen counter and decided that was just too far away and that the damn thing could just keep ringing. I was in sloth mode, after all. I went back to reading, but my phone seemed to be going off every minute, distracting me. After the tenth ring and the fifth ding of a text message, I gave up reading and glared at the phone, willing it to shut up with my mind. When that didn't work, I got up from my couch and cursed the whole way.

I snatched the annoying gadget, swiped my finger across

the screen, and of course, it was Jackson. Without even checking the texts, I switched the phone to silent and tossed it back on the counter. I was already up, so I grabbed the chips, my vegetable for the evening, before making my way back to the couch.

Twenty minutes later, while my left hand was deep in the bag and the bottle of wine was to my right, the buzzer to my apartment started going off. My head snapped in that direction right as Razor dove off the couch and started doing circles around the welcome mat while barking so hard his body was lifting off the ground.

Motherfucker. I put the bottle of wine to my lips and took a huge gulp. I was not answering that door. It wasn't happening. I didn't care if it was some famous hot guy standing outside that door waiting to fuck me into oblivion; I wasn't getting up.

I sank down lower into the pillows on my couch to muffle the noise a little, but it didn't help much. Between the buzzer and Razor's barking, the noise level in my tiny apartment was at an all-time high.

Suddenly, it stopped. Razor tilted his head to the side while I mimicked the movement. Both our ears perked up as we listened for a second. I breathed a sigh of relief when it didn't start back up. Razor laid down on the mat while I flipped my magazine back open and continued my reading. Just as I brought the bottle back to my lips, a knock on the door scared me enough to make me spill the red wine all down my chin and onto my shirt.

Razor started back up again, and I wanted to scream. *What's a girl gotta do to get her recluse on?*

"Cassie? You in there?"

Are you kidding me with this shit? That voice belonged to no other but Jackson the Farter.

I sank back down into the pillows and pulled the blanket up higher until it almost covered my head. I thought that if I hid, then surely, he would go away. No such luck. There was a little window beside my front door. Originally, I thought it was charming. Added something extra to my small living room since most apartments in the city didn't have that. But right then, I was cursing it all to hell because there he was, looking through the little crack in the blinds.

"I see you," he said like a peeping Tom. He sounded so fucking excited about that little fact, and I didn't know whether to cry or laugh.

The eye I had exposed from under the covers glared in his direction. I couldn't see much of him, but I could see part of his ridiculous smile. Honestly, the man was acting like I should have given him a medal for not only, somehow, getting into my apartment building, but also for finding which door was mine. I had to wonder how many windows he peeked in until he found the right one.

I continued to stare at him in silence, hoping that either this was just a bad dream or that he would go away if I laid still enough.

"I see you have some wine. Are those veggie crisps? I love those."

By this point, he'd smashed his face against the window. Right then, I made the decision that I didn't care how good looking the man was; he was insane.

I took both the bag of chips and wine, pulled them under the blanket, and pretended I was sleeping.

"Are you okay, Cassie? Are you sick?"

I could hear him knocking on my window, trying to get my attention, but I did my best to block him out.

"I'll just be out here if you need me."

Great. That was just fucking great.

I consumed that whole bag of veggie goodness and my entire bottle of wine while under my blanket fort. I wasn't coming out unless the apartment was on fire, and even then, it was iffy.

I must have passed out because when I woke up the next morning, Razor was licking the salt residue off my fingers and I was cuddled up to the empty bottle of wine. I pushed Razor off me and stood up. I raised my arms above my head and stretched.

"Oh, good. You're awake. I was starting to get worried," the voice said from outside.

I screamed like a little girl at the voice, and Razor, who had been eating the crumbs off the couch, started barking. I looked toward the window, and sure enough, Jackson's eye was once again looking back at me.

"What in the fuck are you doing, you crazy son of a bitch?" I screamed. Maybe not the best way to greet someone, but had he been there all night? He was certifiably insane.

"Darling, don't get so upset. You fell asleep, and I thought it would be rude to just leave."

I walked the short distance to the door and grabbed my umbrella. Enough was enough. I unlocked my door and opened it enough so that I could fit the umbrella through the crack and I pointed it at him.

"If you aren't away from my door in less than twenty seconds, I will shove this up your ass and open it."

"Darling, that's a bit extreme."

At that, I wanted to roll my eyes. This guy wanted to talk about extremes? Instead, I started counting. He must have gotten the point and realized I wasn't kidding because, by the time I got to ten, he was gone.

I closed my door and locked it before looking down at Razor, who was looking at me like he approved of my behavior.

I spent the rest of the day happily lounging on my couch in recluse mode. I did pass Jackson on the street one day, but it was raining, and I had my trusty umbrella. He looked like he was going to approach me, but as soon as I went to lower my rain protection device, he changed his direction.

So if you are dating me, I need you to realize there will be days or even entire weekends when I just want to be alone. I want to eat my snacks, drink my wine, and read my trashy magazines or books in peace. If you can't handle that, then you can't be with me because like I said, reclusive sloth mode is good for my soul, and I won't change that for anyone.

On the flip side, please call in advance if you want to do something. My time is precious to me.

18. Must be able to make plans

I don't want to pick where we are going all the time. Actually, I'll probably never want to pick what we are doing. You make plans and tell me or just surprise me. Either way, just make a damn plan! I don't need a man-child who doesn't know how to make a decision; I need one who's Mr. Decisive.

For the most part, I was a planner. That was a total lie—I liked to know what was going on, the exact time it was going on, and have a list of who it was going on with. Not only would I set a reminder the day before, an hour before, and at the time of, but I also kept a little day planner with me open to the current date. My other favorite office supply was Post-it notes. No joke—my computer was surrounded by the sticky suckers with daily goals. As I accomplished said tasks, I tossed the note. Why? Because it kept me focused, and I never forgot anything, but it was also very satisfying to crinkle up those pieces of paper and say, "Yes, I got that done. Next, please."

When I met Slade, he was running late for an appointment. I was walking out the door of one of my favorite coffee houses when he smacked into me.

"I'm sorry. That was totally my fault. I really need to start setting my alarm earlier," he said as he looked at his watch.

My eyes remained focused on my coffee cup as I was doing the whole three-finger grip and holding it straight out so it didn't get on my dress. Luckily, my coffee stayed put. When he spoke, my gazed darted to him. His voice was on the deeper side, very appealing, and made my ears perk up at attention. Much like Razor "Little Shit" did when I offered him a cookie.

"No harm, no foul," I replied because it sounded cool in my head, but when I actually said it, it sounded terrible.

He was handsomely debonair in his suit. It fit him too well. There was not a speck of facial hair to be found, the hair on the top of his head was neatly combed in place, and his jaw had that chiseled look to it. I never truly said I had a type before, but if I did, he was it. The man looked like he could own a boardroom, which usually meant he was equally controlling in all things. He offered to buy me another coffee, even though mine was full. I head to the trash and threw away almost six dollars.

We walked up to the counter to order, but Slade seemed to be having a hard time deciding. The barista was rather annoyed and finally suggested he just stick to his regular. Since I had only just ordered, she asked if there was anything wrong with my drink. I, once again, faked that I was in desperate need of caffeine if I was going to get through the day at work. After we had our order, we sat at one of the tables and talked for close to two hours.

"I thought you were late the way you came barreling through the door," I said to Slade.

He looked at his watch again. "I was, but it can wait. It's Saturday, after all, and I'm supposed to be off. I just needed to tie up some loose ends at the office."

He told me he was a stockbroker at a large firm, and that turned me on more than it should have. It was a powerful and risky position, putting your money in today's market. I was getting to an age where I was going to have to invest money in my future, and it was like some divine intervention that Slade was sent to me. I totally could date the guy and secretly get some investments tips on the side. That was what I did too, and we dated for close to a year.

On the first date, Slade was about five minutes late. Not a big deal. It gave me a little extra time to get my A-game on. When I asked him how I should dress, his response was, "Let's wing it."

Here's a little clue, men—women did not like to wing it on the first date. We want to impress you. I wanted to know if we were going horseback riding because I was going to find a spectacular pair of jeans that fit my ass just so. Or maybe we were going to a casual bar where I could wear my pocket dress because pockets made it causal, but it still clung to Peaches and Rose just right. And if you told me we were going to a hot new club, you could be damn sure I was going to wear a low-cut top, so when we danced, my boobs would be ever so slightly on display for you. I needed details.

I made a judgment call. He was a clean-cut guy in a suit, and I figured he was not the type to do any of the above. The little black dress I chose could be multi-functional, depending on the shoes I wore. I had three different pairs set up by the front door, and once I saw what Slade was wearing, which was a suit minus the jacket, I chose the four-inch red satin peep toe pumps. I also had matching lipstick in my purse, just in case.

"Have you decided where we are going?" I asked him as I slipped into his sports car. It was the color of smoke, lush, leather, and sexy. I didn't know what model it was, but it screamed money.

"A dinner cruise around Manhattan. We have to hurry if we want to make it. I scored the tickets last minute from a client of mine."

Although we weaved in and out of traffic, the car handled it like a champ. Plus, the way Slade expertly handled the car was hot. He kept one hand on the wheel and one hand on the shifter all while keeping up small talk. We made it to the dock just in time. Slade even held my hand as we ran up the ramp.

Dinner was elegant. After dinner, we had cocktails on the main deck. The scenery was stunning, and Slade was the perfect balance of gentleman and touchy. I even got to make out with him in his hot car when he dropped me off that night.

The first date went so well, I was quick to accept a second. Slade was ten minutes late for that. And once again, he didn't give me any indication of where we were going.

By the third date, he was fifteen minutes late. Do you see a pattern?

After almost a year of never knowing if he was going to show up, be on time, or ask me what I wanted to do for the night, or even if we had any definitive plans at all, I grew bored. Slade always complimented me on my organizational skills. Mainly, my Post-it collection and how it was such a great way to stay on task. I put my skills to work that night.

At seven o'clock, I made sure I was dressed in my best yoga pants and my practically see-through college t-shirt. My hair was thrown up in the messiest of buns with one of those old-time scrunchies while my face was void of any makeup—not even a swipe of ChapStick was on my lips. Take that, Mr. Can't make plans or show up on time.

At eight thirty, an hour and a half late, he showed up. The door buzzer informed me of his arrival.

"Can I help you?" I asked as I looked out the peephole.

"It's me, Cass."

"I'm sorry; did you see the note on the door?"

I had put a little Post-it on the door promptly at seven.

"Yes," he said.

"Did you read it?"

"Yes. What am I supposed to do?"

"Read it again," I told him.

"Okay, I just did."

"No, read it out loud."

"If this is my boyfriend of almost a year and you are late tonight, don't knock."

"And are you late?" I ask him.

"How can I be late if I didn't let you know when I'd be here?"

Ding, ding, ding.

I opened the door slightly and put another note on the door.

"Call first and make plans," he reads. "You should know that we always have plans at seven."

I picked up the marker I had waiting and wrote. Then I did the same; I opened the door and stuck the note on it.

"It's eight thirty, you ass . . . Fuck, Cass, come on. Open up. So I'm a little late. What's the big deal?"

I was prepared for that response. This time, I slid the note under the door. It said . . .

I've added together all the minutes you've been late. I want you to take that number and subtract it from the number of times you actually had a plan a day ahead of time, and you know what the total is?

I looked through the peephole and saw him calculating. His eyes were so far rolled back in his head as he tried to come up with a number, and this was the answer I got, "Five."

Where in the hell did he get five? Like five minutes, five hours, or five days? Over three thousand seven hundred was more like it.

I broke it down for him on the next note.

Over sixty hours of my life was wasted on not knowing if we actually had a date. That's too much for me. I could have been painting my toes, getting a facial, or even deep conditioning my hair.

"That can't be right?" he questioned.

I finally open the door. "It's totally right. And I'm not feeling up to rushing and getting ready for wherever you want to go tonight. So have fun."

"Are you breaking up with me?"

I handed him my last note attached to the gifts I got him. A planner, calendar, Post-its, and colored pen. The colored pens were a lot of fun when you color coordinated with activities.

He opened the card that simply said, "Yes."

For about two weeks, I kept getting messages from Slade. How he would change, be more punctual, and how he was even using notes on his computer.

My reply was simple. If you could remember to text me every night at eight o'clock, I'd consider it.

He tried. He also failed miserably. Right then, I decided I

needed a man who was a planner. And not just one who was a planner, but one who also owned a planner and used it. I was just anal like that.

After that, I decided a man in a suit was not my type. Okay, maybe he still was, but I really needed someone different. A bad boy.

19. Talk dirty to me

When a guy tells you exactly what he's going to do to your body before he even touches you, that's hotness on a whole different level. Make me squirm, make me beg, make me wet all over, but for the love of all things good in bed, please make sure you know what you're talking about. Talking sexy is one thing; completely unsexy talk is just plain wrong.

Noah and I met at a mutual friend's Christmas party while, unknowingly, we both walked under the mistletoe. Apparently, at that ugly sweater party, there was a rule that you must kiss if you and another person, either sex, were caught underneath.

"Want to give them a memory to last?" Noah asked me.

I was game for spreading a little holiday cheer. "Ho, ho, ho."

He quickly grabbed the back of my head and brought my mouth to his in a lip lock to die for. I wasn't expecting his kiss to affect me like it did, but it was raw, dirty, and made what I had under the mistletoe very excited. The kiss only lasted for about three minutes, far too short for me, but probably too long to be appropriate for not even knowing his name.

Once the lip lock moment ended, he held me close as he introduced himself. After I had given him my name, we parted ways and mingled with the other guests although the two of us kept stealing glances at each other until we finally got some alone time.

"Come here, little girl, and sit on my lap. Tell me all the dirty things you want for Christmas."

I hadn't realized what his sweater said with all the kissing, but it made me laugh and made what he just said a little less creepy. It said, "I'm not Santa but feel free to sit on my lap." Me, I just found a sweater that I bedazzled to death.

Nothing happened that night. Just a lot of conversation and some more mistletoe action.

It was two weeks before I saw Noah again. With the holidays, he traveled back home to be with his family. There was a lot of hot texting, though, and two weeks of foreplay was thirteen days too long.

I was more than ready to get down to business tonight. My dry spell lasted from my breakup with Slade until, I pray to God, tonight. This morning's text from him had me raring to go.

I can't wait to have my lips on yours again and your body wrapped around mine.

I had drinks ready, along with something baking in the oven for when he arrived. I only sampled a sip or three of the wine to calm my nerves. Okay, maybe it was a few big gulps that added up to a glass, but I was jittery and pacing, waiting for him to show. Which he did right on time too—scoring big points.

"Hi," I said almost shyly. My heart started racing out of excitement and complete lust for this man. I leaned against the door while he leaned against the frame.

"Hey, gorgeous," he said, and I swooned or moaned; it could have been a little of both.

I quickly stepped aside to let him inside. He looked around the apartment.

I looked at him. He looked at me.

I pointed at the wine. He grabbed the glass and chugged it. I did the same.

He raised his eyebrow. I raised mine back.

It was all so very intense. This was all the buildup we needed.

"Enough of the small talk. Let's just clear the sexually charged air, shall we?" Noah asked as he moved a step closer to me. Then he took another step. On the third step, he lowered his mouth to mine in a steamy kiss. It was aggressive and needy with a hint of kapow.

When we broke apart, I finally got to respond. "Are we just going to make out all night?"

The corner of his mouth turned up in a knowing smirk. He lowered his head and whispered in my ear, "No, Cass. I think it's time we fuck."

Not wanting to waste any more time, I led him to the bedroom, more like he led me while I directed the way. As we walked down the hall, he kissed the hell out of me. Most of our clothes were on the floor because they weren't needed anymore. All that remained was our underclothes. Like I said, two weeks of foreplay was enough.

It took me by surprise when he pushed me on the bed and climbed on top of me. Okay, that wasn't the surprising part; it was what he said next that gave me pause.

"Who's your daddy?" he asked as he gave me an awkward

slap on the thigh.

"What?"

"Who's your daddy, baby?"

There are two words that shouldn't be said in the same sentence while getting ready to do the deed: daddy and baby. But I decided to roll with it. "You are. And what are you going to do to me?"

Here's the thing, when we texted, it was hot, but here in person, I wondered if I was texting the right number.

"You want daddy to talk dirty? Tell you what I'm going to do to this hot body?"

What I really wanted was for him to not to refer to himself as daddy again, but the second part sounded good. Wrong.

"Are you moist?"

No, he didn't. That was the third word not to be said. Because gross.

"You mean wet?"

"Is your flower dripping?" he asked. I almost gagged and laughed simultaneously.

"Oh, god," I groaned, but he took it the wrong way.

"Yeah, baby. But it's daddy when we're in here."

The bile from my stomach rose up more.

"I'm going to lick you with my tongue until you're gushing. Then I'm going to put my erect penis in your petite flower, screw you until it blooms, and fill you with my spunk."

This time, I actually burst out laughing. He went from hot to gross to talking like a junior high teacher—which he was, by the way—to gross again in a matter of seconds.

Noah pushed up on his hands while mine wiped the tears from my eyes.

"What? I thought you like dirty talk," he said. That only made me laugh harder.

"You thought that was dirty?"

"You seemed to like it when we text," he said as he moved off me.

The moment was gone. I was going to stay in my dry spell a little longer.

"I don't even know where to begin. That was just wrong on so many levels. I'm sorry, Noah. I'm not ready for this."

The junior high teacher in him took that the wrong way too. "I can wait until you're ready. No rush."

We got dressed, and he kissed me on the cheek good night. The next week, he tried to have phone sex with me. When the words member, vagina, and squirt were used in the same sentence, I hung up.

There were now officially thirteen words not to be used while talking dirty to Cass, all of which were mentioned above. Use them and you were guaranteed not to get any action.

After writing my list and the memories of the ghosts from dates past, I actually shook. It took finishing off the wine and passing out from exhaustion to get me over the trauma of remembering everything.

Part Two

When fantasy and reality collide, literally

The sound of Emma's ringtone on my phone wakes me. She knows if I get woken up, I tended to be a little less than happy, but it's already ten o'clock so she's mildly safe.

Emma is one of those girls who wakes up with a smile on her face. I, on the other hand, have perfected my resting bitch face until I drink at least one cup of coffee. Sometimes two. Since I was up until three in the morning writing that list and traveling down memory lane, it's definitely a two cup kind of morning.

"Good morning, sunshine." She says it in a way that it was more sung than simple words.

My response was more of a grumbling sound than actual words, but somehow, she understood it.

"Someone had a late night." She says like she's talking to

a baby. It's a good thing I love her, or I would have hung up by now.

"Grab your coffee, and I'll pick you up in an hour. I want you well caffeinated and showered. We have plans."

The smell of my favorite morning beverage hit me as soon as I enter the kitchen. Buying the coffeepot with a timer was the best idea ever; it's always ready right on time and stays warm for as long as I need it to. The only thing it can't do is deliver it straight to my bed. That and add my required amount of creamer.

After the first cup, I find the energy to shower. Since I have no idea what we were doing, I walk around in a t-shirt, bra, and panties, my usual around the house wear. Pants and I do not get along. Whoever decided to make the offending garment should suffer a life of wearing constricting clothes in hell. Yes, I wear them when I go out. Even those tight ones that make my ass look superb, but it doesn't mean I like it. Not one bit.

Emma bounds through the front door looking beautifully low maintenance. Her dark brown hair was piled on top of her head in one of those knots she does. Whenever I try to do my hair like hers, it looks like I lost a fight with the hair tie. What puts a smile on my face is that she is not dressed up; she's wearing her signature leggings and a simple t-shirt to match. Mentally, I did a happy dance that jeans will not be involved in today's activities.

"Here, I brought you a present," she said as she handed me a gift bag filled with tissue paper.

"What's the occasion?"

Em loves presents. In high school, she used to leave gifts in my locker. Usually on Mondays. It would be anything from a new pen to a flavored lip-gloss, but she wrapped it up all pretty to make me feel special.

"It's what you are wearing out today."

I pulled the paper from the bag and threw it on the nearby counter. Inside was a pair of leggings similar to the ones she was wearing. Where hers were red with wine glass images covering them, mine were teal. It just happened to be each of our favorite colors.

"Thanks. I think."

"Just put them on."

For months, she was telling me to try these leggings, but I kept refusing. They just weren't me. Remember, I prefer to be pantless.

"First, tell me where we are going."

She gets a big, excited smile on her face while she magically produces a bottle of wine. "Drunk painting."

"What the hell is that? It's only eleven in the morning."

"It's one of those classes where you bring wine and they teach you to paint. I figured we would eat some breakfast first. Then we can Uber it. It's at one, so you need to get dressed."

Actually, that sounds fun. While I get dressed, Em starts cooking our healthy breakfast.

"Why didn't I try these things sooner?" I scream as I come out wearing my new favorite pants.

"Told you so."

"I had to check twice just to make sure I was wearing pants."

She laughs. "Didn't I tell you it's as close to being nude without actually being naked?"

I totally get it. I fear I might be switching my yoga pants for some of these funky patterned leggings. Damn her.

After we finish breakfast and got to the class, we sit at our easel. The room is filled with women, and a male or two of every age, looking for a day away from reality. The sound of corks popping fill the room. The instructor, Chandler, is hot. Sadly for us, he is taken, and his boyfriend is there to help, who is also equally hot.

We are informed that we would be painting a tranquil forest scene of birch trees and falling leaves. Chandler's painting is exquisite.

"I don't think I can paint like that," I whisper to Em.

"It's about the journey, not how well you paint."

I look at her like she has two heads. She sounds like a fortune cookie. We both bust out laughing.

"I can see we already have our troublemakers of the class." Chandler looks at us with a raised eyebrow.

"Sorry," we both say in unison.

"Remember, this isn't about being the best artist, or how well you paint. It's about letting your creative juices flow, and of course, your wine can flow as well," he says as he raises a glass.

The first thing we were to paint was the sky background. It was easy enough, and it allowed people to talk, drink, and paint.

"Why were you up so late?" Em asks me.

"My dating adventure with Dustin inspired me."

She gives me that look, the one that says elaborate, please.

"I'm tired of going out with the wrong men."

"Amen, sister," the woman next to me says. She clinks wine glasses with me then goes back to her painting.

"So last night I started a list," I continue.

"What kind of list?" Em asks.

"Basically, the qualities I want in a man."

"How are you going to find that man? Are you planning to put an ad out in the paper?"

That is an idea, but it is turned out to be a mini novel. The price alone for that ad would cost me a mini fortune. "I haven't thought about it yet. I only got as far as starting to write it."

"Jeez, Cass. How long of a list are we talking?"

I roll my eyes, trying to remember how long it is at this point. "I think I filled my journal."

"My god, that sounds like it's more of a contract."

The woman next to Emma adds her two cents as we move to painting the sky "I signed a dating contract once."

Em turns to her. "No shit, like a 'dating' contract."

"Like the kind that allowed him to tie me up, blindfold me, and spank my ass all night."

"That's hot," I say.

"Best night of my life."

"Only one night?" Emma asks.

"Yep, one night of pure ecstasy was what the contract was for. The asshole ruined me for all other men," she says with slight sadness.

Lucky lady.

"Anyway, you don't need a man list," Em says to me.

"Yes, I do."

"No, you don't."

"Why's that?" I ask curiously. She has the same write it down and solve the problem personality.

"I have a feeling you'll meet someone when you least expect it. He's going to sweep you off your feet and rock your world and bed at the same time."

"You're such a romantic. And I highly doubt it," I say as I take a sip of wine.

"You doubt me?" she says as she feigns being offended.

"I do, oh great one. Besides, I'm not looking for anyone."

"Then you'll definitely be meeting him soon," the woman next to us says.

"Okay, everyone. We are going to move on to the trees." Chandler explains the mixture of brushes, colors, and paint strokes we would be using. It seems simple enough. He is great at making painting look easy.

Between painting, Em and I chat with everyone near us. The last part we paint is the leaves on the trees the autumn scene. The colors are amazing—oranges, reds, and yellows. When I feel like my painting is complete, I grab a second glass of wine. Em finishes around the same time as I do. We stand to stretch. Sitting for almost two hours on a less than comfortable chair is killer on the derriere.

As I turn to look at my picture, I almost spit out my wine. Then I glance back and forth between my and Em's pictures, and I end up choking on the sip I had just taken.

"Are you okay?" Emma asks.

It takes a second to recover from the coughing slash laughing fit. "Look at our pictures."

"What? I don't think they are that bad."

I pull her back a few steps to help her see what I see. "You don't see it, do you?"

"No, Cass."

"Oh, my god, Em. Mine looks like a vajayjay on display in full bush mode, and yours looks like a penis ejaculating." I point out the shape of my trees, and it totally looks like a vagina. When I start pointing out hers, Emma's eyes go wide.

"Well, shit. I see it now. At least it will be a conversation starter. I'm totally hanging this in my entryway."

I could see it, each of us hanging our painting for everyone to stop and study it. They would wonder if they are imagining seeing dick and pussy pictures. Was it on purpose? I would play dumb and say I don't see it.

The entire class stops to check out our masterpiece of profanity. Everyone agrees they look like male and female parts.

"Best paintings ever," I say as I high-five my best bitch.

20. Accept my crazy

I have many personalities. Sometimes, the crazy in me comes out more than other times. I don't necessarily mean hit you with a frying pan crazy; I'm talking about those random thoughts that pop in my head that make you look at me with wide eyes. Be one with my crazy. Embrace it. Join it.

Every Monday morning, I feel out of sorts, and today is no exception. My hair won't do just right, my hands seem to have forgotten how to put on makeup, the zipper to my favorite skirt will break, a button will pop on my shirt, exposing the girls, and I'm almost guaranteed not to be able to find my phone or keys.

It takes me almost thirty minutes longer to get ready to leave my house than it does on any other day of the week. I usually walk to work, but this morning, I decide to risk my life in a cab just so I can try to finish my makeup in the backseat. It's all about time management. The cab driver swerves all over the New York streets, and I swear he's doing it on purpose. After I poke myself in the eye with my eyeliner pencil for the third time, I shoot him a dirty look before deciding to hell with it.

The only benefit to his erratic driving is that I arrive at my building five minutes early, and I manage a cat eye look with my eyeliner. Maybe the cab ride wasn't for nothing after all.

I take the elevator to the tenth floor where the advertising firm is located. Our receptionist, Bettie, is always the first to greet me with a wave as I pass.

"Looking good, Cass. And I love your makeup today."

Bettie must be ninety years old. Not to mention, she's blind as a bat. Throughout the day, you can see her raise and lower her glasses to look at the numbers on the phone. But she's sweet and makes the best pound cake, which is exactly why I should keep walking here.

I sit down at my desk and start shuffling through the papers I left lying in an organized folder on Friday. That's when my phone dings to remind me I have a meeting across town in an hour. Only it isn't for VYBE. It's for my company. I haven't told my boss, but I am trying to start my own agency, Quinntessential advertising. I only have a grand total of one client, the same one I'm supposed to meet in an hour, who I will lose if I don't get my ass in gear. Running my own agency was always my plan, and, usually, I'm way more organized and would have scheduled this for after work, but apparently, I didn't with this one. I think the excitement of getting a perspective client made me say yes.

Another thing, on the days I have appointments or at least plan to have them, I will drive to work. Of course, today is the day I forget that and not bring my car to work with me. Not only do I have to get all the paperwork together, but I also have to figure out how to get myself all the way across town in less than an hour.

"You've got to be shitting me. Fucking motherfucker," I mumble to myself.

"What did you say, dear?" Bettie asks. She's also slightly hard of hearing.

"I said what a lovely day. Fantastic, Mother Nature."

"Oh, yes. It's supposed to be a lovely week."

I need a plan. I don't even know the person's name of who I'm meeting with because they only put the company name down, Lase Designs. No phone number, nothing. Canceling is not an option. It would only look bad on my part. Why didn't I use my sticky note system to prepare yesterday? Today just keeps getting better and better.

Think, Cass. Think.

I send Emma a quick text to bail me out once again. I had her fake that she passed out and I was her only way of getting home.

I have fifty minutes to get home, get my laptop, and meet my client. I can do this.

In record-breaking time, and after a hefty tip, the cab gets me to my apartment. After gathering my papers, hailing yet another cab, and almost having three heart attacks in the backseat of the death trap, I somehow make it to the trendy coffee shop right on time.

I smooth my hair down and check my teeth for any lipstick smudges before walking inside. It makes me a little nervous that I don't know who I'm looking for. I mean what am I supposed to do, walk up to every person and ask them if they are with Lase Designs? I don't even know if I'm meeting a male or female, so that's not happening. I choose a table in the corner and start pulling out the paperwork I'll need.

Today's meeting should be quick and simple. We are

basically just going over what the company is looking for, and how I can help them expand their business.

I'm leaned over in my chair, digging through my briefcase, when I feel someone standing beside the table. Naturally, I assume this is the waitress, and without glancing up, I place my order.

"I'll just have a double caf, non-fat, caramel mocha swirl latte with no whipped cream, please."

I continue shuffling through my papers, but after a minute, I notice the figure still hasn't moved. I'm in no mood for this today, and I need that damn coffee. At the office, I usually have my second cup by now, but with my stupidity, I didn't get it. It makes me moody. I glance up, ready to ask what the problem is, but when my eyes meet his, I almost swallow my tongue. Jesus, this waiter is hot and extremely overdressed.

I let my eyes travel back over him a moment. I mean he's just standing there in his black suit pants, herringbone tie, and a blue dress shirt—which all look like they are made just for him. The way fabric stretches across his wide chest is extremely distracting, but I figure I might as well appreciate the beauty before me and toss him a good tip for just being so damn pretty.

I'm not normally attracted to this kind of man, though. He has the whole bad boy look with dirty blond hair that is cut long on top and shaved short on the side and motorcycle boots. Seriously, he looks like he stepped off the cover of one of my books, and he looks so familiar.

He clears his throat and tucks his hands in his pockets while I look back up at his face, which is equally fun to admire. A neatly trimmed beard covers his strong jaw, and his eyes are the lightest shade of blue I think I've ever seen.

One perfect eyebrow quirks up, and his luscious mouth forms into a smirk.

"Hello, Cass."

His voice sends a tingle to places I most certainly don't need to be tingling in, especially in the middle of a busy coffee shop. I shake off my lust-filled thoughts and try to figure out how he knows my name. I've never been to this coffee shop, so I know he's never served me before.

I fall into the nearest chair as the realization of who he is hits me like a bucket of cold water. It's been a long time since I've seen him, and damn, he grew up to be a fine specimen of a man. I would remember those eyes from anywhere. My eye starts twitching as the recognition of who he is sets in.

"Jason? Jason Carter?" I ask in shock.

He smiles, sits down in the chair across from me, and places his notebook on the table. His long legs take up a lot of room and brush against mine. I have to stop myself from checking him out again because when he grazed my leg, parts of me wake up. Parts that should not be awake at a business meeting.

"Actually, I go by Jase now. Jase Carter, the owner of Lase Graphics; part owner, to be exact." He smirks again and nods toward the papers in my hand.

"That's a terrible name. I thought I was meeting a woman." My face heats up, and I glance down at the paperwork. The siren goes off—I took on this job because their name sounds more like a lingerie shop than a graphic design company. Then the it hits me that I was just checking out my client. My client who I was convinced I was in love with in elementary school. The client who is hot as hell and who is still looking at me with that cocky smirk. The one who said I had cooties and threw sand in my eye because I professed my love to him.

I'm still staring down at the papers, hoping the ground will swallow me up, when the waitress appears at our table. Where in the hell was she a minute ago?

"I'll have a black coffee with two sugars. The lady will have a double caf, non-fat caramel mocha swirl latte with no whipped cream." He lets out a low chuckle as he looks over at me again.

"Sorry about my comment," I tell him. I really need this contract since it will help me with my initial startup.

"You were just telling the truth. So, Cass, how have you been?" Jase asks as leans back in the chair. All smooth, calm, and collected.

"Fine. Do you want to get right down to it? I have your form here of what you are looking for from me." I start thumbing through my papers, and I'm literally all thumbs. The waitress comes to deliver our coffee and feels the need to help me with my mess of a meeting because the coffee sloshes over the side of the cup and spills on my neatly written plans.

Fuck my life. Like seriously, fuck my life. First, I forget that I have this meeting. Then I have to travel clear across the city at the speed of light. Oh and Mr. Universe wasn't done with me yet. No, he wasn't. He sends me my first ex-boyfriend as my client. Got anything else for me today? Bring it. It's on.

"I think the universe should apologize," Jase says with a serious tone.

"What?"

"You had a rough morning, and I'd like to apologize on

the universe's behalf. And for my six-year-old self's behavior. He was a jerk that day."

"What?"

"You just said the universe is fucking with you."

"No, I didn't." I swear I didn't say it out loud. Did I? That would just add to the perfectness of my perfectly hellish day.

"Yes, you did."

"Clearly, you are mistaken. I said no such thing. I had a great morning, and the universe is perfect. See look at my horoscope." I pull up my horoscope app to prove a point. "My stars are aligned. Great opportunities are coming my way. My aura is fucking flawless." I totally covered that.

"Okay," he says.

"Okay."

"It must have been the waitress." He smiles.

"What?"

"That had a fuck my life moment. She seemed like she had a bad day. Right? Not you, though. You look like you are having a fucking amazing day."

"You shouldn't swear at a business meeting," I tell him. Really, I find it charming that he can be so relaxed with me.

"Fuck, I'm sorry."

"Is it okay if I swear then?"

"Fuck, yes. Swear away." He gestures with a circle of his wrist.

"Good because I was the one having a total fuck my life moment a minute ago. Can we start over?"

Jase grabs his notebook, pushes back his chair, stands, and walks away. My jaw drops. He left. Like literally walked out the door and left. My horoscope lied. There will be no opportunity today.

Jase

I walk out the front door of the coffee house only to walk back in a minute later and head right back to the table where Cass is sitting. The papers she was fumbling with are now put away in her briefcase. When she spots me, her eyes go wide.

"You must be Cassandra. I'm Jase Carter of Lase Graphics. Before you say anything, the first thing I need is a new company name. Ours is terrible, very unmanly. Can you help me with that?" I say as I stick my hand out to Cass.

"I totally can help you with that. In fact, Mr. Carter, I have some great ideas for you," she says, playing the role of all business Cass. I like this new version of her already.

I open my planner and we get down to business.

21. Hold my purse and rock that look

Seriously, hold my purse. If I see some shoes I must try on, you need to be confident in your manhood and hold my fucking purse. You want me to set my six-hundred-dollar bag on the floor? Not happening. Don't look at me like I'm crazy when I hold it out to you. You put that purse on your arm like it was made for you, and you tell me how amazing those shoes make my calves look.

It is the second time I'm meeting with Jason, I mean Jase. I need to stop thinking of him as the boy I knew and more as a client, but I seem to be having a hard time with that. The image of me telling him I love him keeps flustering me. He hasn't said anything about the words I said all those years ago, but it feels like the elephant in the room to me. A five-ton elephant.

This should be our last meeting, in person at least. For the past week, I created four different ways we could go with his ad. He said he wanted to hit a wide market; people of all ages need graphic designers. He isn't keeping his company's focus on one area either; he says he's willing to do anything from simple business card design to full-on website design for a Fortune 500 company.

I keep asking him what he needs me for. If he can design websites, why can't he make a simple ad? Jase's answer was simple. "I'm shit at the hook, line, and sinker aspect."

Makes sense. I can work with what he already has laid out. Taglines come naturally to me but to sit and design all the other stuff? I can't do that. That's why big companies have a department for everything under the sun.

I pull into the coffee shop where we are meeting. It was his suggestion to come here again. He says he lives on caffeine; at least, it's something we have in common. When I get out of my car, Jase is parked right next to me. He steps out, looking too good. Even better than he did last week.

I grab my purse as he heads toward the driver's side door of my car. As I step out and lock the door, he leans in and kisses me on the cheek. It flusters me for a second. Should I do it back? Is it one of those things I'm supposed to do because we know each other from way back? And, goddammit, why does he have to smell like he just stepped out of the shower and fresh baked cookies and all things manly wrapped into one pheromone package?

I go to give him the same greeting, but he turns his head, I'm guessing to gesture to where we are going, even though I know where we are headed, and I end up kissing him on half of his lips. It was like one of those bad kiss moments where the corners of each of your mouths smash together then there's the whole slobber effect because you didn't see it coming and the saliva just spills out. Not cool, Cass. Just not cool.

"Well, that went wrong," I say like a moron, just adding to the moment.

"Your landing could have been better. Hi, by the way. Did

you hit a lot of traffic?" he asks me.

"It wasn't bad." Move on, Cass. Nothing to see here. Just forget it and change the subject.

"How was your morning? Did you sleep well?" he asks me. Like genuinely asks me.

"Umm. Yes, and it was fine." This is not what I meant about a subject change. When he asks me about sleep, I picture a bed. More specifically, him in bed. Abort, abort.

"That's good. Ready to head in?" He places a hand on my back, and I glance over my shoulder just to make sure it wasn't something else. Nope, it's his hand, and if he moves it just a few inches south, that hand will be touching my ass. For a second, I think that might be nice since it's been a while since anyone has squeezed my cheeks.

"Yep," I say like I've lost my complete sense of vocabulary.

Once again, his behavior and my thoughts stump me. So much that I forget my entire presentation in the car.

"Crap," I yell as I come to a complete standstill.

"What?" Jase asks.

"You made me forget everything in the car."

"How did I make you do that?"

By just being you. "I was supposed to meet you inside, and you showed up too early. It messes with my system."

I step back to my car, but for some reason, I can't find my keys. I like my purse, it's beautiful and leather, and it's my baby, but I can put one thing on the top, and it will disappear into the bottomless pit. Once I find them, I open the back door to get everything I need. I found this perfect rolling cart that helps me keep everything organized.

"Hold this," I say to Jase as I hand him my purse. There is no way I'm putting it on the ground. A purse like this deserves better treatment than that.

He takes it from my hand without any protest. Quickly, I take the crate out and push the button to magically make the handle appear. As I once again lock my car, I chastise myself.

Idiot. You just made yourself look like a fool in front of your client just because he smells good and looks even better. I mean he's wearing so many layers, yet I can still see his muscles. Fucking muscles doesn't even describe them. Even that shirt, tie, and sweater over them still show his ripples and divots. Are divots even a way to describe those things? Jesus Christ . . . then the whole almost kiss thing. What the hell, Cass? You might as well have licked his face.

As we near the front door of the coffeehouse, I hear Jase make this sound. It's a cross between a chuckle and a cough.

"What?" I ask without looking at him.

"Nothing. I think I heard that waitress having a moment again all the way out here."

I turn to look at him because I have no idea what he's talking about. In one of his hands is my rolling cart and over his other shoulder is my purse. Dear lord. I go to reach for my bag, but he stops me.

"I got it." He even manages to open the door for me and doesn't put everything down until we get to our table.

At this point, I realize what he means by the waitress comment and I'm so pink with embarrassment that I excuse myself.

"Do you want me to order you a drink?" Jase asks as I stand up.

"Yes."

"Double caf, non-fat, caramel mocha swirl latte, with no whip. Biggest size, right?"

The man needs to stop baffling me. "How did you know? That is really freaky."

He laughs, pulls out his phone, and points. It was my post on social media from early this morning about a craving.

"That's stalking."

"How is it stalking when you post it in plain sight?"

"I don't know."

"It's what you want, though?"

"Yes."

"Okay, I'll order it for you. And a cranberry scone?" he questions.

"Now, I know I didn't post that. How did you know that's my favorite?"

"I didn't."

"You didn't. Then why did you say it like that?"

"What, like a question?"

I sigh. "No. Like you knew I'd want it."

"You look like a cranberry kind of girl."

What the heck does that mean? How does a cranberry scone girl look? Maybe she looks like a crazy person because I'm pretty sure that's what I am.

"What does that even mean?" I ask him.

"I just meant would you like one because I'm ordering one, and they are really good here."

"Oh. Yes then."

Jase laughs. "Did we just have our first fight?"

I don't bother to answer him. "I'll be right back."

I swear I hear him say, "Maybe she's still a little mad."

Maybe I heard wrong. He could have very well said, "Maybe I should order the crab." But that makes absolutely no sense because they don't have crab here.

When I reach the bathroom, I see a sign on the wall by the door. *Best crab cakes in the city.* I make a face at it because I think there is something about this coffee house, and not Jase, that messes with my mojo.

I walk in the door and lock it. After grabbing a few paper towels, I lower the diaper changing table to put my purse on top. Now, under normal circumstances, I wouldn't lay my beautiful purse there, but I need to find some essentials. It's time to get my professional side on. I find my personal wipes and freshen up. It takes me a good five minutes to fix my makeup, hair, and lotion up. Yes, I carry all the essentials in my purse. You never know when you will need them.

By the time I finish, I'm sweating, so I run my wrists under the cold water to cool down, only the water goes haywire, spraying left, right, forward, and back and causing the front of my dress to get wet. Not just wet but soaked. Straight through to my panties. I look around the bathroom to see what I can do. Luckily, I keep a tiny hairdryer in my purse. Don't ask. I plug it in the outlet and go to town. Just as I have it aimed up my dress, pointing directly at my hoo-ha, the door busts open. Jase is staring directly at me.

Could this day get any worse?

"I just had to use the . . ." he says, pointing at the toilet. "Are you okay?"

"I spilled water. The door was locked. This is the girls' room. And don't you knock?"

"I did knock, but no one answered. It's unisex. The knob turned. And why do you have a hairdryer?"

"Don't worry about that." I open the door, hair dryer in hand, and point at the picture. There in their stick figure glory is both a picture of a man and a woman.

"I'll just use the other bathroom and leave you to your drying."

If one could die of embarrassment, I totally would right now. After I get myself together, I gather the courage to go back to the table. I'm positive I just lost his business. Judging by the way I made a complete fool of myself, why would he trust me to grow his business? I think even the clowns in the circus would be leery of hiring me.

"Look, I know this has been a less than impressive moment. It's you. Being around you has really stirred up something in me. It's like the six-year-old comes out in me again. Speaking of which, the whole sand in the eye thing needs some discussion. Not today but eventually. Preferably, after I win you over with my skills. I mean we haven't even gotten to the presentation yet, and I am really fucking this up. And there I go with my mouth. So I'm going to sit down and shut up. Or maybe try to conjure up some superpowers and teleport back in time to start this day again." I take a deep breath after I finish my rant and shove half the scone in my mouth. He's right; I am a cranberry scone kind of girl.

Jase pushes the cup of coffee toward me. "You want to show me what you got in that cart of yours?"

Only it sounds so hot the way he says it. I take a sip of my drink to cool off, only it's not cold. It's piping hot. And those little bumps start to form on my tongue. This is so bad. Way to go, Cass.

After I close my eyes and take a deep breath, I somehow manage to get my act together. I think it was after I drank my coffee. Unlike most people, caffeine doesn't make me jittery; it helps me focus. My presentation was epic. Jase said he loves it, and he couldn't wait to show it to his business partner.

As I start packing my paperwork away, Jase asks me, "Would you want to get a drink one night?"

"Like another business meeting with you and Lance? I could do that." Lance is the other owner of the company. I pull out my planner and look for a date. "What works for you?"

"Ummm . . . I guess. Saturday night, eight o'clock? I could pick you up."

"Sounds good." I give him my address then stand to leave.

He follows me to my car, and just before I get in, Jase says from his driver's side door, "Thanks for the entertaining day. Oh, and wear something casual nice on Saturday. I'm taking you to New Illusions."

"Okay."

"See you then, Cass."

"Okay."

He drives off, but I'm still sitting in my car going through my horrible yet amazing day ten minutes later.

22. Must adorn at least one tattoo

Tattoos are a form of art. I don't want the random tattoo you picked off a wall either. I want to know the story behind it. An amazing story of how you walked through a burning building to rescue a squirrel and that's why you have a picture of him on your ass.

On Saturday night, I'm dressed and ready by seven thirty. I give myself one last look in the mirror and decide that I look hot. Not that I'm trying to look hot for a business meeting.

"You are so full of shit, Cass," I mumble to myself.

I turn again to look at the back of my dress. Jase said to wear something casual nice; this isn't exactly casual, but it's nice. That counts for something.

I'm wearing a conservative black dress with a little something extra, and by extra, I mean part of it is missing and dips down really low to the small of my back. I'm not showing off cleavage or a lot of leg, so it can still pass as business attire. I'm wearing my favorite black Louis Vuitton shoes and carrying a new Kate Spade clutch that Emma surprised me with last week.

Okay, maybe I went a little overboard with my outfit, but

every time I've seen this man, I've made an ass out of myself. I need the upper hand.

After applying another coat of pink lip-gloss, I make my way to my kitchen, deciding I need a glass of wine to calm my nerves before he gets here.

At eight o'clock on the dot, the outer door buzzer goes off, and I press the button to let him up. When Jase knocks on my door a minute later, I have to take a deep, calming breath before opening it. I give myself a little pep talk

As soon as I see him, I decide I should have had two glasses of wine because holy shit balls. I've only ever seen him in his business suits, and he flustered me then, but in his faded jeans riding low on his hips and his tight black t-shirt, he is a wonder to behold. I take longer than necessary checking him out, letting my eyes travel over him, and that's when I see the tattoos.

Kill me now because I think I just moaned out loud.

My eyes go to his face when I hear his deep chuckle.

He's giving me a full-blown smile, and I have to make an effort not to attack him.

Business meeting. This is a business meeting. You cannot think about sex and fucking and licking those tattoos, Cass.

"Hi, Jase. Come on in. I just need to grab my purse."

"Hey, Cass." He drops the cocky smirk and gives me a soft smile.

I open the door wider to let him in. As I turn to walk toward my kitchen where I laid my bag down, I hear what sounds like a cross between a moan and a choking noise. I peek over my shoulder at him, but his eyes are focused on my exposed back.

Well, at least I'm not the only one.

He clears his throat and points at the wall. "Nice trees."

"I know, aren't they?"

"They're very lifelike," he says with a straight face.

"That's what I was aiming for. Realistic, bushy trees."

"I have a feeling this is going to be an interesting night."

"Me too. Now let's go. Unless you want to examine my bush further?" Good fucking God, Cass. I really need a brain to mouth filter with him. "You know what I mean." I grab my purse and lock my front door before we make our way downstairs to his truck. Who drives a truck in the city? It's not just any truck; it's big, dark with tinted windows, and very Jase. I don't know a damn thing about trucks, but this one is sexy as hell.

He holds the door open for me as I slide inside, and I find it charming. I mentally berate myself again. Enough is enough. This is my client. I will stop thinking inappropriate thoughts about him right now.

I watch him walk around the hood of the truck, and I can't help but watch how his body moves as he slides into the driver's seat. He turns and smiles at me, then turns the key, and puts it in drive.

Fuck. I'm screwed.

We arrive at New Illusions a short time later. As Jase drops his truck off with the valet, I notice the line to get inside wraps around the building. When I look down at my shoes, I curse under my breath because there is no way I will be able to stand in these things for that long.

When Jase leads me toward the front entrance, I'm surprised when his hand lands on my lower back. The slight touch is burning my skin—maybe my skin is burning up from him—and I almost swat it away. I don't need these distractions, dammit!

We walk straight up to the door, and I listen as he gives the bouncer his name. The large man checks his clipboard then lifts the rope to let us in.

"You must have some good connections," I say, turning to him with my eyebrow raised.

He chuckles. "Something like that."

I've never been to a bar like this; upscale is an understatement. It's hip and trendy, but also has an air of wealth. There is a fucking chandelier at the entrance, for Christ's sake!

As we step up to the roped-off stairway, Jase doesn't even have to tell the hostess his name, and I wonder what kind of people he associates that he can get us into the VIP section. The hostess smiles a little too widely at him, which bothers me at first, but before leading us toward the stairs, I realize that's just crazy because I'm the one he's with.

"I think Lance is already here." Jase waves his hand, indicating for me to go up the stairs first.

I'm not too proud to admit that I add an extra sway to my hips.

The upstairs area looks much like the downstairs, except it's a little more private and not quite as loud. The overly smiling hostess leads us to a table that has a man already seated, and I assume he's Lance. When he notices us approaching, he stands and offers me his hand.

"Cass, this is my business partner, Lance Williams. Lance, this is Cassandra Quinn," Jase says, gesturing between us, but that damn hand has found its way to my back again. I'm trying so hard not to focus on that one spot, but I'm failing miserably.

"It's so nice to finally meet you, Cassandra," Lance says

while giving me a wide smile. Let me just say, these two to-gether are potent. While Jase has the bad boy look going on tonight, Lance is clean cut and extremely attractive in that *GQ* type of way.

I reach my hand out to shake his back. "Please, just call me Cass."

The two of them start talking about some deal they just finished. I'm only half listening as I survey the area again. Our table overlooks the downstairs, and I start moving to-ward the chair furthest away from the railing. Before I can sit, Jase pulls out the chair for me then chooses the seat next to me. I'm a tiny bit scared of heights, and I'm not sure I could sit here all night thinking about plunging to my death while carrying on an intelligent conversation. I nervously wiggle for a second as silence falls over the table. Luckily, the waitress picks that moment to come over and take our drink orders.

Yes, wine. I need wine.

I order a glass of Pinot Grigio, and the guys both order a whiskey neat.

Lance asks a little about my company as we wait for our drinks, and I fill him in on what all I can offer to his and Jase's company.

"What made you go into advertising?" he asks, as the waitress sets our drinks in front of us. I give her a smile in appreciation before taking a much-needed sip.

"I always knew I would take this career path. I love the fast-paced work environment and thinking of new inventive ways to promote people's brands and products. I like to meet new and different clients and find out what they like or dis-like. While I'm not trying to sound like I'm bragging, I seem to have a gift for spotting certain elements in the products or

brands I'm representing and making them more successful." I
wink when I deliver that last part, and Lance sits back in his
chair, chuckling at me.

"You're hired," he jokes.

"She was already hired, dip shit." Jase laughs.

I just take in their banter as I take another sip of my wine.

I had already gone over my plans with Jase in our earlier
meetings, and I get the feeling he handles that side of the business and me meeting Lance tonight was more of a formality.
By the end of our discussion, we've agreed on two things: one,
the new company name will be J&L Graphic Designs, and
two, their slogan will be "Graphics that design your future."

We each have a few more drinks, but unlike me, Jase
stops at two and switches to water. It wasn't my fault, though.
Between the two of them, I seem to never have an empty
hand while we get to know each other a little better. Well,
Lance and I do at least. Jase is mostly quiet, and every time I
sneak a glance at him out of the corner of my eye, his gaze is
already on me.

By the time we get ready to leave, I am feeling more than
a little buzzed and kind of regretting my decision to wear
Louis Vuitton. We say goodbye to Lance who stays behind. As
we make our way down the stairs, I clutch the railing like my
life depends on it because it kind of does. Jase takes notice of
my distress when he looks over at me; he offers me the crook
of his arm, and I gladly take it. Once my arm is in his, I can't
help but give it a little squeeze.

I hear him chuckle again, but I ignore it. Any woman
would have done the same because his arms are solid and so
large that my hand only reaches halfway around.

We wait in silence by the valet for his truck to be pulled

around. Under the bright lights outside the bar, I can't help but admire the tattoos on his arms again. They are bright and colorful and fit him perfectly. I run my finger down one, which causes him to tense beside me.

Bad, Cass. Let the poor man go before you maul him. But I don't let him go. Nope, I continue to feel up my client under the guise of looking at his tattoos.

His truck pulls up too soon for my wandering hands' liking, and Jase once again opens my door. Once I climb inside, I'm not sure if I'm hot from all the wine or Jase, so I take it upon myself to take control of the air and let it blast in my face.

He seems a little tense when he gets in the truck, but I'm feeling quite relaxed in my happy wine-induced bubble.

"I like your tattoos."

"I couldn't tell," he snorts and says dryly.

"Hmm . . . yes, I like them a lot. What do they mean?"

This time he chuckles out loud. "They are memories from all of the cities I've traveled to. I couldn't carry a lot when I was traveling, so I thought, why not get it inked on me. Do you have any?"

"Me? No, I'm a scaredy cat when it comes to pain, but they look hot as fuck on you."

Oh, god. Did I just say that? Did I just tell my client his tattoos look hot as fuck? So unprofessional. The damn wine is giving me no brain to mouth filter, or maybe that's partially Jase's fault too.

"I'm glad you like them, Cass." His voice is gravelly, and it's doing things to my body. Things that don't need to be happening.

I stick my face closer to the air vent and decide to keep

my mouth firmly shut for the rest of the ride home.

Jase

I keep sneaking glances over at Cass as I speed down the city streets toward her apartment.

Every moment I spend with her makes me like her even more. How that's possible, I'm not sure. She's smart, charming, and so fucking beautiful it hurts, but I also find her weird little quirks and the way she can't control that mouth of hers sexy. She's funny as hell, and the fact that she even had Lance eating out of the palm of her hand within two minutes of meeting him is a miracle.

I want more, though. I shouldn't want that since we are working together, but I couldn't care less. I also know she will try to stick me firmly in the friend zone because of that, but that's not happening.

As I walk her up to her door, I have to fight to hold back my laughter as her eyes linger on my tattoos again. It seems my girl has a tattoo fetish.

My girl. When did I start thinking of her as mine? It doesn't matter. She is mine whether she knows it yet or not.

When we arrive at her door, I bend down to kiss her cheek and let my lips linger a little longer than appropriate on her soft skin. Before I force myself to step away, I take a moment to inhale her vanilla scent that is driving me crazy.

"Good night, Cass," I say as I finally move away from her.

She looks back down at my arm and actually lets out a sigh of appreciation when she says, "Good night, pretties."

I'm almost positive she just told the ink on my sleeve

good night. I chuckle quietly as I watch her walk into her apartment and shut the door behind her.

Yes, that quirky girl is mine, and I'm not going to let her get away.

23. Washboard abs, that 'v', and arm porn makes me happy

Strong arms equal a strong man, and I don't mean because you spend hours in the gym either. I want them to be from manual labor, a hard day's work. Tattoos just enhance said arms. The rule is his arms must be thicker than my thighs. Do I need any explanation on what a six-pack and that V thingy does to a woman? If you have these three features, you are sure to get lucky . . . often.

"So how did your date go last night?" Emma asks me from the other end of the screen. She's hunched over with her feet propped up on the coffee table holding a bottle of nail polish in her one hand. We always video chat when we talk since it makes us feel like we are still living together; it's part of our daily routine. Just like Martini Bar Monday, Tequila and Taco Tuesday, Wine Wednesdays, Thirsty Thursday, Fucked-up Friday, Smashed Saturday, and Sober Sunday—because you always need a day of rest in there—are all our things.

"It was a business date, not a date, date."

"Formalities. Seriously, how was it?" She starts fanning

the toenails she just painted.

"Cute color. It went fine. His business partner is cute," I tell her with a wiggle of my eyes.

"Do tell."

I tell her all about Lance; at least everything I learned last night. I'm trying not to mention Jase. If I do, I know that she will see I have developed a secret crush on my newest client.

"There's something you're not telling me," she says.

"About Lance?"

She squints her eyes and looks at her tablet closer. "No. What happened last night that has you twirling your hair?"

"I am not twirling . . ." Shit, I look, and I am. I haven't done that in years. Probably since high school. I put my hands down and sit on them to keep me from doing it again.

"You like Lance."

"What? No," I quickly say back. I mean he's cute and all, but he's not the one who sends tingles down south.

"Oh, my god. You still have a thing for Jase."

I laugh the fakest laugh in the history of laughs. "No, I don't."

"Yes, you do."

"Don't."

"Yes. Admit it. Come on, Cass. It's written all over your face. And you've been avoiding telling me anything about him. Like what he drives."

"A truck."

"In the city?"

"That's what I said."

"That's hot."

"I said that, too."

She disconnects the video and minutes later knocks on

my door. You see, when I moved out of our apartment, we didn't want to be far from each other. So the day the smaller apartment across the hall became available, I took it. Yes, we video chat even though we live across the hall from each other. We like our personal space, but when I'm having a crappy day, it's the best feeling knowing that your best bitch is right there if you need her. Or she can bang on my door when she's going to call me out, and I can open my door, and she's right there. Literally, like right now. Giving me her signature "don't lie to me" look, she walks inside and turns to me as I relock it.

"Cassandra Quinn, if you had a middle name, I'd use that too, but you don't, so I will go on. Cassandra and Jase sitting in a tree. K-I-S-S-I-N-G."

You get the picture. My best friend came over to mock me. "Shut up."

"You like Jase," she says in that teasing way.

"Stop it, Emma."

"Come on, Cass. What happened that was so bad?"

So I spill it. I tell her how I didn't get dressed up to impress him, but how secretly I did. Then I tell her how he made a t-shirt and jeans look like they were the sexiest outfit under the sun. How his tattoos made me wet the minute I saw them—so unbelievably wet that I was crossing and uncrossing my legs all night. That when I touched his arm it was so firm and strong that it was such arm porn that I heard "Bow Chicka Wow Wow" playing in my head. That I had three drinks, maybe five, which she knows any more than two makes me a little loose in the lips, and then I said good night to his arm porn. Oh, yeah, then there was the kiss on the cheek. One little touch of his lips against my skin shouldn't feel so damn good. I swear I felt him sniff just below my ear, and I wanted to lean my head to the right so he would put those damn kissable lips against my neck. Last, but not least, how I threw out one of my favorite BOBs because he's just not cutting it anymore.

"No, not the pink one," she gasps.

"Yes."

"With the . . .?"

"Yep, it's in the trash."

"That's just wrong."

I sigh and plop down on the couch next to her. "What am I going to do? Seriously, Em. I can't have sexual thoughts about this guy."

"Why not?"

"I need this account."

"Okay. So keep the account and the guy."

That's not possible. Working with someone and sleeping with him is not good. But then again, having him bend me over the computer desk . . . "It would be very distracting."

"Then go for a run." She points at my running shoes by the door.

"Like now?"

"No, not now. I mean when you start to think about him sexually." She rolls her eyes like I should have known what she was thinking.

"Like now. Besides, you know I hate running."

"Then why the hell did you buy a pair of a hundred and fifty dollar running shoes? And you are picturing having sex with him now?"

"They are cute and teal. And yes because my brain just won't let me forget him, it seems."

"So then don't run. Put those teal bitches on, and power

walk that man out of your system."

I can do that.

Emma walks on the heels of her feet to keep from mussing up her polished toes out of my apartment. As for me, I put on my black sports bra, tight stuff tights, and my fresh track jacket from Lululemon. Then I put on my kicks and grab my headphones. It is time to sweat out all thoughts of Jase and his sexy as fuck tattoos.

Although the walk to the park is quick, it gives me enough of a little warm up before I crank some music to get me moving. Here's the thing, though; in the city, people here take their power walking seriously. Once, I thought I would go for a casual stroll in the park, but this seventy-year-old woman with her two-pound weights in each hand yelled at me to get out of her way. I learned quickly there is no strolling. You must go with the pace of the person in front of you or risk life and limb.

By the third mile, sweat pours down my back, and I am panting. It's working, though; I'm not thinking of him at all until I slow enough to take a sip of water. I feel the breeze first as another person passes me. Not just any person, though, a man. I power walk a little faster, but he is running at a good speed. And let me say, nothing on him is jiggling. He stops to tie his shoe, and I stop to pretend to tie mine, but really, I'm just admiring the view of his ass in the gray sweats he is wearing. In fact, that's all he is wearing. I lick my lips in admiration while watching his back muscles and tattooed arms move as he ties those shoes like a pro.

Apparently, I'm not far enough off to the side because someone screams, "Watch it."

Then next thing I feel is a leg or a knee hit me, which

makes me ungracefully trip forward right onto the shoe tier.

"Sorry . . . Jerk . . . Some people are so rude," I say to the poor man who I just toppled. I fall directly onto his back, his solid back, his extremely muscular back. If there was a back in the history of backs defined as panty melting, this is it.

"Cass?" he says as his head turns toward me.

Mother Fuck. "Hey, Jase. Fancy falling on you here."

Of all the million people to land on, it has to be him. The man I'm not supposed to be thinking about. The man I'm still practically on top of. And, now, seeing him close up, I want to lick his half-naked body even more.

To make matters worse, I lose my balance and fall backward, only to land directly on my ass.

"Shit, Cass. Are you okay?" Jase hovers over me.

I go to sit up, but awkward Cass just keeps popping up. My head makes direct contact with his.

"Mother dick," I say a little too loud. "I'm fine. Shit, that hurt. What's in your head?"

He stands then offers me his hand. And no lie, it's perfect, the way the sun is glowing around him while he stands there all shirtless and, my god, does he have an eight pack? Is that even possible? I count them as I rise to my feet. Yep, eight of them. All ripped, sculpted, and perfectly defined. I glance down again, just to look my fill. This time, I notice the V shape that points to his low riding sweats.

"Uh, Cass?"

"Huh?" I'm not looking at his face; my focus is still on his muscles.

"I just asked how your head is."

"So good." I'm no better than Steve, the breast talker.

A hand reaches under my chin and gently pushes upward.

"You have a red mark. Are you sure you're okay? You seem a little dazed," Jase asks me.

I am dazed but not from my head-on collision. "Is it hot? All of a sudden, I'm really warm," I say as I unzip my jacket and start waving it open and closed to cool off, which is not going to help. The wave of heat was not from the sun, or my walk, but from this man.

"Here, drink some water." Jase hands me a bottle of water, which I have no clue where it came from.

I take two large gulps then hand the rest back to him. I finish taking off my jacket because my body, along with my panties, feels like it's on fire.

"Thanks."

"You sure you don't want more?"

"I'm good," I say as I tie the garment around my waist. What I'm really trying to do is avoid looking at his face or abs or arms. But I can't help looking when he takes the remainder of the water and dumps it over his head like in one of those cheesy commercials—only this is live. It's like my own personal sort of strip show. For a second, I wish I had a dollar to stuff in the waistband of his sweats. Thanks for the show.

"It did get hot. I think I should have stopped after the second lap," he tells me as he wipes the excess water from his hair.

The man is just trying to put me in a permanent state of arousal. Because now I'm back to studying the tiny droplets of water dripping down his eight pack and wishing I could lick them. One by one. "Wait, you're on your third lap around the park?"

"Actually, I'm starting my fourth," he says like it's no big deal.

"That's like eighteen miles."

"Yeah."

"That's a lot."

"Yeah."

"And you're still breathing?" I question.

"That's nothing. Back when I was in the Air Force, we used to run thirty miles a day."

"Air Force?" He's just full of surprises.

"Yes."

"So you can fly airplanes?"

"No, I'm a computer guy."

"So you worked on computers in the Air Force?"

"Yes. Is that so strange?"

"Nope. Seems about right." I needed to get away from him and fast. If I see or he tells me another hot thing about him, I'm going to be digging out BOB's brother, The Womanizer. I know—terrible name but great delivery.

"Cass?"

I look at Jase as he says my name and want to kick myself for once again getting lost in thoughts of sex because of him. "Sorry."

"You're ringing," Jase tells me as he points at my pants.

"Shit." I grab it from the pocket in my pants and see it's Emma. "What's up?"

"Cass, you need to come home. I heard a noise in your apartment."

"What kind of noise?"

"It was this eeerrrr grrrr clunk clunk clunk whoosh kind of sound. There is water shooting out of your kitchen sink. I tried to turn the knob thing, and it only seems to have angered it. The maintenance man is out of town, and the landlord is not returning my calls."

"Shit. Fuck. Okay, I'll be right there. Throw some towels on it and start looking up plumbers. I'll be there in ten, nine if I run."

I turn to Jase. "Gotta go, emergency."

As I round the corner to the block my apartment is on, I notice Jase is right behind me.

"Why are you following me?" I shout at him.

"I heard you say plumber."

"You're a plumber too? Is there anything you're not?"

I don't need him turning a stressful situation into a sexual one. Having Jase in my apartment will put him too close to my bedroom, the sofa, or even the kitchen counter. God, him picking me up and putting me on the counter would be so hot. I shut the door on that thought and pick up the pace of my now super power walk.

"My dad is a plumber, but I worked for him during the summers after I turned sixteen," Jase says as he barely is jogging right by my side. Goddammit, his legs are longer than mine are; for every three steps I take, he only jogs one.

"Fine," I huff.

Jase

When Cass took off her jacket in the park, I had to think of all things unpleasant to keep myself in check. The curves of her body are unbelievable. A man would drop to his knees for a chance with a girl like her.

Every day, I see women in their little running outfits, but Cass just took a sports bra and running pants to whole different level.

When I heard her in a panic on the phone, the need to fix whatever was wrong overwhelmed me. I caught words, but the two words that stuck out were towels and plumber. I can handle that, and maybe, if I can fix whatever's wrong, she'll forget about my asinine sandbox days.

24. Must be good with his hands

Not just in the bedroom. I want you to know how to fix shit around the house. Screwing in a light bulb every six months does not make you a handyman. You need to know what to do when the sink clogs or when a screw falls out of the chair.

I'm power walking down the last block that leads to my apartment like my ass is on fire. Well, I'm stumbling while my lungs are burning, and I'm trying to remember why I thought working out was a good idea today in the first place.

Oh, yeah. The infuriating man currently running beside me is the reason I decided to torture my body today.

He stops when we reach my building and looks at me. I can only imagine what I look like—red splotchy face, sweating like a pig, and gasping for breath. Really attractive, I imagine.

I use one hand to prop myself up against my building and bend at the waist.

"Just go on without me," I gasp out.

He chuckles and looks at me like I'm joking. Right then, I decide he needs to get his eyes checked because I'm serious as heart attack.

"Come on, Cass. Just a few stairs and then we'll be there. I don't want your apartment to flood."

Shit, stairs. I forgot about the fucking stairs. Just when I'm thinking of lying on the nasty street, a thought comes to me that has me moving again.

"Little Shit!" I wail, as I take off running into my building and up the stairs.

"Little shit?" Jase asks in confusion, but there is no time to explain.

My poor puppy is inside my apartment that is probably now flooded.

I make it to my door and shove the key in the lock. I can hear Jase coming up the stairs as I push my way inside.

Holy fucking hell. I could swim in here. Not really, but it's a little scary how much water has pooled in the kitchen in such a short time. The sink in my kitchen is busted, and the water is spraying in every direction at an alarming rate.

"Razor," I scream as I run through my living room and head for my bedroom.

This is fucking ridiculous; I was only gone an hour!

Razor is standing on my bed looking absolutely terrified. I scoop him up and give him kisses. From the doorway, I see Jase make his way to the kitchen. I set Razor down and follow him. He's going to need help to control this madness.

"What do I do?" I yell.

He turns and looks at me with a raised eyebrow.

"Why are you yelling?"

"I don't know. It seemed more dramatic."

He chuckles and shakes his head. He pushes the towels around, that I guess Emma left there, to try to cover the pipe.

Dear God in heaven. The muscles in his back are flexing

again, and I can't take my eyes off them. I really do need to lick him.

Lick him? Your apartment is flooding, and your only thought is licking a man?

"Cass."

He must have been trying to get my attention because he is staring straight at me in either amusement or annoyance.

"Yes?" I question, licking my lips.

Abort mission! I repeat, abort mission! There will be no licking Jase.

"I need some more towels and a wrench."

"Sure, yeah." I nod my head but don't move.

"Baby, your apartment is flooding."

Baby? Did he just call me baby?

No time to overthink. He's right; my apartment is leaking, for Christ's sakes!

I run into the bathroom and grab the rest of the towels before going back into the kitchen. I watch his muscles move again as he messes with the pipe. The water is no longer shooting everywhere, but it's still leaking pretty quickly.

"The wrench?" he asks.

Instead of answering him, I dive toward the sink and drop to my knees in front of the cabinet. Bad idea. Such a bad idea because, when I turn my head, my face is directly even with his crotch. His sweats are wet and molded to his body, and I can tell that he is well endowed, so well that I swear I can see every little detail.

"Well, hello there."

Yes, I just spoke to his penis. What else am I supposed to do with the big guy, ignore him? I think not.

"Cass, did you just speak to my junk?" He sounds like

he's either going to laugh or he's trying to figure out if I'm crazy. And junk? I don't think I would classify what he's packing as junk. More like a prime grade A piece of man meat.

I look up at him and it seems like all of the air is sucked out of the room. He looks down at me, and all humor is wiped from his face as he stares down at me on my knees.

"Umm, no."

"Jesus fucking Christ," he breathes.

"Wrench," I supply helpfully. Lifting up the gadget I came down here for in the first place.

He visibly shakes himself as he takes the tool from my hand.

"Watch out."

I scoot to the side, and he lowers himself to the floor and crawls beneath the cabinet.

"Do you know what you're doing down there?"

He lifts his head enough so that he can look at me. "I could go so many different directions with that question, Cass. But yes, I know what I'm doing down here."

Well, alrighty then. I'm still on my knees beside him, and I watch his arm muscles flex and move. I'm curious to know what he's doing, so I scoot a little closer, but I still can't see because it's so dark under that cabinet.

With his big body in the way, the only part of me that can fit under there is my head.

"What are you doing?" I ask.

"What are you doing?" he says as he stops again to stare at me.

"Don't stop working, Jase."

"Cass, you are laying on top of me with your head shoved under the cabinet." He says this slowly like I'm the crazy one, but he's the one taking forever on the pipe.

Now that I think about it, though, I'm not sure how I got in this position. I must have blacked out from the trauma of it all. I am laying directly on top of him. One of my hands is resting on his firm stomach, the other hand is on his chest, and my lady bits are precariously close to his manly goods.

Hmm . . . While I'm here, I might as well see what these crazy muscles feel like. I slide my hand over his abs, and I hear him suck in a sharp breath and mumble something about "Death of me." He must be talking about the water.

I watch as he pulls hard on the wrench, and suddenly, I don't hear the water anymore. He wiggles a few more things under the sink.

I'm not sure what to do, so I just remain completely still.

Jase clears his throat. "Water is turned off."

"Yep."

He lifts his head and looks at me. "You should probably call your landlord to have someone replace the hose under there and get someone to come clean the water up."

"Yep."

"Cass?"

"Yeah?"

"You've got to get off me, baby."

His voice is all deep and dark, and it makes me shiver. Or maybe that's the cold water soaking through my clothes.

"Oh, yeah. Of course."

I move too quickly, and the back of my head slams against the cabinet.

"Fuck."

Jase's hand immediately comes up to the back of my head. "Shit, Cass. Are you okay?"

His hand is rubbing circles on the back of my head, and our faces are dangerously close. *I need out of this cabinet! This was a bad idea. Like the worst idea ever.*

I slide down, but in an effort to get away, I make things considerably worse. My lady bits make direct contact with his very large, very erect penis.

Both of us still at the contact. I look up at him while he looks down at me. He looks like he's the one in pain, even though I'm the one who keeps getting hurt. I have no clue what to do.

"Looks like someone is happy to see me. He's a big fella, isn't he?" My foot in mouth syndrome comes back again.

Jase stares at me a second longer before throwing his head back and laughing.

Oh, I like that.

I decide to take the opportunity to climb off him, and I stand up. In all of the excitement—and by excitement, I mean the huge thing in Jase's pants—I completely forgot about my scared puppy.

I watch Jase slide out of the cabinet before I walk over to my bedroom and pick up Razor, who is whining uncontrollably.

"Poor baby. I bet you were so scared," I say in that baby talk he likes so much. He makes a little whimpering noise as if he agrees.

"Who do we have here?" Jase asks, walking over to where I'm holding Razor.

I wait for my sweet puppy to completely lose his shit like he does with every other man, but he doesn't.

Jase reaches out his hand and pats the top of his head.

"Huh. He must have PTSD from the water incident," I mumble.

Jase chuckles as he continues to stroke Razor's back. I think Razor actually sighs. "What makes you say that?"

"No reason." There is no way I'm telling him about Razor's antics.

My phone picks that moment to ring. "Here, can hold him while I go answer that?"

He takes Razor with no problem, and I stare at them in shock for a second before going to find my phone.

I find it by the front door and answer it when I see Emma's name flashing on the screen.

"Hey, a plumber is on the way. Just come here."

"I got it under control for now. I'll pack a bag and be there in a minute."

"What does that mean? Should I come over?"

"No!" I say a little too quickly, and I can practically feel her suspicion through the phone. "I'll be there in a second."

I turn and look at where Jase is still standing holding Razor. The little shit looks thrilled at the attention, and that only adds to my confusion when it comes to this man.

"I need details, bitch," Emma says before hanging up.

I chuckle to myself as I slide the phone back onto my table before walking toward my closet to grab my overnight bag.

"Where are you staying?" he asks.

I pause, reaching for the bag, and turn to smile at him. "Do you remember that girl you tried to ditch me for?"

He looks up at the ceiling like he's trying to recall that memory. I decide to help him out.

"You tried to impress her the day you fell climbing the monkey bars." He visibly winces at the memory. "Anyway, she's still my best friend and lives right across the hall."

"I'm glad my horrible childhood behavior brought you a lifelong best friend. And it wasn't her trying to impress." He smiles at me before looking back down at Razor. I look too, and that's when I see that little shit sprawled out on his back while Jase rubs his belly.

Is it possible to be jealous of your dog? Because I'm pretty sure at that moment I am. I turn around and continue pulling my bag down so I can get packed.

Emma is never going to believe this.

Jase

I watch Cass as she starts packing a bag to go to her friend's house. I wish I could ask her to come to mine, but I know there is no way in hell she would agree to that. We don't really even know each other, but I want to get to know her a hell of a lot more.

When she was sitting on top of me under that cabinet, all I could think about was flipping her over and tasting every inch of her. All fucking night long. I wonder how she would have responded if I had pulled her lips to mine and kissed the fuck out of her? Would she have pulled away or would she have leaned in closer? That thought alone has me walking over to the other side of the room and discreetly adjusting myself. I decide that my next plan of action is to get Cass to agree to go on a date. No business, just her and me. I have a feeling this isn't going to be easy.

25. Must love my best friends

Yes, I know they are crazy, but they are mine, and if you're with me, then you must accept the fact that they will know everything about you. Some of our moments will be ours, but if you hurt me, there is always a chance they will find you and bury you. Best to get on their good side now.

Emma and I have had a slumber party for the past two nights. My landlord, Mr. Crammer, couldn't seem to get his act together and get my kitchen sink fixed. He was afraid that my apartment would flood again, so he completely shut off the water. At least he knocked off a half a month's rent to compensate me. The cleanup crew came immediately, but that was only because I footed the bill, which I then handed to Mr. Crammer

I just got off the phone with him a minute ago, and it seems that I will be bunking at Emma's for the next week. Turns out, this isn't the first time this has happened. It seems that this time they found some mold under the cabinet and will have to rip it out along with replacing the pipes. Good news, I get a new kitchen; the bad news, the construction will last about a week.

"You can stay with me as long as you need, Cass." Emma and I are having an early lunch at our favorite diner. Once a month, we splurge, forget all things diet, and get a taylor ham, egg, and cheese on a fresh baked bagel with hash brown on the side and a chocolate shake to wash it down.

"I appreciate that, but does Carson mind?" Carson is her new steady man; so steady that I think he's going to become a permanent fixture in her life. He's nice but just a little too formal for me. For Emma, I think he's perfect.

"Not one bit. Besides, I can just go to his condo if I get sick of you."

"You'll never get sick of me."

"Probably not, but there's a first time for everything," she jokes.

I take a bite of my sandwich, and I look over to see Jase standing right next to me. Here I am with a sandwich the size of my head hanging out of my mouth when the unthinkable happens. Did I mention my healthy breakfast is also loaded with salt, pepper, and ketchup? Big boob problem 101—when you eat, something always seems to drop and fall on the same spot. For me, it's my right boob, the one closest to Jase. This time, it was ketchup on my white blouse.

"Good morning, ladies," Jase says to both of us.

"Good morning, handsome," Emma says. She widens her eyes at me like I was holding out.

"Emma, you remember Jase, don't you?" I ask as I dip the napkin in my water and start wiping away, which only makes the stain worse. Not only is it spreading it, but the brown paper napkin is also shredding and embedding in my shirt. I give up and start unbuttoning my blouse since I have on a little camisole underneath. And my jacket I keep at the office will cover me just fine if I keep it buttoned. When I look up, Jase is watching me like a hawk.

"As in Jason Carter," Emma squeals.

Jase finally stops staring at me to look at Emma. "Emmaleigh Lewis? Wow, you look fantastic."

He bends and gives her a kiss on the cheek. Emma is sitting on the inside of the booth, and Jase makes himself at home and slides in to join us. He takes his healthy gluten-free bran muffin—I'm not sure if it is that, but it looks healthy all filled with oats and nuts, and he's so in shape I'm sure he doesn't eat anything gluten—and puts it on the table along with his coffee.

"You don't look so bad yourself. Cass, you've been holding out. I mean I know you said he's hot, but seriously on a scale of one to ten, he's like a twenty," Emma says.

"Only a twenty?" Jase jokes back.

"Maybe slightly higher, but don't tell my boyfriend I said that. He may get a little jealous."

"On a scale of one to twenty, where's your boyfriend?"

Emma takes a second to think. "A nine."

Jase makes this pfft sound. "A nine? That's disappointing. What makes him only a nine?"

"He can be a bit stiff sometimes." She's not joking. Stiff is not the word I would use, though. Boring with a capital B is more like it.

"I thought you women like it stiff," Jase says, and Emma cracks up. Me? My jaw hits the table. What the hell is going on? They are going back and forth like Emma and I do, and I get jealous. Not jealous that he seems to have hit it off with her, but jealous that my best friend is hitting it off with Jase. Back off, bucko, Emma is mine.

"Make yourself at home. Ha, ha, ha, stiff. That's so funny, Jase. Don't mind me. I'll just sit here and enjoy my breakfast while you two reconnect," I say under my breath, but it probably wasn't as under my breath as I thought since they are both looking at me like I'm the child who just had a temper tantrum. Which I am and I don't care because I'm supposed to be having lunch with Emma, not Jase.

"Cass." The way Emma says my name makes me want to hide under the table.

"Sorry, I didn't mean that," I apologize.

"How's the apartment?" Jase asks me as he lifts his muffin to his mouth. I'm watching as his mouth opens to take a bite, but I'm transfixed on his tongue. It's thick and long, and I wish at this moment that I was that muffin. Because I'm almost positive that Jase eating me would be spectacular.

The apartment, Cass. He's asking about the apartment. "It's still being worked on. I should be back in it next week." I go on to explain everything then realize I never really thanked him for helping me out.

"That's crazy. I could have done it for you faster than that."

"Replace my kitchen?" I ask.

"Yeah, it's not that big of a deal. I just finished remodeling my apartment a few months ago."

"On your own?" I question.

"No, a few buddies of mine helped out. It made the flooring and tile work go faster."

"Jesus, is there anything you can't do?"

"I can't pat my head and rub my stomach." Which he tries to do, but he's all rub and no pat.

It makes me laugh for a minute. Emma is still laughing.

I'm not anymore, though because I'm watching him rub his stomach while remembering how deliciously hard it is. Then I remember other things that were just as hard. Now I'm turning pink from the memory and starting to sweat, not sweat sweat, just a little glisten, but still, it's not good. To cool off, I take a big gulp of my chocolate shake, only it gives me brain freeze. My hand instantly grabs my forehead as I wince in pain.

Jase hands me a spoon.

"What is she supposed to do with that?" Emma asks since I'm sitting here with only one eye open because the pain is in my right eye and traveling oh so slowly down, down, down.

"Put the rounded side to the roof of your mouth." He says this like that's supposed to do something. "Trust me, Cass, it works."

I do what he says, and lo and behold, the cold tension starts to subside. I take the spoon out of my mouth. "You're a genius."

He just nods his head like it's no big deal.

"Jase, thank you."

"It was nothing. I just gave you a spoon."

"No, I mean for the apartment the other day. If you hadn't come to my rescue, it would have been so much worse. How can I repay you?"

Jase

The way she uses the word rescue has me feeling more than proud. I feel like I am King Kong standing at the top of the tallest building with my chest puffed out and my hands beating it like a badass. Until I come up with the perfect way for her to pay me back.

"I know how you could thank me."

"How?"

"Go out with me."

"You mean another business meeting?" she asks.

"No, like a date."

"A date date?" she asks and really starts squirming before looking at her best friend for help. Emma just turns her head as if she's ignoring the whole thing.

"Yes, a real date."

"I can't."

"Can't or won't." Can't means not now, but maybe another time. Won't means it's completely off the table, but fuck it, I don't care if she says that. This will never be off the table.

"Won't."

My heart jabs, but it's not over. I pick up my garbage and get ready to leave. Before I do, I bend toward Cass' ear. "I'm not giving up yet. I remember the way you felt lying on top of me under that sink. That woman wanted me, and you know what, Cass? That guy wanted her right back."

I pull back, and I hear her draw in a breath. I dip my head toward the two of them. "Ladies, thanks for letting me join you."

Instead of going back to the office, like I should, I call Lance and tell him I'm taking the rest of the day off. I've been on edge since the first meeting with Cass. She's stirring something in me, something so deep, something exciting, and something I know would be so fucking amazing.

Two hours at the gym was what it took to work Cass half out of my system. Thirty minutes of running then thirty minutes of lifting weights followed by an hour boxing. After the five-mile run home, I was barely thinking of her. My thoughts were moving to food, shower, and bed.

As I'm getting ready to go to sleep, my phone buzzes.

I change my answer.

Cass. And just like that, I'm not as tired as I was just a few seconds ago.

Jase: Remind me again what the question was.

Cass: Can't or won't remember? Which both mean that you have no memory of asking me on a date and me saying that I won't go on said date when, in fact, I really wanted to say yes to the date because I remember what it felt like being on top of you under my sink.

I smile at her rant because everything about this woman is fucking cute.

Jase: And what did it feel like?

Cass: Stiff.

Jase: I knew you women like it stiff.

Cass: Jase.

Jase: Cass.

Cass: Will you ask me that question again?

I'd ask her a million times over if I had to, but I know what the answer will be this time, so it's a no-brainer. Only there is no way I'm going to text that shit. I hit the call button, and she answers immediately.

"Hey," she whispers.

"Will you go on a real date with me, Cassandra Quinn? No business partners or work talk. Just you and me, dinner at my place, this Saturday at seven?"

I wait for her answer, and she giggles exactly like she did way back when. "Yes."

She doesn't give me any time to reply because she just hangs up. I'm once again standing on top of the building feeling like I just saved the world, all because I got a date with the most beautiful girl in the universe.

26. Pursue me

Call me old fashioned, but I don't think a woman should have to chase a man. If you're interested in me, show me. Otherwise, I will never know. I want you to pursue me; I want you to make me feel special and just plain wanted. I'm a strong, independent woman, but that doesn't mean I don't want to be wooed.

I arrive outside Jase's apartment building five minutes early. The doorman opens the door for me, and I give him a quiet, "Thank you," before walking to the bank of elevators.

I'm jealous that he not only has a doorman but an elevator too. My legs are thanking the building owner too because twenty flights of stairs would be a bitch to climb.

The woman next to me gives me a once over as I enter the elevator and press the button for the twentieth floor. I give my hair a fluff in the mirrored door and pull my red lipstick out of my purse. I'm so nervous that my hand actually shakes a little. This is my client. Am I making a huge mistake? This could go south quickly, and I really need this job. Just as I'm thinking about riding this elevator right back down, the doors to his floor open.

I don't move. I stand as still as a statue while I continue to overthink.

"This is your stop, dear," the helpful elderly lady beside me says.

I give her a quick smile. "Thank you."

Really, I'm just refraining from saying a smart-ass comment. It's not her fault I decided to date my client, and now, I'm rethinking that decision.

One right turn and I find Jase's door rather quickly. Lucky me. Before knocking, I wipe my hands on my dress and take a deep breath.

This is just one dinner, Cass. You can do this. If you change your mind, you can go home, have some wine, and forget this ever happened.

Except when Jase opens the door, all thoughts of forgetting this ever happened go straight out the window. Holy hell, the man is hot as sin. I swear he gets more attractive every time I see him. How is that even possible? He's dressed casually in a pair of faded jeans that hang low on his hips, a black t-shirt is molded to his chest, and I can see each and every mouthwatering muscle that lies underneath it. Those sexy as sin tattoos are on display for me again, and I feel my mouth go dry.

He smiles, and he bends down to kiss my cheek. "Hey, Cass."

"Hi," I breathe.

Get your shit together, Cassandra. I mentally berate myself. He is just a man. A fine ass man but still just a man. You have been on plenty of terrible dates with attractive men. This one may not be any different.

He pulls back and opens the door wide enough for me to

walk through.

"I just have to grab the bottle of wine, but everything is already set up on the roof."

I follow him to the kitchen and tilt my head to the side in confusion. "The roof?"

"Yes. It's one of the reasons I bought this condo. There are heaters. I promise you won't get cold." He winks, and I think I actually swoon before I get control of myself again.

I take the opportunity to look around his space as he gets the wine and the glasses.

It's beautiful in here. The floor-to-ceiling window offers a beautiful view of the city lights. It's decorated tastefully: masculine, modern, but not cold. Its warm tones and inviting accents suit him well.

"Ready?" he asks, walking over to me. He's carrying a bottle of wine and two glasses, and he has that ever-present sexy smile on his face.

"Yep." I nod my head.

We ride the elevator up to the roof, and honestly, I don't know what to expect. I fiddle with my dress as Jase stands beside me, looking as cool as a cucumber.

Jeez, does nothing affect this guy?

When the doors open, I'm stunned speechless.

It looks like a garden. Plants and flowers are scattered around, and lights are strung everywhere, giving the space a soft glow. He was right; there are heaters up here. The view is absolutely amazing. Even though I'm scared of heights— when he first mentioned the roof, I was apprehensive—he has the picnic blanket set up far enough away from the edge, so I don't feel like I'll be falling to my death tonight.

"This is so beautiful," I whisper.

"I'm glad you like it." His voice is close, too close. I turn my head, and he is right there, close enough that if I leaned in just an inch, my mouth would be touching his.

I clear my throat and step toward the blanket he has spread out on the ground.

"What's all of this?" I gesture to the dome platters.

"Food," he says simply. I watch as he slips his shoes off before sitting down. "Come join me, Cass."

That smile he's aiming my way is potent. It makes me feel like I would probably do whatever he wanted if he just keeps looking at me like that.

I slip out of my heels before sitting down on the blanket with him.

He pulls the cork out of the wine bottle and pours each of us a glass. As he passes me a glass, his fingers brush mine, and just that slight touch makes me blush a little.

"Do you make all of your dates sit on the floor?" I ask as I bring the glass to my mouth and take a sip of the rich red wine.

He laughs, but I'm serious. "Nope. As a matter of fact, I've never had a woman up here before."

Why does that little tidbit of information make me so happy?

When he pulls the lids off the platters, he reveals an assortment of finger foods. I reach for the little meatballs first. I pick one up by the toothpick and pop the whole thing in my mouth.

"I love these little balls," I say once I've chewed and swallowed.

Jase coughs a little into his glass of wine and smiles. "Cass likes balls. Noted."

I roll my eyes a little before reaching for the plate that holds crackers and cheese.

"Did you do all of this?"

"Yes. Am I impressing you yet?"

I know he means it as a joke, but honestly, I am. I don't tell him that, though, because I wouldn't want to overinflate his ego.

"So what made you want to be a graphic designer?"

He smirks at me like he knows I'm avoiding his question. "I'm not exactly sure what first pulled me to graphic design. I was always into computers. After I had spent four years in the Air Force, I decided to go back to school to learn about programming and graphics. I met Lance my freshman year of college and we both had the same goals. When we graduated, we both worked odd jobs for a while, but the plan had always been to open our own business together."

"Lance seems like he's the hard ass out of the two of you."

He laughs. "Yeah, he most definitely is, but he's also really good at what he does."

You can clearly see the two of them are like brothers, and I smile as I reach for another meatball.

As we talk, I find that Jase is not only interesting, but he's also attentive. As he asks me questions about my life, he actually seems to be interested in my answers.

After we've eaten, he pours more wine into each of our glasses and moves the empty trays to the side. He leans back against the pillows and stretches his long legs out in front of him.

He looks so comfortable that I do the same. It's quiet, and each time our shoulders bump, I swear I can hear my own heartbeat. Why am I so nervous? Oh yeah, because this is my client and anything that happens here tonight could affect my business.

Jase turns to look at me. His eyes drop to my lips, and the air around us suddenly fills with tension . . . of the sexual variety. My mouth goes dry, and I lift the wine glass to my lips, taking a much-needed drink.

"Did you know that the blue whale has a penis that is about eight feet long? That's enough dick to feed a small country."

Where in the fuck did that come from? Oh, Jesus. Did I really just say that?

Jase's eyes widen for a second before he throws his head back and laughs. It's a deep belly laugh, and I feel all tingly that I'm the one who made him do that, even if he's laughing because I'm talking about a whale's dick.

Suddenly, I want to kiss him. I want to kiss him and feel that smile against my mouth. I come to the realization that maybe, just maybe, if I give in to the sexual tension, I can free myself of this crush I have on him. I bet he's a terrible kisser. His outward appearance is too perfect. Something has to be wrong with him. I set my wine glass down and decide to test my theory.

He stops laughing but is still chuckling a little as he looks at me. I lean in to kiss him, but I move a little too quickly. My mouth breaks my landing, our teeth clank together, and I basically head-butt the poor guy.

"Shit. Sorry." As I pull back, I curse under my breath and rub my head.

I don't dare look at him since my cheeks are now the same bright red color as the wine is. Oh god, I have turned into the bad date. I just became my own worst nightmare.

His hand comes up to my face, and he lifts my chin until I'm forced to look into his eyes. They twinkle with humor but are also soft as he studies my face.

"Let's try that again," he whispers.

He leans in slowly and tilts his head. When his lips press against mine, a thousand butterflies take flight in my belly. The kiss is demanding, but at the same time, his lips are unbelievably soft and full. The fullest lips I've ever felt against mine. When he swipes his tongue along my bottom lip, I immediately open for him, but when my tongue meets his briefly, I pull back.

"I taste like meatballs," I mumble.

This time he doesn't laugh; his hand just goes to the back of my head to pull me back to him.

"No, Cass. You taste delicious."

This time, he takes the kiss deeper. He explores the inside of my mouth like he can't get enough. The entire time, he grips my hair with one hand, like he's scared I'll pull away, while his other arm comes around my back to pull my body closer to his.

My hands come to rest on his hard chest before traveling up to loop around his neck. I don't know how, but the next thing I know, I'm straddling his lap and grinding myself against his hardness.

His hands drop lower to my ass and pull my lower body tightly against his. I can feel his hard length beneath me, and it makes me gasp into his mouth. Jesus, he's big. Like really, really big.

Everything escalates so quickly that I don't even have time to care about my career or anything for that matter. One minute, we're talking about the eight-foot whale dick, and the next minute, I'm rubbing against what feels like an eight incher. Correction, nine.

He groans and flips me onto my back. I let out a little squeak at the unexpected change in position, and he breaks his mouth away from mine.

"Fuck, Cass. You feel so good against me."

I let out a little whine at the loss of his mouth and try to pull his lips back to mine, but his hand travels up my thigh and under my dress. Every inch of me perks up and takes notice that a hand is very close to my . . . say it, Cass, say it . . . pussy.

"Is this okay?" he asks, as his hand travels up and down my side, making me shiver.

I nod my head, not caring one bit that we are outside and anyone could walk out and see us; it's been so long since someone touched me, and his hands feel so good.

His lips move down my neck where he begins to lick and nibble on my sensitive skin. To give him better access, and for my own personal pleasure, I tilt my head back. He kisses down to the tops of my breasts before making his way back up to my mouth, which only drives me more insane.

I know my panties are soaked to the point of embarrassment, but when his hand slides from my hip to exactly where I need it, I can't find it in myself to care. He pulls back from my mouth again, and I blink open my eyes. His are dark and intense, and he continues to study my face as he dips his hand into my panties and zeroes in on my clit.

Damn, he's good.

"Well, thank you, Jesus." I say that out loud and could give two fucks that I did.

"Goddamn, Cass. You're so wet."

I know. That long finger slides through my wetness before going back to my clit and rubbing tight circles.

"Oh, my, god," I breathe.

"Do you like that? Because this is me touching you, Cass. Jesus and God have nothing to do with what I'm doing to you."

"Yes." I swear to God if he stops, I may have to kill him.

Lucky for me, he doesn't stop; he keeps rubbing and teasing until I'm biting down on my lip to keep myself from screaming out in pleasure. I can feel his hardness against my hip as he grinds against me all the while he fingers me to the best orgasm I think I've ever had.

His lips meet mine again, and I let out a long moan down his throat. My body is shaking and trembling, and I think I may have blacked out for a second. Only I saw white, so technically, it was a whiteout. When I come back down to earth, he's smiling down at me, looking very satisfied with himself.

Well, that was fun. I just let my client finger me on a roof where anyone could walk out at any second and see us, but I can't find it in myself to care one bit. All I can think is that I want more.

"You have magical hands. I wonder what you can do with that big boy in your pants?"

Sweet Jesus, he's turned me into a wanton slut.

He chuckles and rubs the side of his nose against mine. Oh, that's nice.

"Come on." He pulls his hand out of my panties and helps me sit up. I smooth down my dress and my hair before taking his outstretched hand and let him pull me to my feet.

"Where are we going? Do we need to clean this up?"

He bends, sets my heels in front of me, and as I slip into

them, he slides into his shoes.

"Nope, I'll do it later. Right now, I want you. Alone. In my apartment." His hand tightens around mine, and my pulse accelerates again.

I'm totally about to have sex with my client, and I don't give one shit.

Jase

I know I'm practically dragging Cass to the elevators like a caveman, but I can't seem to stop myself. As soon as her lips touched mine, I knew I needed more. The way she felt when she exploded around my fingers almost made me come in my pants like an adolescent teen. The things this woman does to me is like nothing I've ever experienced, and I keep having to remind myself to take it slow. But I want nothing more than to take her downstairs and fuck her into oblivion. At the same time, I don't want her to regret this. I want to take my time and explore her body. I want to make sure that we are on the same page as to where this is going. This isn't a one-night stand. This is the beginning of us, and I want to make it memorable for her.

We enter the elevators, and I pull her close to me as I kiss the top of her head. I'm going to make sure she's as addicted to me as I am to her by the time she leaves here. I want to make sure she never forgets how good we are together. Because I know without a doubt, I never will.

27. Must outweigh me

I'm not one of those skinny girls. I'm all curves, the womanly kind. I need a solid man, in every possible way you can use that term. If I put in the effort to look good for you, you should do the same. Superficial? Maybe. With that said, I want to feel your weight when you are on top of me, let your body blanket me but not smother me. If I touch your back or ass, I want to feel those muscles working while I hold you.

As soon as we walk through the front door to Jase's apartment, he pins me to it and delivers one more mind-blowing kiss before tapping me on my ass. "Go make yourself comfortable while I get us a drink."

I can't help walking directly to the window to look at that view again. All I get to look at is a brick wall and my much older neighbor, Walter. He's nice and all, but seeing him shirtless every morning when I open the curtains is not the best way to start the day. Jase has a full view of the park and the busy city streets, yet it's utterly silent in here.

"I'm completely jealous of this view. It's stunning," I say.

"Breathtaking is more like it." Jase comes up behind me with a glass of wine, hands it to me, and then wraps his one arm around my waist. He oh so softly nibbles on the sensitive spot just below my ear, and instantly, my body temperature rises again. Not that it ever returned to normal after what he just did to me on the rooftop. I'm ninety-nine percent positive I'm glowing everywhere. "I meant you, not the city, just in case you were wondering," he continues.

My heart picks up another beat. I came here with the intention of working him out of my system, not to get that little butterfly feeling. After what he just said, they are dancing around my stomach like crazy.

"I was strictly talking about the New York view. How did you get this condo? I mean it must have cost a fortune. Not that I'm saying you're poor or rich. Because you never know, and I don't know how successful your business is. Not that it's any of my business. What I mean is, wow, look at the view," I blurt out. I can't stop. And on top of flushing and sweating when I'm nervous, I seem to have developed a case of can't-shut-up-itis. One minute I'm fine and the next I'm a wrecking ball. Jase, on the other hand, is calm as can be.

"I bought it from my parents."

"You mean when you moved all those years ago, you only moved to the city?"

"Yep. My mom got a job in the city, and Dad was able to travel for work, so we moved here. They retired and headed south, but the city is in my veins. They gave me a great deal, so I bought it. As for being rich, what do you consider rich? One million, two million? That I don't have, but I did have enough to buy this from my parents and renovate the entire place without going into debt. I invested all my money I made while in the military, even most of the money I made from my job with my dad."

"They must have been one hell of an investor. I need their name."

"Her name is Margaret Carter, and she also goes by the name Mom." He smiles proudly.

"Well, you know she won't steer you wrong then."

"Cass."

"Yeah."

"I don't feel much like talking about my mom right now," he says as he grabs my cheek in his hand to turn my head more.

"What do you feel like doing then?"

He takes the wine from my hand and puts it on a nearby table. When he comes back, he returns to the same position as before, but his eyes are darker, and his pupils are dilated. That tongue of his darts out ever so slightly to lick his full lips; I could go on and on because he does everything I have read about in books that men do when they are turned on. It makes me even hotter, wetter, and panting like Razor when he sees the female Doberman next door.

"This." He says one word, one word that sounds so unbelievably hot, so powerful, and so final that it puts me in such a state of arousal, I know I can't leave here without having him at least once, maybe twice, but hell, three time's a charm, right? That should last me about a month or two.

Then he kisses me and all thoughts of working him out of my system leave, simply because this man can kiss like nobody's business. Jase has the perfect set of lips for kissing. Full and soft. He does this thing where he leans down, gives a little suck on my top lip, then my bottom before completely claiming my mouth. He's not even using his tongue, and I'm moaning.

I turn my body toward him, just so I can touch him more. My hands run up his chest and straight to his head where I can run my fingers through his hair, which is so soft and free of any product. While he keeps one hand against my jaw, his other lowers to my ass. He doesn't grab it, doesn't squeeze it; no, he just keeps running his hand up and down slowly.

At the same time, he licks the seam between my lips, like he's asking for access, he cups my ass, and his thumb starts kneading my hips with these slow circles. I think I moan or sigh, but I definitely do something that has me granting him access to every inch of my mouth. Our kiss turns from PG to rated R in a flash.

His tongue is red hot. I could be wrong; it very well may be mine. This man puts me in a permanent hot flash state everywhere. He does this amazing twisting thing with his tongue as he moves in and out of my mouth; it's almost as if he wraps his tongue around mine for a second before pulling away. I don't want him to pull away, though. I want him to do it over and over a million times more—it feels that good.

My hands tighten in his hair the more turned on I get. Tighter and tighter, I pull; he lets out this groan, and then I'm off my feet. With one hand, Jase manages to lift me off my feet, my legs wrap around him, and he pins me to the glass window I was just looking out. I wonder simultaneously . . . what man can lift a woman with one hand? And god, that's hot. I haven't found one unsexy thing about this man so far, which makes me equally excited and nervous. Because if he's just this good with his hands and his kissing, then he has to be just as amazing with all his parts. Suddenly, I can't think again. Jase wraps his hands around my hair and tugs, exposing my throat to him. For a moment, he doesn't even kiss me;

he just runs his nose from the base of my neck up to my ear.

"You smell so fucking good, Cass. I can't get enough of your scent. Now, every time I smell vanilla, I'm going to get hard."

When he starts kissing my ear and neck, much like he was my mouth, my legs squeeze tightly around him in an attempt to release the building pressure. My panties have gone from damp to I need to take them off in a matter minutes.

"Jase," I whisper.

He pulls back, sets me on my feet, and looks into my eyes. Mine are pleading with him to take me already while his dance back and forth trying to make sure I'm on the same page as him. Which I am. I am on the page where the guy tosses the girl on the bed and takes her right here on the floor. But Jase doesn't do that.

"Are you sure?" he asks me.

"I'm beyond sure."

"Cass, I'm not talking about a quick fuck. I'm talking about one that is going to last from now until you go back to work on Monday. I may even try to convince you to call in sick then because I have a feeling that forty-eight hours of complete access to your body won't be enough."

Remember what I said about my panties? Well, now they are so uncomfortably wet that I have to get them off. I reach down under my dress, hook my fingers in the lacy material, and drag them down my legs. With one hand on Jase, I step out of them, one leg at a time. I let them dangle on my finger as I hold them out to him.

"I think that sounds perfect. I've been saving up my sick time in case something important came up. So Jase . . . you'd better not disappoint me."

What happens next is my fantasy come to life. He grabs the lace from my fingers, breathes in my scent, and then puts them in his pocket. When he begins to stalk me like I'm his prey, I'm forced to walk backward. My back comes into contact with a set of stairs, and he cages me in with his arms on either side of me.

"Once we go up to my bed, Cass, you're mine. Do you think you can handle that?"

I can't talk because I'm biting my lip, so I just nod, when I really want to scream, "Yes. Please, Yes."

"Climb up for me, baby."

I was slightly disappointed that he wasn't going to carry me until I turn. These are not stairs; I'm looking at something closer to a ladder than an actual set of stairs. There is no possible way he could carry me up these. And let me tell you, climbing this is not that easy with heels on.

From behind me, I hear a stream of soft-spoken curse words. I stop on the fifth step to check and see if Jase is okay. Knowing my luck, he very well could have fallen off the ladder that he hadn't even started climbing yet. But there he is, one hand on the side of the ladder, one foot on a step, and he's staring straight up.

"Are you okay?" I ask.

"Just keep climbing. You're giving me quite the view up your dress, though. And since you seem to be taking your dear old time sashaying up my ladder, my next project is to put in a set of fucking stairs so I can carry you up there myself."

At that point, I was ready to climb the remaining fifteen or so rungs and get down to it. I grabbed one heel and tossed it somewhere. The second one goes a little rogue and breaks a corner lamp. We both watch as the lamp does the whole *timber* motion then listen as the bulb explodes next.

I wince. "Sorry."

"Fuck it; it was a cheap piece of crap."

"Shouldn't we clean it up at least?"

Jase takes two steps, moves his hand up the back of my thigh, and then touches me between my legs.

"Fuck the lamp," I say.

I'm a girl on a mission. If I could, I would take the steps two at a time. I finally make it up after what seems like hours, and Jase is right smack dab behind me. I barely have a second to look at his room, which is very masculine and clean. He doesn't waste any time; he picks me up right from where I'm standing, which is in front of him, and carries me straight to his bed.

Before he completely lets me go, he holds me just under my chin, turns my head to the side, and whispers—no, more like gravels—in my ear, "Did I tell you how much I love dessert, Cass?"

The way he's holding me won't allow me to answer; all I can do is shake my head once.

"It's my favorite meal. And you know what else?" He pauses for a moment to slowly lower the zipper on my dress. After he gives the straps one good tug, it pools at my feet while I hold my breath, waiting for him to answer his own question. "I think you'll be the best fucking dessert I've ever tasted."

Good god, my heart, my breath, and my limbs stop working all at the same time. I have no clue how I'm going to make it on the bed, but Jase does it for me when he scoops me up, wraps my legs around him, and gently lowers me onto the softest bed I've ever felt in my life. Then to make it even better, Jase lays his weight on top of me—not in a crushing way, but in a way that I can feel his muscles touching me, and it makes me want them to be against me completely, flesh to flesh.

As he lowers his mouth to mine this time, his kiss is different, more powerful. He cups my face in both his hands and does this whole lip and tongue dance. That's the only way to describe it; each nibble, each lick, and each suck of my lip is a perfectly choreographed dance that has my body trying to move against him. It can't, though, because his weight isn't allowing me to, which just makes it hotter.

Suddenly, he's not laying on me anymore. I want to scream no when he stops, until he takes off his shirt, and then I want to sing. When he stands to take off his jeans, I want to call his mom and say thank you over and over again for making this beautiful man possible and give him an Academy award, or whatever the sexy body version would be, for being so perfect.

He watches me watching him, and even that is hot; the way he licks his lip as if he's dying for a taste of me. And by god, I want him to taste me so fucking bad. I might burst into flames just thinking about it. I'm that hot. I sit up to unbutton and remove my bra because one: it's the only thing I'm wearing, and two: I don't really want to keep dragging this out. I'm beyond ready for him. I drop the annoying, push-up, wired, devil-made material on the ground. And my boobs are so happy to be free at last.

"Goddamn, you're beautiful," Jase says as he looks at me with this his thumb pressed against his lip.

He is over me again in a flash, cupping me in each hand.

Between his thumb and forefinger, he pinches and teases Peaches and Rose, and they are in heaven. When he lowers his mouth and licks, a sound I've never heard myself make escapes me. I'm pretty sure I just purred, if not very close to it. The more he sucks on each of my nipples, the louder my purrs become. Then he starts heading south.

When he kisses down there once, I think any coherent thoughts leave me. I become one big ball of oh-my-god-this-feels-too-good, I could die happy right now if you just keep doing that right there.

Only, it keeps getting better and better. The man has a talented tongue to go with his talented fingers. He brings me to the edge only to make me beg for more when he starts kissing my inner thighs. Jesus Christ, that feels good too. The only thing for me to grab is his head and hair because I really need something to hold once he starts doing this thing with his mouth. It's this whole suck, kiss, lick thing, and it feels so fantastic that I know I can't hold on much longer. I pull his hair harder, which makes him moan against me, and I know I'm going to burst in less than ten seconds.

"Don't stop. I'm so close," I all but beg.

It only takes one more flick of his tongue, and the heavens burst open. The angels start singing "Glory Hallelujah," and I have the second best orgasm of my life. I'm hoping there will be a third because I'm pretty sure that will be epic. But right now, I'm just trying to catch my breath.

Jase rises to his knees, licks his top lip, and then lowers his boxer briefs. Good fucking God, Jase has the human equivalent to a whale's penis. He's large and not just in length, either; he's thick, and holy fucking shit, he's pierced. There's this bar running through the head of his dick, and it's hot.

Like really hot. He strokes himself as he says, "Chocolate cake was my favorite dessert until now. You just took its place, and I really love chocolate cake."

Just like that, I'm ready for him. I want to explore his body, but he doesn't let me. When I go to touch him, he stops me.

"I want to touch you, Jase."

He groans. "Fuck, Cass, I want that too. But seeing you, here on my bed, naked and sexy as hell, if you touch me, I might come undone, and when I come undone the first time, I want it to be deep inside you."

Shit, everything he says is so sexy. My answer is a simple, "Yes, please."

He reaches in his nightstand and comes back with a condom. If he won't let me touch him, then he needs to let me do this. I grab it from his hands with my cat-like reflexes. I put the wrapper between my teeth and give a good tug.

"Fuck." He groans as I slowly roll the latex over him. When it's on, he doesn't give me another second to touch him. My hands get pinned above my head, his body comes over mine, and he uses his legs to spread me wide.

"Cass, I want to take my time, but I'm desperate to be inside you. Desperate to feel your pussy wrapped around my cock as I fuck you. If this is too fast, tell me now before I'm too far gone. And, baby, I'm right on the edge."

"Jase . . ."

"Yeah."

"Just fuck me already."

He laces our fingers together, and with one thrust, he's in. We both let out a stream of incoherent, jumbled curse words that have no clear definition. He stills above me, kisses the hell out of me, and then releases my hands, which I'm glad for. I have a feeling I'm going to need to hold on to something for dear life.

When he ends the kiss, he rolls his hips once and then again. Slowly. Torturously slow, and by god that piercing is a miracle worker. I try to move, but his weight is on top of me, and even that feels good. I'm on the verge of another mind-blowing orgasm, but I don't want this to end just yet. I want this feeling, this tingling all over my body, to last forever.

One by one, he lifts my thighs. His legs spread slightly under me, which lifts my ass at an angle that only makes him go deeper, deeper than I've felt any man.

"Fuck, Cass, you feel so fucking good."

I can't think straight, so I say the first word that comes to mind, "Ditto."

His movements speed up, and I'm one step closer to my release. Remember when I said I needed to hold onto something? Well, it turns out Jase's ass is perfect for holding onto. You could bounce a quarter off his ass, all tight and round. My nails are most likely leaving marks, but he doesn't seem to mind because the harder I dig, the harder he thrusts.

"Feels so good, Jase."

"Goddamn, Cass, your pussy was made for my cock." He raises one of my feet and places it on his chest. Things just keep getting better. The man must have read a book titled *Ways to make a Woman come in Minutes* because that's what I'm about to do. At this point, I think he's getting close too. The grip he has on my leg keeps getting tighter and tighter until my leg is thrown over his shoulder and I'm practically bent in half. Thank God for those yoga classes.

I know I'm going to lose control. I feel it over every inch

of my body, even the hairs on my head are tingling with the anticipation of this orgasm.

"I'm going to come, Jase. Oh, god, I'm going to come." I don't care what I sound like, even though I probably sound like some cheesy porn movie, because it's true. The whole room sounds and smells like sex. I'm on the edge teetering and trying to wait for him to get off too.

"Come for me, baby. I'll be right there with you." He moves faster. I can see his face straining to hold on just like I am. He pounds into me harder, and I'm gone.

For a second, I get that "I'm at the top of a rollercoaster and I'm about to fall" feeling. My toes curl, and my whole body stiffens for a moment until it goes to that all over tingly sensation. I think I say, "Yes," but I can't tell you if it was out loud or not.

Jase thrusts three more delicious times, which prolongs my orgasm. His jaw goes tight, his arm grips my leg like it's his lifeline, and then he stills and says, "Fuck."

He strokes inside me a few more times before pulling out and falling beside me on the bed. We turn to look at each other, and we both look like we just ran a marathon.

First, I say it. "Holy shit."

Then he replies, "I'll raise you with a holy fucking shit."

I don't know if I should laugh or cry because that was singularly the best sex of my life.

Jase

I'm lying next to Cass. What I'm really thinking is, *Holy shit, I'm lying next to Cass.* The girl I never forgot. There's always that one girl who stays in the forefront of your mind, and she's it for me.

Don't get me wrong, I'm also thinking, *I just had fucking amazing sex with Cass*. Sex I intend to have multiple times. That was just the warm-up for what's to come. And I plan to make her come a lot.

I turn off the light, thinking she may need a little rest before round two, and pull her chest against mine. When she rolls onto her back, I'm disappointed. I know most men aren't into the whole cuddle thing, but I personally love when a woman wraps her body around mine. But she's not pulling away. No, she lies on her back and pulls me on top of her.

"Cass?"

"Yeah."

"What are you doing?"

"Going to sleep."

She baffles me.

"With me on top of you? I'll crush you." And that's the last thing I want to do.

"Perfect. It'll be like having my own personal Jase-sized blanket." She kisses me one last time and closes her eyes.

She's going to be the death of me. But all it really does is give one more reason to fall a little more for this woman.

28. Must be able to make me laugh

I don't want to giggle girlishly at your lame jokes. I want to laugh so hard with you that I snort. And then I want to laugh some more because of that. You must have an odd sense of humor and accept the fact that I do too.

Monday morning, I wake up and immediately call into work. This is what personal days are for, right?

After I set my phone down on the bedside table, I cuddle back into the warmth behind me. Jase's arm comes across my stomach to pull me closer to him, and then he starts kissing my bare shoulder.

He didn't lie when he said he would keep me naked most of the weekend. It's not as if I'm complaining, though, because naked Jase is a sight to behold.

"Good morning, baby," he mumbles against my skin. His voice is husky with sleep, and the deep gravel makes me shiver.

"Morning."

"How about we shower and actually put on some clothes so we can go grab breakfast?"

I pout at that thought. He rolls me onto my back, looks

down at my face, and chuckles, until my look changes to something else, and he groans. You'd think after so many orgasms that I lost count, I'd be completely satiated, but with Jase this close to me, I can't help thinking one more would be great.

"We need food, baby."

After giving my lips a little kiss, he pulls back and rolls out of bed. I watch his firm ass as he walks across the bedroom floor into the bathroom.

"Cass?"

My eyes lift to his face where I see him smirking at me.

"You coming?"

Hell yes, I'm coming. Hopefully in more ways than one.

An hour and an orgasm or two later, we slide into the booth at the diner across from each other. It smells like syrup in here, and my mouth begins to water just thinking about the pancakes I'm about to order.

Jase grabs a menu, but I don't bother. I have a singular focus: coffee and pancakes.

The waitress comes over to take our order, but Jase gestures for me to go first. I think how very gentlemanly of him, but then I think about this weekend, and I know he's not a gentle man when he's in bed and how much he seems to like when I go first. I turn pink at that thought because now I've turned into a pervert.

The waitress walks away after she takes our order. I look over at Jase and ask, "What do you want to do today?"

He wiggles his eyebrows at me, and I laugh lightly.

"We've already gotten dressed and left the house. We might as well enjoy the land of the living while we're here," I tell him.

"I just needed breakfast. I had planned to haul you back to my cave and have my way with you all day."

The waitress, who is pouring our coffee, clears her throat, blushes, and quickly walks away.

"I think you embarrassed her."

He shrugs his shoulder. "Is there something you want to do today?"

"I feel bad that I called into work. I never do that. I need to try to work from home at some point this afternoon."

"Such a workaholic."

"Aren't you? I mean you seem like the type who would be chomping at the bit to get into the office."

"Usually I am, yes. But I have the entire day to spend with a beautiful woman, so I think work will survive."

I blush a little at that and pick up my coffee cup to take a sip.

"He's late for work and just realized he has a meeting across town in thirty minutes. He probably spent all weekend working on the project but also forgot it at home," I say, nodding out the window where a guy about our age is walking swiftly down the busy street.

Jase looks at me and tilts his head to the side before looking out the window. He smirks when he spots the guy.

I see him scan the street before pointing out a woman who looks like she's dressed for a night out on the town.

"She woke up this morning in what she thought was a millionaire's penthouse. She thought she had hit the jackpot with Mr. Armani suit until she realized the guy didn't pay for the room, the suit was a knockoff, and the hotel came to kick him out. Now she's doing the walk of shame while she comes up with an inventive way to make his life a living hell."

"Wow. Good one."

He looks so pleased with himself. Emma and I play this game all of the time. While we people watch, we like to make up little stories about them as they walk by. Not to be mean, but it just makes life more interesting while passing the time until the food comes. Yes, it's a little odd and strange, and I have never played with anyone but Emma, but I secretly love the fact that Jase looks like he's enjoying this as much as I am. He gets my humor! Oh, my god!

He gestures to me, indicating that it's my turn.

I scan the street for a second before finding an elderly man. "He ran out to get coffee for his wife. He's been doing the same thing every Monday morning for the past thirty years because he knows Hilda, his wife, doesn't like Mondays. This morning, he decided to stop for some flowers because Hilda is in an especially bad mood, and he knows lilies are her favorite."

"Cassandra Quinn, you're a romantic."

"Every woman is a romantic, whether they want to admit it or not."

"Noted."

We continue to play this game as we eat our breakfast and drink our coffee. Once we finish, Jase pays the check, and we head out onto the crowded city streets.

"Want to go take a walk?" he asks as he takes my hand.

"It's like you're trying to torture me," I grumble.

He gives my hand a tug and starts walking. "Take a walk with me."

I nod my head in agreement. "Where to?"

"It's a surprise."

We walk in silence for a few minutes. I look around at

the hustle and bustle of the city, and I can't help but smile. I love it here so much, and when I look up at Jase, I see that he has the same smile on his face as me.

"What was it like growing up here?"

"Exciting. I loved every second of it. People think that raising kids in the city restricts them; they don't have a yard to play in, but my playground was Central Park, and anything I wanted was within walking distance. What more could I ask for?"

You can hear the love he has for this city in the way he talks, and it just makes me like him even more. "Have you ever heard of the Whispering Gallery?" I ask.

He looks down at me curiously and shakes his head.

"You New Yorkers think you know everything about your city," I joke, causing him to laugh.

"Tell me about it, oh wise one," he insists.

"It's an archway in Grand Central Station. Someone can stand on one side, and whisper into the tile and the other person can hear them while standing on the opposite side."

He hums and seems to contemplate something. "I'll have to look into that."

Knowing that I shared some of my useless knowledge with him excites me more than it should. I also realize I've been smiling the entire time we've been walking, which only makes me smile more.

He comes to a stop, and I look around at where we are.

"A playground?" I ask.

"Yes."

"Are you going to throw more sand in my eye?"

His smirk turns into another smile. "No. I was such an ass. I'm sorry, Cass. Will you ever forgive me for that day?"

"Everyone called me a pirate for like a month."

His hand comes up to touch my cheek, and he runs his finger across my skin. "Does Princess Cass want me to build her another sand castle?"

I tilt my chin up in the air and give my head a little nod. "Yes, yes she does. And it'd better be the best fucking sand castle ever. Maybe then, I'll consider it."

He leans down and gives me a brief kiss on the lips. "Yes, ma'am."

He takes my hand in his and leads me over to the swings first. There are only a few people here, and I'm kind of thankful for that. No sense in scaring the kids. I hop on, and he moves behind me to push.

"Higher!" I yell, and I can hear his laughter in response.

He gives me several hard pushes, and I really get going. The only problem is when you are an adult, and you are swinging really high, it's scary as fuck. And when I get the sensation that I'm flying, I also remember I am terrified of heights.

I'm a brilliant woman. *Death by swing.* I can see my headstone now.

My hands tighten against the metal chains.

"Jase!"

"What?" he yells back.

"I want down. Now."

"Well, get down, Cass."

He says it like it's so easy.

"I can't."

"Why can't you?"

Is he really going to make me say it out loud in front of these people? And why is this goddamn swing not slowing down?

"I want down," I repeat. My heart feels like it's going to explode any second. Yes, I may be being a little dramatic right now, but I don't care. I want out of this death trap.

"Baby, get down then."

"I'm fucking scared!"

Yes, that was me who just yelled the word fuck at a playground with children present, but I'm scared and possibly starting to have a panic attack at the same time.

"You're scared?" He laughs a little like he thinks I'm kidding.

"Don't you dare laugh at me, Jason. I am scared out of my motherfucking mind. Get me down! I'm going too high."

And apparently, I'm still dropping f-bombs.

"Baby." The word sounds like he choked it out to hide his laughter.

Asshole. This is his fault.

"Catch me. I'm jumping down."

He comes around to the front of me and shakes his head. "You are not jumping. Just set your feet down."

"I can't."

"Why?"

"Because I'm jumping."

"Cass, jumping is not the best way to do—"

But his words are cut off as I jump out of the swing toward him. His eyes look as wide as saucers, and he quickly unfolds his arms to try to catch me.

"Holy shit," I scream, thinking right at the last minute that this probably wasn't such a good idea.

I'm sure I look like a drunk starfish with my arms and legs spread wide. Jase catches me but stumbles back a bit and almost takes out a kid who is running past.

It takes both of us a second to adjust to what just happened, but when we do, we both explode with laughter. I'm snorting and laughing harder because, well, I just snorted. Jase is bent over at the waist holding his side, and it takes us a good five minutes to get control of ourselves again.

"What was that?" he asks, wiping the corner of his eyes where tears caused from his laughter are falling.

I shrug. "I don't know. I had a moment, but I think we should probably do that sand castle another day."

I incline my head to the army of pissed off mothers, and his eyes briefly flick that way before he grabs my hand and leads us out of the park.

"Never ever change, Cass," he whispers, as we make the walk back to his apartment.

"Not planning on it," I say with a wink.

Jase

I hold Cass's hand tightly in mine as we walk back to my condo. I don't think I've laughed that hard in years, but that's just one of the many reasons I love being around her. There's never a dull moment with my girl.

When I'm with her, I feel alive in the best way possible. It doesn't matter if we're at a meeting, she's underneath me in bed, making up silly stories about people on the street, or watching her fly at me from a damn swing. Whenever I'm with her, I don't ever want our time together to end. Is this what love feels like? It's too soon for me to fall in love with her, but as I look down into her smiling face, I know that if I'm not already in love, I'm falling damn fast. I just need to come up with a plan that allows me to keep this amazing woman forever because now that I have her, I can't imagine a day of my life without her in it.

29. Must compliment me

It took me two hours to get ready for dinner. When I walk out of that bedroom, the heavens had better part, and the red carpet had better roll out. I want to know that you appreciate my effort, but that's not the only time I want compliments. I want compliments on my mind. Rarely do men do this, and why is that? Yes, I know my ass looks fine in these jeans. Yes, I know my eyes are a beautiful shade of brown, but did you hear anything that just came out of my mouth? Compliment my brain, and you will get to the fun times much faster.

"Cass, I need you." Jase sounds like he's begging me for help. I'm almost scared that something happened to him.

"What's wrong?"

"I have to go to a party tonight, and I need a plus one. I just took out the invitation and right there on it, it says Mr. Jason Carter plus one. You can't let me go as a negative." He's really adorable when he begs.

"Bring Lance as your plus one," I tease.

"Lance already has one, and I can't go as a third wheel. I know it's late notice, but you have to save me from a life of forever being the guy who came dateless."

How could I say no to that? I don't. In fact, I take the rest of the day off from work to get primped and ready. He said it's a cocktail party release event for a video game he and Lance did some graphics for. It's projected to be the game of the year, according to what I read up about the company. I needed to know a little about what I was walking into, so I did a little research on TnA Games. This party is the talk of the city, at least in the gamers' world.

I had a dress I was saving for a wedding that I was going to—which was canceled after the groom claimed on the eve of their wedding that he tripped and fell inside the wedding coordinator's vagina in the bathroom—that would be perfect for the occasion. It's smoky gray and sleek. From one side, it looks like an ordinary drape dress, but if I turn the other way, one shoulder is exposed. And let's just say, if I wasn't wearing sticky tape, Rose would be making an appearance. She's already peeking out just enough since both her and Peaches are free flying tonight. Also, this dress gives me an excuse to wear my teal, peep toe Louboutin shoes.

Promptly at five, Jase shows up. He's barely knocked, and I have the door open when my jaw hits the floor. Everything he's wearing makes him look successful and just downright hot. His dress pants form to his thighs and hips so tightly that I want to touch the fabric and feel what they're made of, a white dress shirt hugs his arms, and I'm only a little sad that his tattoos are covered because either way, he's total arm candy. Instead of a jacket, he went with a tie and vest combination that is sadly covering his washboard abs, but damn, he looks just as good with clothes as he does without.

He's standing there doing that whole one arm supporting his elbow and thumb to the lip thing that turns me on. He's studying me and my body, and something is so sexy about it that my body flushes. When he lifts his finger, indicating he wants me to twirl around, I do so gladly.

When I have my one side facing him, I pause and glance over my shoulder at him.

"Fuck, Cass. This place is going to be filled with gamers who never get out of the house, so I'm not sure I want them looking at you and for you to become their fantasy."

"I'll just change into a burlap sack then," I joke.

"Fuck no; I'm going to have the sexiest date tonight. I just don't know how I'll keep my hands off you."

I give a little extra bend when I reach for my wrap and clutch from the table. As I walk past him and out the front door, I pause to say, "Who says you have to keep your hands off me? In fact, I'm counting on the fact that you will be touching me . . . often."

I think I hear him say something like, "Better be careful about what you ask for," but I could have heard wrong.

It's a thirty-minute ride to the venue. The hotel did a fabulous job of transforming the hall into a video gamer's dream. All along the outer walls, consoles are set up with each of the games that TnA has out on the market, but the rest of the area looks like an upscale club. There is a dance floor with television screens displaying the new release of Sapphira and The Seven Swords. Sapphira is a medieval princess whose seven swords give her a different ability.

The first time I looked up the game title, it took me to the wrong site. Let's just say, Sapphire and the Seven Swordsmen is not the family fun night game being featured here. *Don't click on it*, I kept telling myself. I did, though, and it wasn't pretty.

This game will be a hit with both male and female video gamers. Girls will gravitate to the female hero while boys will love the whole swordfight aspect and the fact that Sapphira is hot for an animated chick.

Jase takes my hand and leads me to the bar area, where Lance and his date are, along with a few other people. As I look around, it strikes me as odd that no one is dancing. Everyone gathers around the televisions and are playing the games, and I think, quite possibly, a tournament of some kind has been organized too for money.

"Here he is," an older silver-haired man says to Jase as he sticks out his hand to him.

"Mr. Mercer, thanks for having me. This is my girlfriend, Cassandra."

"Well, now, you've been keeping secrets, haven't you?" The female next to Lance says, "I'm Doreen, Lance's friend. Nice to meet you."

Jase moves close to me. "Mr. Mercer is the owner of TnA Games. The guy over there is the lead designer of TnA and on his right is the programmer."

Everyone introduces each other while Mr. Mercer orders a round of champagne—the good kind too. I'm talking Cristal for everyone.

"Here's to a successful release and to starting the sequel next week," Mr. Mercer says as he raises his glass.

I take a sip of the champagne along with everyone, and when the bubbles hit my tongue, it's delicious. When a second round is ordered, I gladly take it, along with Jase's since he switched to a more manly drink of whiskey.

"So, Cassandra, what do you do for a living?" Mr. Mercer asks me.

"I work for VYBE."

"The advertising agency?"

"So you've heard of us."

"Yes. I've been thinking of taking someone on from there. You'll have to give me your card."

Jase chimes in, "Cassandra is actually working with Lance and me through her own company. She's brilliant when it comes to slogans."

"Is that right?" Mr. Mercer asks.

"Did you know Mr. Mercer owns a share in the aquarium in New Jersey? Like you, Cass also has a love for sea life. What were you telling me about whales the other night, baby?" Jase grins as he asks me.

I rack my brain because I can't use the word dick here. This is a semi-formal event, and I do have some decorum. I'll get him for this later, though. I have an ah-ha moment. "It was about the blue whale, I believe. Did you know their heart can be as big as a small car, and its heartbeat can be detected as far as two miles away? Not only that but their mouths are also big enough to fit a hundred people inside."

Jase leans down close to my ear. "Well, it needs to be that big to accommodate all that dick."

"I did not know that," Mr. Mercer says.

Waiters keep walking by with cocktails and food for the next two hours. When we've heard one too many jokes involving computer parts, Jase says, "Excuse us."

He takes me by surprise and starts to lead me out on the dancefloor. He pulls me close and starts moving to the music. I begin to wonder if my theory is right; if a man can dance, he knows how to move his body in bed.

"I can't believe you did that to me," I say.

"What?"

"You put me on the spot and wanted me to talk about whale dick to a CEO of a company that may contact me about a job."

"Well, you handled it like a champ. I mean I knew you were smart."

"You think I'm smart?"

"No, Cass, I know you're brilliant," he says as his hand moves to my back.

"And talented." Then he traces small circles on the skin, and I sigh.

He leans in and nibbles on my ear while he says, "And sexy as fuck in this dress."

He can't say things like that in my ear and expect me to not get turned on.

"Is it too soon to go home?" I ask.

He looks at his watch. "I think we've schmoozed enough for one night. Don't you?"

We say a quick goodbye to everyone, and Mr. Mercer takes my phone number. He promises to call in the morning and set up a meeting with my company. This could be a huge break for me. I'm on cloud nine, and I want to thank Jase for this amazing night, and for making me feel special, and last but not least, for calling me his girlfriend.

My apartment is closer and finally repaired. Jase takes the keys from my hand to open the door. He pins me to the kitchen counter, kisses me on the neck, but then stops too soon.

"Nice kitchen and counters," he tells me as he lifts me on top of my brand new granite.

Razor takes this moment to let us know he's there.

"I should take him out." I'm annoyed that whatever was

starting has to stop for now.

"I'll do it. You get comfortable," he says as he grabs the leash from the rack by the door. "And, Cass, by that I mean dress off, but those shoes can stay."

I do just that too. I tried to sit on the counter again, but it was too cold, so I decided to just wait in the entryway. When he comes back inside, I'm ready and waiting in only my heels.

"Look who I ran into," Jase says then stops when he sees me. Emma is right behind him.

"Hey, Cass."

"Hey, Em."

She starts to make herself at home like she doesn't even realize I'm naked.

"So what are you two up to tonight? How did the gaming thing go?" she asks.

Jase is not moving. In fact, he still has a hold of Razor's leash, and Razor is furiously trying to get to Emma.

"Fine. Hey Em, do you think you could come back like, say tomorrow? I'm sort of in the middle of something."

"Sure. How about I take my little buddy with me? He and I haven't had a sleepover in a while."

She's one of the few people Razor likes.

"That'd be great."

She walks over to Jase, takes the leash, and starts to leave. She stops at the open door, replying, "By the way, I'm totally borrowing those shoes."

Jase

What the fuck just happened?

30. Must know my favorites

I love ice cream or wine, so it would be nice if you would remember my favorite brands. You should be able to order my drink at a restaurant with confidence because that shit is sexy as hell. I want you to cook my favorite meals because you know it makes me happy. Know that I adore sunflowers and why. Learn my favorites, and I'll learn yours, even the naughty ones.

The morning after the party, I wake up a little later than normal. Instead of getting out of bed like a good little girl, so I'm not late, I wait while Jase makes coffee and brings my much-needed cup to me in bed. I don't get this sort of treatment when I'm alone, so I might as well enjoy it. After my first cup of the nectar of the gods is finished, I finally get up and get my lazy ass moving.

Sharing a bathroom with Jase is quite the distraction. I'm applying my makeup while I watch his naked ass in the shower. When I see the soap bubbles running down his chest, I almost lose an eye to the mascara wand.

Focus, Cass. You have to go to work.

I steel my resolve and focus on the task at hand, when all

I really want to do is jump in that shower and lick him, but there's no room for more sexy time.

"You ready?" Jase asks thirty minutes later as he pockets his keys and wallet.

I slide into my heels and nod my head. "Yep. But I need more coffee."

"Of course, you do." He laughs. "We can stop by the coffee shop on the way."

I grab my purse, and we take the stairs down. When we step out onto the busy sidewalk, I realize I love the fact that Jase walks with his hand on either my lower back or holding mine. This morning, it's the hand on my lower back, and I secretly smile.

We both decide the coffee shop that's between our offices would be the easiest. Jase holds the door open, and I smile up at him as I slide under his arm. As I walk inside, the smell of freshly baked goods and coffee hits me, and I'm positive this must be what heaven smells like.

The line is short, especially for this early in the morning. When we reach the counter, I open my mouth to place my order, but Jase beats me to it.

"She will have a double caf, non-fat caramel mocha swirl latte with no whipped cream, and I'll have regular coffee, cream, no sugar, please. Do you want one of those scones you were looking at?" he asks, glancing down at me.

I seem to be having a deer in headlights moment and forgotten how to speak, so I reply with a nod of my head.

He turns to look back at the cashier. "And a cranberry scone and a bran muffin."

I watch as he pulls his wallet out and pays, but I'm still somewhat stunned that he remembered my drink. He puts his hand on my lower back and leads me over to the pickup counter where the barista hands us our coffees and the bag of pastries. When we walk out of the coffee shop, Jase hands me my scone then kisses me on my cheek.

"Have a great day, beautiful. Want to meet for lunch?"

How does he remember my coffee order? It's not like it was a simple order. I could understand him remembering a simple vanilla latte, yet even though my drink name is ten miles long, he still got it right.

"Yeah, lunch sounds good," I murmur.

"See you then, beautiful." Jase walks away looking proud; so proud he starts whistling.

Not me, though, I'm still standing on the sidewalk watching him head down the street until I can't see him anymore. I shake off my shock and turn to walk in the direction of my office before I'm late. *It's just coffee, Cass.* It's not a big deal. He's heard you order it twice so calm the fuck down.

I end up having to cancel lunch plans with Jase because work has me swamped. So when Bettie buzzes my office phone and tells me a food carrier is here to drop something off for me, I'm a little surprised.

I close the tab on my computer and make my way out of my office to where the courier is standing by Bettie's desk. In his hand is a brown paper bag, just like the one my mom use to pack for me when I was a kid.

"Cassandra Quinn?" he asks.

"That's me, but I didn't order anything."

"I'm just the delivery boy, and it's already paid for. Have a good lunch," he mumbles.

"Hey, wait. Your tip," I call after him.

"That's taken care of too, ma'am," he says over his shoulder.

I ignore Bettie's curious expression and head back to my office. I set the bag down and stare at it in confusion for a second before figuring to hell with it. I won't figure out this food mystery until I unpack what's inside.

I pull out a turkey and Swiss on wheat, a cup of fresh fruit, a fruit punch juice box, and two Hershey kisses. My mother used to send me this exact lunch to school every day, but why in the hell is my mother sending me lunch? Has she lost her mind? Has she gone senile? Maybe I need to call my dad and have him look into moving her into a home because she's clearly going crazy.

Before I can jump off the deep end and make the call to have my mother committed, I pull out the last item. It's a napkin, but what's written on it is what catches my attention.

I hope you have a great rest of your day, beautiful. Since I know you won't stop for lunch, I'm making it a priority to feed you. That way I know that busy brain of yours is working at full capacity. - Jase

He's good. And sweet. I hold the napkin to my chest like a little girl who just got a note from her crush, which I guess is a pretty accurate description of what this is anyway.

I immediately pick up my phone and type out a text.

Thank you so much for lunch. I love it.

I tap my finger impatiently against my desk as soon as I see the little dots pop up, knowing that Jase is texting back.

Jase: You're very welcome. I hope you still like turkey and Swiss.

Cass: It's still my favorite. Can I make it up to you having to cancel lunch?

Jase: What did you have in mind?

Cass: Lots of things, but for now, how about a drink

after work?

I smile to myself. Text flirting is fun.

Jase: Sounds great. I'll be out of here at around 6:00 tonight . . . How about we meet at that new martini bar on Welch Ave?

Cass: Yes. See you then!

I lay my phone down and start unwrapping my sandwich. He's spoiling me, and I could totally get used to this.

As luck were to have it, I'm running late to meet Jase. My last client would not shut the hell up, and I kept having to assure him that I had everything handled. The cab pulls up outside the hip new bar, and I rush to hand him the cash and climb out.

I had already text Jase and told him I was running a little behind; he said not to worry, that he would go ahead and get us a table.

I scan the dim bar until I see my man. My man. When did I start referring to him as mine?

He wore a suit and tie to work today, but he has ditched the tie and rolled up the sleeves of his dress shirt. His hair looks like he's run his hands through it a million times, and he looks sexy as hell.

"I'm so sorry I'm late," I say as I approach the table, and he stands.

"You're fine, Cass." He smiles then lowers his lips to mine.

Oh, that's nice.

His mouth leaves mine all too soon, and he pulls out my chair for me to sit.

I look at the drink in front of me in confusion.

"Whose is that?" I can't keep the jealousy out of my

voice. Was another woman just sitting here?

He chuckles as he sits. "It's yours. I ordered it when you said you were on the way. They just delivered it."

I turn my head to the side. "I didn't tell you what I wanted."

"You drink a cranberry martini almost every time you order a cocktail. Do you want something else? I can send that back." He waves his hand in the direction of who I am assuming is our waitress.

"Wait. That's not necessary. This is what I would have ordered."

He looks back over at me and gives his head a quick nod. "So how was your day?"

I want to answer him, I really do, but I'm still stuck on the fact that this amazing man actually notices things about me. He pays attention. Not because I had to ask him to, but because he wants to. There is no telling what he's noticed about me, and we have only just started dating!

I get up from my chair, and he lifts an eyebrow at me in confusion. I quickly make my way over to his side of the table, sit on his lap, bend my head, and touch my lips to his. For a second, his are still and I'm sure I've shocked him, but he quickly snaps out of it and kisses me back. One of his hands comes to my head and tangles in my hair while the other finds my cheek. He holds me to him and moans down my throat when my tongue comes out to swipe against his lips.

Maybe I should have waited until later to show my thanks because now my panties are getting soaked in the middle of a bar, but I can't say that I really care about that right now.

Jase

I know Cass isn't one for over-the-top public displays of affection, so I'm not sure what caused her to kiss me in this bar, but I'm not complaining. Anytime I can have her touching me, I'm good with that. I missed her today, even though we were only apart for a few hours. What I really want to do is carry her back to my apartment and spend the rest of the night with her naked body wrapped around me, but I want her to know that's not all this is for me. She's mine. Every part of her is mine, but I'm hers too. I hope she knows that. She slows the kiss down but doesn't pull all of the way back yet.

"Thank you," she breathes against my lips.

I'm not sure what she's thanking me for, but whatever it is, I want to make sure I do it as much as possible if that is going to be her reaction.

She stands up, takes a step back, and smooths down her hair and dress before sitting back across from me. She takes a sip of her drink and hums in delight.

"My day was fantastic. How was yours?"

I chuckle at her. God, I'm so in love with this crazy woman.

31. Be the alpha

I don't want a pushover. I want someone who will wrap his arm around my waist and show the world I'm his and be damn proud of that fact. I want to be kissed in public, and I want your hand on my ass when you see another man looking at it. I don't have time to reassure you that you're all I see. I want you to be the one to make sure I don't have a reason to look anywhere else.

Jase and I are just leaving the movie theater. He said he wanted to take me on a real date—not to a bar but for pizza and a movie. And that sounded great.

"How did you like the movie?" I ask him. He let me pick the movie, which was a romantic comedy.

"I won't admit this to anyone but you. I liked it, though." Jase takes my hand in his as we walk to the exit.

"Cass? Is that you?"

I look to my left and see who's calling me. "Oh, my god, Chip?"

"Yes. Wow, Cass, you look great."

"Thanks. Chip, this is my boyfriend, Jase. Jase, this is my umm . . ."

"I haven't heard that name in years. Hey, I'm Randy. Cass and I dated way back in high school," Chip, or Randy rather, says as he holds out his hand to Jase, which Jase shakes then quickly wraps his arms around my waist and pulls me close.

"It wasn't that long ago," I joke.

"Ten years," Chip reminds me.

"Crap, we're getting old."

"Well, you still look amazing."

Jase's grip around me tightens so much that I have to squeeze his arm to let him know.

"So, Chip, what do you do?" Jase asks him in a condescending tone.

"I'm a heart surgeon."

I think Jase may have said, "Well isn't that goddamn fucking perfect."

"That's great. I told you, you were good with your hands in Biology," I tell him, and I hear Jase growl next my ear.

"Well, listen, I'd better get going. It was great seeing you again. We should get together sometime and reminisce."

"Sure, sounds great."

Chip hands me his business card, and I stuff it in my pocket. As we reach Jase's truck, he reaches into my pocket and takes out the card with Chip's number.

"You're not getting together with him, Cass."

"Why not?"

"Did you see the way he looked at you? He wants in your pants."

He tosses Chip's card in the nearby trashcan, and I think he's being ridiculous. There was no look, just a friendly conversation. Okay, so what, we dated—that doesn't mean any old feelings are there. And as for wanting in my pants, he wasn't going to get in there again.

"It's not like that, and he does not."

"Do I have to remind you who you belong to now?"

The way he's pressing his body to mine is making me hot. "Maybe just a little."

"I'm not joking, Cass. I don't want to hear you tell a guy you used to date he has great hands because I may have to break them."

"He was my lab partner and he was good with a scalpel. Besides, yours are better." To prove to him how much more I love his, I raise his hand to my lips and kiss each one of his fingers.

He growls again. "Fuck."

He presses his lips to mine, and it's as if his whole body is part of this kiss. He's possessive, controlling, and leaves me wishing we were in my bed. "Take me home and show me I'm yours, Jase."

As we drive the few blocks, I can't stop touching him. First, his arm, and then I move to his thighs. I never knew a man's legs could be so sexy, but Jase showed me something new I like on a man. Every inch of him is powerful, not just his arms. Just thinking about his body has my hand moving to the left and over his zipper.

"Cass."

"Mmm?"

"What are you doing?"

"Touching my man." When I say that, I feel him harden more. He's both a grower and a shower, by the way. When I reach for the button on his jeans, his hand stops me.

"Two more blocks. As much I would fucking love for you to touch me, I'm not in the mood to get in a wreck. Plus, I want to be able to watch." Jase presses my hand firmly against him one last time before bringing my mouth to his lips.

We pull into the garage below the building and make it to the front door. His body presses against my back as he starts kissing my neck. It's all so very distracting that while I'm trying to press the numbers into the keypad entry, I keep fumbling. Jase takes over and opens the door on the first try.

Before we make it inside, another person calls my name.

"Cass, long time, no see."

Oh shit, it's Jackson, and he's walking a dog.

"Since the weather is so nice, I decided to take Shadow for a walk. Doesn't look like we'll be getting any rain, since you seem to be without your umbrella you used to like so much. Isn't it funny that he led me here? I guess you left your dog upstairs," he casually says.

Jase is still against me. In fact, I've buried my head on his shoulder in an attempt to hide.

"Another ex?" he asks.

"We went on one date."

"Do I have to rip off his hands too?"

"No. It was a bad date."

Jase swoops down and tosses me over his shoulder. He turns to Jackson. "Cass is busy indefinitely. If you don't mind, I'm about to take my woman upstairs and show her what a real man can do. You can just turn your ass around and fuck off."

Jackson looked like he was about to piss himself. His dog, on the other hand, was ready to leave and pulled him forward. I should have been a little angry, but for some reason, that just made the whole carrying me up the stairs over his shoulder hotter.

"Jase, I can walk."

"Not happening."

"It's four flights."

He slaps my ass, and good god, that sends a shiver up through my body.

"Do you doubt me? It could be fifty flights, and I'd still carry you because I can."

He doesn't even let me open the front door; he just demands my keys and takes control of everything. He sets me on the couch, walks back to the door, whistles, and Razor comes running. I didn't even know he could do that—the dog, I mean. I've tried to teach him a million tricks, and he would just look at me like I was crazy.

Jase takes him outside and comes back. He points at the dog bed in my office that he bought for Razor after one too many times of whining at the foot of the bed, and the little shit obeys. He trots right in there climbs in, spins around twice, and lays down.

"How did you do that?" I ask him.

Jase just gives me that lopsided knowing grin of his and stalks toward me. "Maybe I'll show you someday."

He takes off his shirt then mine along with my bra. "Right now, I'd like to show you something else."

This time, he takes off my jeans first then his.

"What's that?" I say practically panting.

"How we fit perfectly together." He sits, pulls me on top of his lap, and grinds against me. "That you are mine in every way."

He touches each of my breasts, and my nipples grow hard. "Peaches and Rose."

"What did you say?"

He touches my left breast. "I've named her Peaches because your skin reminds me of peaches and cream."

He gives a gentle squeeze to my right nipple. "And this is Rose because your nipples remind me of rose buds when I touch them."

There's no way I've mentioned that before. More than ever, I want to show him I am his. To show him just how much it means to me to hear him say these things. Because I feel them too. I'm falling for Jase, and that both scares and thrills me.

I start kissing his strong jaw covered in the scruff that I love so much and down to his chest that I equally love. When I reach his abs, I take my time kissing and nibbling each of his eight rippling muscles.

His fingers rest between the strands of my hair when I take his thick cock in my hand, and when I give him two long strokes, he tugs my hair.

"Kiss it," he both tells and begs me.

I stick my tongue out and give him one gentle lick, and when I kiss the head, I hear him take in a slow deep breath.

"Fuck, Cass, do that again."

This time, I circle my tongue around his piercing twice before lowering my lips over him. I never even considered a man with a piercing before, but I'll never want anything different. But then again, I don't want any other man besides Jase.

Gently, he presses his hand on the back of my head, silently asking me to take him fully, which I do gladly. His taste invades my mouth—it's manly, musky, and now, he's become my favorite dessert or appetizer. The combination of his hardness and cool metal against my tongue, the softness of his skin, and the way he's moving his hips has me beyond wet.

"Your mouth feels so fucking good."

I look up to see Jase watching my every move, and I can't take my eyes off him. I move faster, suck him harder, and use my hand to massage him at the same time.

"Keep doing that. Feels so good. Going to come."

When he says that, it makes me want to get him there now. I take him in as far as I can and swallow.

"Goddamn, Cass."

I smile as much as I can with his cock in my mouth and do it again because I don't think he's really complaining.

His hips start moving back and forth, and I know he's going to come soon. And for the first time, I want to taste a man—not any man, only this man—in my mouth.

"Don't take your eyes off me, Cass. I want you to watch as I come between those lips of yours."

I raise and lower my mouth only twice more when I feel the first twitch.

"Gonna. Come. Now."

His words are short, broken, and then the first taste of him hits my tongue. It's salty, sticky, and smooth all at the same time, and I decide I love giving my boyfriend head. I'm going to do it as often as he lets me. It makes me feel powerful to know that I can bring him to his knees and that I can make him come undone like he always does to me.

I give his beautiful cock one last kiss before climbing back on top of him.

"You're so goddamn beautiful," Jase says as he caresses my cheek.

"You're not so bad yourself."

"Thank you," he says.

"For what?"

"For coming back to me." He doesn't let me answer, and I really don't think I can because my heart just did this whole jolt thing, like it finally came to life, but I know since Jase, it's been working overtime. Every time I see him, talk to him, or we're together, it's working overtime from beating so fast.

He lifts me once again to take me to my bedroom where he shows me over and over that I'm his. I'm so completely his that I think for the second time I may be in love. The funny thing is it's still the same man, and that's not really funny at all.

Jase

I've never been a possessive man before, but something in her brings it out in me, especially at the thought of another man who has touched her.

She's sleeping now, and I can't stop watching her; it could be because I'm lying on top of her, but it seems to be the only way she'll actually fall asleep. It's not the most comfortable way for me to lay, but if she wants me on top of her, I will give her anything she wants. I know I said tonight that she's mine, but the truth is this woman owns me. She owns every piece of me—my heart, my soul, and my body—and I wouldn't have it any other way.

32. Must know how to make tea and know that pajamas or no pants are acceptable attire whenever I feel like it

He doesn't have to be British, but is it too much to ask for a goddamn cup of tea when I'm feeling less than perfect? I mean what's a girl gotta do to find someone who remembers her period is coming up soon, and the bitch probably needs a hug or maybe some chocolate?

Also, I don't want a man who is going to bounce up in the morning, get dressed, and be ready to go at the butt crack of dawn. I'm not the rise and shine type, especially on my days off or when I'm feeling off. It doesn't bother me to spend my nights and days trolling around in my panties and tank top, so it shouldn't bother you.

I'm in the seventh circle of hell. Okay, not really, but I did just start my period. Which is pretty much the same thing. My uterus feels like it's trying to claw its way out of my body.

I get it, Mother Nature. I'm not pregnant, which is great to know, but could you maybe send an email next time?

I had plans with Jase tonight for dinner, but I had to cancel. I feel terrible that I had to do that, but as I mentioned, I'm burning up in the fiery gates of hell and probably will for the next few days. So I'm kind of busy.

I'm currently lying in a bitch ball on my couch. The whole on your side position, head to the pillow, knees pulled up as far as they can go with your arms wrapped around them. It's comforting. My heating pad is across my lower back, and I have my comfiest pajamas on. Netflix is streaming my favorite TV show, and a bar of chocolate is shoved somewhere near my head. The first day of my period is always the worst, and lucky for me, mine started on Saturday this time.

I hear a knock at my door, but I already know who it is, so I don't bother to get up. Jase called to check on me about thirty minutes ago since he knows I don't usually cancel our plans. He must have heard me whimpering because he said he would be over shortly. I didn't try to argue because hell, if he's going to stick around for the long-term, he's going to see me like this eventually.

"Come on in," I yell out. I'd given him a spare key when he offered to take care of Razor for me one day when I was working late.

His big body appears in the doorway a second later. He's holding a brown paper bag, and he has a worried expression on his face.

Razor greets him with a happy bark as he dances around in circles under Jase's feet. This development still fascinates me. Apparently, little shit loves Jase. Who would have thought?

"Hey, buddy," Jase says, scooping him up with one arm and tucking him against his side like a football. He gives Razor a couple of scratches on the head while he studies me in my current state. He seems to come to some type of realization because the worry leaves his face a little, and he gives me a look of pity.

"Are you not feeling good, snookums?"

Did he just call me snookums? I want to throw something at him, but that would require moving, so instead, I just give him my best glare.

He sets Razor down and heads toward my kitchen. I can hear him rooting around in there for a while and then I hear my bedroom door open and close a few times.

I have no idea what he's doing, and I don't really care because Satan is currently living in my ovaries and trying to kill me. I just continue to watch my show, and I nibble on my chocolate, ultimately deciding I don't care enough to get up.

He finally comes out wearing a pair of pajama pants and a t-shirt.

"What are you doing?" I ask as he hands me a cup of tea.

"I'm getting comfy with you. I made you some of the chamomile tea you like so much, and I want you to take these."

He passes me two ibuprofens, and I quirk an eyebrow in question.

"I know you haven't taken any." He's looking at me like he's daring me to say otherwise.

I sit up with a groan as I take the pills out of his hand. When I take a small sip of my tea, I taste that it's just right.

He sits down on the couch where my feet just were. "Now, do you want pizza, Chinese food, or both?"

"Both." I sigh happily into my cup of tea. The warmth hits my belly, and it feels good.

He chuckles and puts his cell phone up to his ear.

I listen to him order our food as I study him a little closer. He looks good in his lounge clothes and the red pajama pants he's wearing look so soft that it makes me want to rub my face against them. His white Air Force t-shirt looks like it's been through the wringer with a few small holes on one side. I love that I get to see him like this, and I love that he is comfortable with me seeing him like this.

I set my tea down and crawl toward him, bringing my blanket and heating pad with me, of course.

He glances over at me and smiles as he moves his arm to make a spot for me to lay on him. He scoots down farther on the couch and props his feet on the old trunk I use as a coffee table. With my head resting on his chest, I place my hand on his stomach as I listen to his voice rumble while he finishes placing our order. At the same time, I feel his hand come up and fingers start playing with my hair, and I'm pretty sure I start purring again.

When he finishes the calls, he drops his phone on the table beside him.

"I'm sorry you don't feel good, Cass," he says quietly after a minute.

"I hate Mother Nature," I mumble.

I feel his chest move as he chuckles lightly in response.

"Thank you for coming over," I say as I kiss his chest through his shirt.

"Always, baby. There is nowhere else I'd rather be."

The damn thing is I know when he says that, he really means it.

Jase

When I first got the text from Cass canceling our plans to-night, I was worried out of my mind. I rushed over to her apartment as quick as I could, only to find my girl in pain. This is the first time I've felt the need to comfort a woman. When I saw Cass on her couch looking so pitiful, all I wanted to do was make her as comfortable as possible.

I run my fingers back through her hair again because she seems to like that. She has my shirt balled up in her fist like she doesn't ever want me to move. The feeling is mutual.

I wasn't kidding when I said there wasn't anywhere else I'd rather be. It doesn't matter what state she's in; I'll be there for her.

She moves and lets out a little painful moan. I reach down and adjust the heating pad so that it's back on her lower stomach. She sighs and cuddles back into me.

I'm so far gone for this girl, and I want to spend the rest of my life having little moments like this.

33. Must learn me and don't forget the little things

Let me elaborate. Learn the shape of my body with your hands. Remember that I have a scar on my back and five birthmarks. Kiss each of my freckles and tell me which one is your favorite. Know what makes me sigh and what can make me moan.

If you really want to keep me, you have to learn not only my body but also remember something random I said yesterday. I'm not talking about the fact that my grandmother had a sister named Sue. I don't care if you remember little facts like that, but if I say something on the fly that I want to do, don't forget.

"Wine?"

Does he even have to ask? He's still looking at me like wants an answer, which is a yes.

We decide to have dinner in tonight at Jase's place, and guess what? He's cooking. I think I'm having more fun watching him cook than I am anything else. He had already started by the time I got here a few minutes ago, but from the few minutes I've seen, he's a sight to behold in the kitchen.

Razor barks at his feet, begging for a scrap of food, which is a definite no. When Jase called earlier and asked me to come over for dinner, he also asked me to stay the night. Usually, when one of us stays over at each other's place, it's been kind of assumed, not asked. He said he wanted to ask this time so I could make plans to bring Razor since the two of them seem to have formed this special bond, which also earns him huge points for wanting to make sure my sweet puppy was taken care of.

He passes me the glass of red wine, and I tip my lips up to meet his.

What I was thinking was going to be a little peck turns into something more quickly. I have to set my wine glass down before I spill it on the both of us. His hands skim down my sides and around to my ass, as he pulls me to the edge of the counter. With my arms wrapped around his neck, I pull him to me and tilt my head to the side so his tongue can slip deeper. God, I love the way he kisses me. I could happily spend all day doing this, but when I feel his length growing hard between my legs, I remember how good he is with that as well.

"I'm going to burn dinner," he mumbles against my lips.

"I'm not hungry anymore."

"Liar." He chuckles.

Okay, maybe I'm a little hungry, but he feels so good that I pout a little when he pulls away.

"So needy." He says it like it's just me.

Hell yes, I'm needy, and I know he is too. We haven't been intimate since Mother Nature paid me a visit last week. Sure, we had some heavy make-out sessions and some over the clothes petting, but I need the real thing, and luckily, I will be getting it tonight.

I sip my wine as I watch him move around the kitchen with ease. Something is insanely sexy about watching a man cook for you. I mean not only is the view amazing but also when food is involved, everything is always better.

We eat sitting on the barstools in his kitchen, and I have to say, his chicken mozzarella pasta with sun-dried tomatoes is better than at any restaurant where I've eaten. So much so, I eat a second helping before sitting back in my chair and rubbing my belly.

"That was delicious."

"I'm glad you enjoyed it." He smiles as he picks up my plate and rounds the counter, walking toward the sink.

"I'll do cleanup since you cooked," I protest.

"There's no way you are doing my dishes. I'll do them later. Let's go have a drink and relax."

After he tops off my wine glass, he grabs himself another beer, and I follow him into the living room where I practically collapse on the couch. He starts flipping mindlessly through the channels until he shuts off the television and tosses the control on the table in front of him.

"Come, take a walk with me."

I look over at him with my wine glass halfway to my lips. "Another walk? Why do you want to torture me so badly all of the time?"

He smiles and leans forward. His hand comes up, and he skims his fingers down my cheek. "I want to show you something. Will you please come take a walk with me?"

I sigh. "All right."

Since I can't seem to say no to him, I slide my shoes back on and quickly finish off my glass of wine. I have no clue where he could possibly want to take me, especially when I thought sex was a given tonight.

Razor lets out a cry, and I look over at him. "We'll be back soon. Be good," I say in my best stern voice, which only makes Jase laugh.

"How could he not be good?"

"Oh, he has you fooled. There are many ways Razor 'Little Shit' Quinn cannot be good."

When we get downstairs, I'm surprised when Jase hails a cab.

"I thought we were walking?" I ask as I slide into the backseat.

"This place isn't far, but maybe walking isn't the best idea."

He looks like he's up to something, but I shake off the feeling. Instead, I cuddle under his arm and watch the bright city lights pass by my window. About ten minutes later, we come to a stop, and I look around at where we are.

"I told Razor we would be right back."

We're at Grand Central Station, and I'm not prepared for a train ride. I don't even have my purse. What is this man up to?

"Come on, Ms. Curious." He grabs my hand, pulls me out of the cab, and we make our way inside.

I've always loved the way the inside of this station looks. Even though it's been renovated, it feels classic and kind of romantic. If you think about all of the hellos and goodbyes that have been said in here over the years, it's inconceivable.

I let Jase lead me down to the lower concourse, and for a second, I think we are going to the oyster bar, which makes no sense because we've just eaten, but he takes me over to a wall instead.

"Stand here."

"What? Like I'm in timeout?" I turn to look at him over my shoulder, but that's when I realize where I am. The Whispering Gallery. Oh, my god, he remembered.

"Jase," I say his name softly.

"Turn around and put your ear up to it. Let's see if it works." He gives me a smile as he keeps walking to the other side of the arched walkway.

I do as he says, and before long, I hear my name whispered.

"Cass?"

I squeal in delight and turn and look at him across from me before whispering his name back.

"Jase?"

I keep my ear next to the tile to see what he will say next.

"I love your brown eyes," he whispers.

"They're green," I joke back.

"No, they're not. And I love the way you laugh."

"What else?" I ask.

"I also love your useless knowledge."

My heart flutters.

"And, Cass," Jase says.

"Yeah," I choke out because I have this feeling something big is about to be said.

"I love you."

Three simple little words, three little words that make me feel like breaking down and crying happy tears as I hear them whispered across the archway by the man I am so hopelessly in love with.

"I love you too," I choke out.

Before I can even blink, I feel his heat at my back, and he's turning me around to look down into my face.

"Do you?" he asks.

"So much."

His lips meet mine or mine meet his, I'm not sure who moves first, but I wrap my arms around his neck and his fingers find my hair.

We stay that way for a long time. A minute, an hour, or a day . . . I'm not sure, but we finally break away long enough to take a breath of air.

"Let's get back to my apartment before I'm tempted to slide inside you right here. And I'm thinking that would be a bad idea since the people over there would hear you moaning."

It sounds good to me, but I don't think I want to go to jail tonight for indecent exposure. Instead, I take his hand, and we walk out of the station and up to the sidewalk, where he hails us another cab.

The ride back to his apartment feels much longer than the ten minutes it actually takes. By the time we reach his door, we are pulling at each other's clothes and any finesse that we may have had goes right out the window.

"Tell me again," he breathes.

I don't have to ask what he wants because I already know. "I love you."

"God, Cass. I love you so much, baby. And, honestly, I think I have for most of my life too."

He picks me up and carries me to the stairs he had put in after that first night I stayed here. True to his word, my man wanted to be able to carry me to bed.

My back hits the mattress, and he finishes peeling off my clothes while I help him do the same. I don't think I'll ever get used to Jase's body or the fact that I get to touch it anytime I want. Which I do when I slide my hands down his chest to his rock hard cock. I give it a few hard strokes, and his forehead drops to mine.

"Fuck, that feels so good."

His hand comes between my legs, and he plays with my wetness before zeroing in on my clit. He bends his head further then licks across first one breast then the other then takes each nipple into his mouth, one at a time.

As my back arches off the bed, I moan deeply. "I need you," I whisper.

"I need you all the time. You call me on the phone, and I need you. You walk in the room, and I need you. But with you like this, I need you so fucking much. It's torture for me to go slow."

He moves his hand and pins mine above my head. I can feel his hardness right at my entrance, and I try to lift my hips to get closer, but I can't without holding him.

At the same time he takes my mouth in a kiss, he pushes all of the way inside me. I feel every inch of him touch me deep inside, and as his tongue tangles with mine, he sets a steady, slow rhythm with his body.

He's not frantic; he's taking his time, loving me and my body, and for the first time in my life, I can feel the difference between sex and actual making love. With each roll of his hips, I feel him going deeper inside me like he can't get close enough. It's slow, it's beautiful, and it's sexy as hell, watching him trying to keep himself in control while I'm having a hard time doing the same.

My inner walls start to close in on his hardness, and he bites down on my lower lip.

"I can feel you about to come, Cass."

He picks up his speed ever so slightly, and his hand that

has mine still pinned to the bed tightens.

"Goddamn," he whispers as he moves in and out of me.

I feel his hips lose their rhythm a little, and I know he's close too. And, God, I'm right there. The first thrust brings me higher, the second brings me to the top, and the third has my body tightening almost to the point of pain. Then I feel like I'm falling over a cliff and I'm coming and coming and coming as I whisper his name over and over and over again. So many sensations are running through my body that I want to cry and laugh at the same time.

I feel Jase bite down lightly on my neck at the same time I feel him start to come inside me. He moves his hips with each pulse of his body, and it only prolongs my orgasm.

While we both attempt to catch our breath, he lays some of his weight on top of me as he gently glides back and forth.

He lifts his head out of my neck and releases my hand so I can wrap my arms around him. His finger traces down my cheek, and he smiles.

I can't believe it took writing a list of all of the things I didn't want in a man to finally come back to the boy who started it all, the one who I knew I was in love with at six years old. If he had just listened to me, I probably would have never had all of those terrible dates or maybe I needed to have the bad to appreciate the amazing man that he is. Either way . . . the moral of the story? Boys are dumb.

Jase

When Cass falls asleep enough that I'm able to roll off her, I climb out of bed and make my way to my kitchen for a glass of water. I notice Cass's purse had spilled in the entryway, and I laugh to myself; she loves that purse and would never leave it laying on a floor, and she would probably get pissed at me if she knew I saw it and didn't pick it up.

I bend down to put all of her stuff back inside, but I stop when I see a journal flipped open with some type of list on the page. I don't want to snoop through her things, but at the same time, I'm curious. That would be crossing the line of invading her privacy, though, so I pick it up to place it inside with her other belongings.

"What are you doing?" Cass's sleepy voice says from behind me.

I turn and look at her over my shoulder. "Your purse spilled. I was cleaning it up."

"Why are you holding my journal?"

"It fell out of your purse. I was putting it back. I promise." Fucking hell, this probably looks bad for me.

She smiles as she makes her way over to me and holds out her hand. "Let me have it. I want to show it to you anyway."

I hand the journal to her and stand up, bringing her purse with to set it down on the table.

I follow her into the living room and sit down beside her as she opens the first page. "I wrote this before I met you for the second time. This was my perfect man list, but I don't think I need it anymore."

"And why is that?" I ask as I wrap my arm around her and pull her close.

"Because I found you," she whispers.

I give her a squeeze and breathe in her sweet scent before looking down at the page she has flipped open. I start smiling widely at the first page.

The L-word.

How ironic that the first thing on the list is something about me. I guess it's time for me to make a list too.

Last but not least . . . love me like I love you

I already explained I won't say these words easily. It takes a lot for me to trust someone. But when you break down the walls of my heart, you're never getting rid of me. I'm in for the long haul. Be prepared. You'd better love me as fiercely as I love you.

It's time . . . time to put the past away for good. The past few months have been scary and unbelievably exciting. While working on a new project with Mr. Mercer, he said, "You two make an amazing team."

Not long after, I left VYBE, and we formed J&L Quinntessential Designs and Advertising. Yes, I work with my boyfriend, and it's the best of both worlds. He works mostly at the office while I work from home most of the time, so it's not like we see each other nonstop, but when we do work together, the lunch breaks are time well spent.

Lance is the moneyman of our little trio. He's amazing at keeping everything organized, even more so than I am. The three of us have become this happy, dysfunctional workhorse family.

As I'm getting ready for bed, dressed in my man's t-shirt and my favorite oversized socks, I head to my nightstand to pull out my perfect man list. It's time to put it to rest. I realize the perfect man doesn't exist, and I'm okay with that. Isn't being imperfect what keeps life interesting?

The journal rests in my hand, and I'm not sure what I want to do with it. It's filled with memories, and all these stories made my life what it is. I shared it with Jase, of course; he winced at some of the things I wrote, got a little possessive, and once again showed me how a real man should treat a woman. It was very, well, Jase. I couldn't help myself as I took one last look inside to remember the me from all those months ago. When I open to the last page, a letter floats to the floor.

A letter to the perfect woman is written on the envelope. Carefully, I tear it open, and the paper inside has a familiar scent. My Jase. I sit on my bed ready to read the filled pages.

To my perfect,

I didn't let you know that even though you shared this with me, I saw this journal one night laying out on your bed and I reread it. Don't get mad. I know you will anyway, but I want you to hear me out first. This is my promise to you.

Whenever we go to the beach, I will build you the biggest sand castle you've ever seen to keep making up for what I did. I wouldn't dare pick you up in a dirty truck; in fact, I'll clean mine every weekend to keep it that way just in case you ever start feeling frisky enough to get in the backseat with me.

I will be happy to divide the chores with you. And if you happen to work late, I will pick up the slack and never complain. The laundry will be folded and put away. The bathroom will be spick-and-span with the toilet seat down. If I ever forget, you're allowed to remind me. Also on my list is to spray the house monthly for any bugs, and I will take care of broken light bulbs too.

If you're sick, you can stay in bed, and I'll run to your favorite diner to get the soup you love so much then I will turn on your favorite movie and tuck you in with your favorite blanket. If you want to be alone, just say the word. If you want me there, say the word then too.

If you think I've eaten one too many of your biscuits, call me out. You can have mine. No matter what you look like, I'll never stop craving you. My arms will always be strong enough to carry you, even when we're old and gray. I'll be making love to you then too. Stopping is not an option.

At work and home, I'll tell you just how brilliant you are because it's not a lie. You're the smartest woman in the world who knows way too much about whales.

Every day, I will make those brown eyes sparkle with laughter, melt like chocolate with lust, or both. As for kissing, I'll never stop because you make my heart rate speed up with your kisses too.

I will always make your tea how you like it, not too hot and not too sweet. In the bathroom, I will keep a thermometer so I can run the perfect bubble bath and promise to use only the recommended capful of soap.

Each night before bed, I want you to put on your glasses, my old t-shirt, and those cute socks you love so much because seeing you like that is a huge turn-on. To help you sleep better, I will read a chapter from whatever book you are currently reading, even if it's one of those smutty ones you like so much, and cloak you with my body, because now that we've been lying like that for so long, I can't seem to sleep any other way.

Lastly, I need you to do something.

The letter ends, and I turn the page over to look at the back. In big letters, it says, *Open your door.*

I hold the letter to my chest and run to open the front door.

There he is, my Jase.

"Hi," I say quietly.

"Hi back."

"How did you know I'd read the letter today?" There's no way he could have known.

"I've been here every night since I put it there."

"Oh." That's romantic, possibly verging on creepy to the neighbors, but I don't care. It's sweet.

"So I wrote my own list. I wanted to share it with you," Jase says as he hands me a leather journal.

For longer than I should, I hold it in my hands. I'm afraid I won't meet his list. What if I'm not his perfect woman?

"Open it."

The first page says, *The perfect woman.* When I flip to the second, the tears start coming. Two words are written . . . *Cassandra Quinn.*

I look at Jase, and he's holding a ring in his hand.

"Don't," I say, and it sounds completely wrong.

"Don't propose?"

"No, yes. Wait, I mean don't yet. Come inside," I tell him.

He takes two steps inside, closes the door, and wraps his arm around me. "I'm in now, can I ask?"

"Yes."

"Cassandra Quinn, I said everything I wanted to in that letter. I had to write it down because I was afraid I would get it all wrong. But I promise to get this question right. Will you marry me and make my life even more perfect than it is now?"

"Wait. Let me see the ring first." He looks shocked but shows me anyway. I said I didn't want anything crazy big, but he went and did it anyway.

"It's perfect. You're perfect, and my answer was yes even before you showed me this."

Jase

"Thank fuck."

The End

Note from the Authors

Thank you so much for reading, *Must Fit the List*. We would love it if you would please post your review where you purchased it or on Goodreads and let us know what you thought.

Below we have included an excerpt of each of our books, enjoy. Emma's story will be coming next! You can contact us or keep up with what we working on now at:

Allie's Goodreads: Allie Able
Allie's Amazon Author Page: Author Allie Able
Allie's Facebook: Author Allie Able
Allie's Instagram: authorallieable
Allie's Twitter: @Allieable1
www.authorallieable.net

Becca's Goodreads: www.goodreads.com/
authorbeccataylor76
Becca's Facebook: www.facebook.com/authorbeccataylor
Becca's Instagram: Instagram.com/rebeccavv76
Becca's Twitter: www.twitter.com/beccat76

Love and hugs,
Allie Able and Becca Taylor

Finding Home

Becca Taylor

Chapter One

Katerina

Just pretend to be asleep. He won't know the difference. This is my nightly routine for when Travis finally comes home. I curl on my side of the bed, pulling the covers up tight around my face, pretending to be asleep. We stay on our sides of the bed, not even touching each other anymore; not a kiss hello or a goodbye . . . and you can forget about holding hands.

Since Travis moved into my apartment, things have changed. On his first night living with me, I thought it would be nice to cook him a big meal, you know, surprise him after work. I sat in the living room for hours after it was cooked, waiting and waiting. When he finally decided to come home, smelling of beer and sweat, I knew the whole thing was a mistake. All I could manage to say was, "Welcome home. Dinner is in the fridge if you want something."

He looked at me. "I already ate. I went out with the boys tonight."

Every night, I eat dinner alone while he goes 'out with the boys'. I know what 'out with the boys' means to Travis. As far as I know, he has never cheated on me. What I do know, however, is that he enjoys checking out the merchandise at the local girly bar. I have no problems with someone going to a strip club. I do have an issue when it happens every night and when they have a woman at home waiting. This is why I never let him know that I'm actually awake.

As soon as he falls asleep, I make my way to the couch. I refuse to sleep next to him after he has been out with his boys.

Tonight, it is different. As I lay in bed, Travis says my name. "Katerina, wake up."

I say nothing.

"Katerina, I need to talk to you. Wake up."

He shakes me gently.

"What is it Travis? I was asleep," I lie.

He is standing by the side of the bed with a duffle bag in his hand.

"I can't do this anymore. I'm leaving for good. I can't handle living here with you." Turning, he walks out the front door, leaving his key on the dresser that I bought for him as a welcome home gift. When I finally take a moment to look around, I notice most of his other stuff is already gone. Not that he had much here. Travis hasn't been living here that long.

After the rumble of his truck quiets as he drives away, I feel fine. Not sad, not devastated or even angry. A slight smile forms on my face, and for the first night in a month, I get to sleep in my own bed.

Chapter Two

Katerina

Here I am, one month later, out on a Friday night, getting my freak on with my girls. That's the kind of mood I'm in tonight, so yes, I said 'getting my freak on'.

We are at the hottest club in downtown Naples, Florida. Club Elements is living up to be everything we expected and more. The music is pumping through the speakers, and the place is a sea of moving, writhing bodies. The club is different from any other place I've been before, which is not saying that much since the only clubs I've been to were to hear Travis's band play.

When we first arrived, I spun around like a kid in a candy store just taking in the view. The walls illuminate red and orange, glowing like flames in a fire. Blue strobe lights above remind me of the Gulf water at night, rippling in the moon light. Every hour, fans blow to create a windstorm. Behind the DJ booth is a set of four giant televisions showing different scenes of each element: earth, air, fire and water. The perimeter of the club is lined with leather, half-circle booths, almost sofa-like, with large oval tables. From the booths, there is still get a great view of the dance floor, so you can people watch or kick back with your friends.

We've been at the club for an hour now. I wore my shortest, curve hugging dress in cranberry red. This is my signature color. It goes good with my bronze American Indian skin tone. My hair looks fabulous – chocolate-brown spirals hang long and loose down to my mid back. My shoes are strappy wedges: I don't need to be falling on my ass while dancing. Yes, it may provide some amusement for the locals, but my intension is not to be the entertainment tonight. I am looking for my own personal entertainment, someone who can satisfy a certain need. Before you get the wrong idea about me, I'm not the type who sleeps around with random men. I've never had a one-night stand; I've never even come close. In fact, I have slept with a grand total of two men.

Tonight is the first night I have put myself out there again. After Travis left, I realized I'd based my life around his. I need my own goals now, a bucket list, although calling it that sounds too boring, like Travis.

My grandmother, to this day, tells me her stories, she calls them adventures. It makes life seem more exciting calling it an adventure, and that's exactly what I need . . .. excitement.

Slowly, I've been forming my own list of adventures. Tonight I am ready to cross some items off that list, and 'pick up guy at club' just happens to the item I am focusing on - that is if someone catches my eye.

Looking for a new man was not originally on my agenda, but I may be persuaded to go to an after-hours party, for two. There is only one requirement . . .. Must be smokin' hot.

For six long years, Travis the Douche (his accurate name) and I went to the same two bars where everyone was his friend. A typical evening's conversation would go something like this . . .

Him: Why can't you dress more like her?

Me: Because I'm not a stripper, Travis.

Him: Why can't your body look more like that?

Me: Because I'm not made to be a size zero, Travis.

Him: I don't like your hair like that.

Me: Well, how do you want it to look? This is the hair I was born with, Travis.

And so on and so on.

Ok, so I lied . . . there is more than one requirement for my new guy. He cannot be a douche, like my ex, this means he must know how to have a good time!

I often wonder why it took me so long to open my eyes and see that Travis is, in fact, a douche. When he told me he couldn't handle living with me, I was dumbfounded. There was nothing for him to handle. I handled all the cooking, cleaning, paying the electric, and the rent. The only job he had was to pay the cable bill.

Aly looks at me, knowing my thoughts are drifting. "If you don't stop that, I'll slap you upside the head." Because that's what best friends say to you when you are being an idiot. I let Travis affect my life for too long. So, that's it. I am stripping all thoughts of The Douche out of my head and moving on.

My girls and I are finally letting off some much needed steam. I brought Alyssa, my best friend for life, and Lexi, who is the resident party girl of our group: she only does one-night stands or keeps friends with benefits, saying relationships are too much work. Then there is Dani, my coworker, and Jade, who I met the night of my twenty-first birthday.

It has been a month since the Douche incident and I feel fantastic. We are dancing, bumping and grinding against anything and everything that is male because it makes us feel sexy.

Elements' serves these amazing signature drinks that

match their theme, and I plan on trying each one. I make my way to the bar with Aly and Lexi. As we walk, Lexi points indicating options for the night, but before I even consider approaching anyone, I need more courage.

When we arrived earlier, I started out light: a fruity drink with edible flowers. This time, I decide to go with the Ocean Blue Martini. As we step up to the bar, Lexi has different plans. The three of us partake in her choice of the literally smoking shots. They serve them in a tray of six, each one different. Once we each have our own set, we toast each other, then down the hatch . . . because that's how we roll tonight.

The effects of the alcohol are definitely kicking in, and I'm ready to hit the dance floor again. The DJ is playing a Ke$ha mix. Blow comes through the speakers. Instantly, I start scanning the crowd for Jade. She points to me from across the dance floor. You know that one song, the one that makes you happy no matter what kind of mood you are feeling, the one that has you turning the volume up full blast in the car so that all the men honk, while the women look at you as if you are completely crazy? That's what this song does to Jade and me. We first heard it on a road trip together. When I reach her, I start my best hip shake. I'm not a dancer by any means, but I know how to shake what God gave me. He blessed me with hips and a set of boobs to match. For the first time in my life, my five foot seven, size ten frame feels sexy.

The DJ goes straight into the hot song of the summer, one with a sensual beat behind it, and while getting into the groove of the music, I suddenly feel two hands on my hips.

I don't look back yet, because I can't bear to be disappointed. I look at Lexi and she does a double wink, our signal that he fits requirement one. A single wink with a hand sweeping the shoulder means 'do the spin and leave now'.

I continue shaking my ass against his length.

The longer we grind, the more I feel him growing, harder and harder. His arm snakes around my waist pulling me tight to his chest, which feels like a brick wall of solid muscle. I move my hands up around his neck into his hair, loving the length: short, but just enough for me to grab.

Please let him be hot.

I don't think my girl would lie to me, and I'm not in the mood for being teased.

Maybe it's the alcohol, but who cares? I never get to act like this. I'm twenty-six and SINGLE.

He moves my hair over my one shoulder. I can feel his warm breath on my ear.

"You having a good time tonight?" His voice has a deep rasp to it that goes straight to my panties. I glance over my shoulder to see the face behind the sexy voice. What I notice first is the full set of kissable lips, and then I see his eyes. They don't disappoint. Green with rim of hazel around the edge, they are surrounded by thick lashes.

Yes, eyes are my weakness.

He gets close to my ear so I can hear him over the music. "What's your name, baby?"

Once again, the sound of his voice affects me, and for a moment I forget my name. It feels like an eternity has passed before I finally lean close to his ear to tell him.

Get it together, Katerina, you got this girl!

"Why don't you turn around so I can properly introduce myself?"

I turn, staring at the wall of hotness in front of me. He is wearing a dark t-shirt that is tight against his chest and arm muscles. His jeans are a dark wash, and I bet they hug his firm ass. I may be a sucker for eyes, but a sexy ass will get me going every time! I think I had a mini orgasm just looking at him. He pulls me hard to his body, thrusting his leg between mine, grinding against me.

Damn, this is hot.

"I'm Caleb. Nice to meet you, Katerina."

The way he says my name instantly, has my body on fire. "My friends call me Kat."

Caleb pulls my arms back around his neck, and they instinctively move into his hair again. Now that I know what he looks like, it is even nicer . . . so freakin' soft, and I momentarily wonder what shampoo he uses.

Either he forgot to shave today, or he always has scruff, giving him that sexy masculine look. His scent, Old Spice Fiji, is driving me crazy. I know it well, from smelling the bottles at work. Definitely all male.

"I guess we will have to become friends then, Kat." Caleb says back to me.

The song ends, but we continue dancing through the next few.

God, it feels so good to be held like this.

He turns me around again, so my ass is snug against his front. My body feels as though it's molded into his.

"Put your hand in my hair again, baby. I liked the way you were touching me."

I'll do whatever you want. Keep it together, Kat.

Caleb puts his hand on my chin, tilts my head to the side so he exposes my neck, dropping his lips first on my shoulders.

He begins trailing light kisses all the way up to my ear. I can feel his tongue making contact with each kiss, leaving my skin slightly dampened. When he hits each sensitive spot, goose bumps form on my skin. The way he touches me has me wanting more. I grip his hair tighter, pulling his lips to mine, and he teases them with his tongue before gently biting, which causes my mouth to open. As if he's tasting me, he grazes my tongue lightly before entangling it with mine.

This is the sexiest kiss I ever had. Panty-melting, toe-curling, chills-down-my-spine kind of sexy good. My ex never kissed like this.

Check on my list, kiss someone who makes your knees go weak.

My grip on his hair tightens as Caleb deepens the kiss, rolling his tongue against mine with each stroke in. My stomach and other female parts quiver in response.

Just when I thought my panties might melt off, I feel someone bump against my side . . . Aly.

Her eyes are bugged out, giving me her best 'what the fuck gesture' because, hello, I don't know this guy! Her bumping into me forces me to stop kissing Caleb, which in turn causes him to groan and squeeze my hip. I look at Aly. I mouth "cock blocker". She just smiles and keeps dancing next to me.

Aly's man, Mike, is with us tonight. He rarely comes out with us, so to Aly this is a special occasion. Tonight they seem to be having a good time. Mike is actually dancing with her. Usually, he sits at the bar drinking and staring at other women. Can you tell I'm not a fan of the jerk? That's a whole different story, and its Aly's, to tell.

I need a break from the dancing. My body is sweaty and

sticky, and I need to cool off. I'm not sure if it's the dancing or the man beside me has me feeling like this.

"I'm going to get a drink." I motion to Aly to see if she wants to join me but she waves me off. She's busy bumping on her man. Mike looks like a fish out of water dancing with her. Aly is all fluid motion, while he is stiff as a board. All my other girls are dancing together, giving me the thumbs up for the hottie next to me.

I make my way up to the bar and Caleb follows beside me. I'm shocked that he does. I figure a guy that looks like him would just dance with the next chick on the floor, but he walks close to the bar ordering our drinks almost immediately from the female bartender. I put the emphasis on female, because she is eyeing him like he's a hot fudge sundae with whipped cream and two cherries on top. He didn't ask what I want, but he orders me the last drink on their menu that I haven't yet tried. It's some red liquid, lit with a flame, and before handing it to me, he blows out the flame, winking.

With our drinks in hand, he motions for me to follow, leading me to a table at the far end of the club so we have a better chance of hearing each other. I'm terrible at the small talk thing. Like I said, I haven't been out in forever. I close my eyes and take a sip of my drink, letting the liquid courage run down my throat. I take the cool glass, running it over my overheated face, then lick my lips clean. Caleb is staring at me.

"You are beautiful, you know that, baby?"

Yeah right.

"How many other girls did you say that to tonight, handsome?"

He pauses for a moment. "I called one other girl beautiful

tonight, but I don't think my mother counts. As for the baby, no one, ever."

Once I feel the alcohol kick in, my words come a little easier. "What do you usually call your women?"

"Never gave it much thought before. I guess I go with the standard 'sweetheart.'" He says as he runs his hands across his jawline.

"Well, I feel honored for the upgrade in status."

"I'm glad you feel that way. You are definitely an upgrade from the usual women here."

"Good line, very smooth."

We finish our drinks and he pulls me up to him.

He smiles. "Well I am saving a few more of those lines for later. Want to hit the floor again, or would you like to get out of here? It's your choice, baby girl."

Can I do this? It's been so long.

I know what my original plan was for tonight, but I also know once we leave, there is no turning back. I fight a war in my head. The good girl says, 'stay, you don't know a thing about this guy; party girl says, 'go, get dirty, let's party. And by party, I mean get laid.'

Who do I listen to?

"Let's go, I just have to tell my girls."

He pulls me back to his front. "Lead the way."

He never breaks contact with my body, the whole way to my friends.

I find Aly first, and whisper in her ear (more like yell), "I'm outta here. I'll call you tomorrow."

She looks behind me asking, "Who's the stud attached to your back? Are you going to introduce me?"

"Aly, this is Caleb. Caleb, this is Aly." I say it quickly

because I know what is coming next. Aly will go all 'protective momma bear' on his ass.

She walks purposely next to Caleb and says, "You take care of my girl. She needs to have fun for once, but you be good to her. If not, you will deal with all of us girls. Now go make some noise."

"Aly, I promise, I will take the best care of her." Caleb says and he winks at her. She laughs and

turns away.

Scattered Pieces

Allie Able

Prologue

The wine glass shatters as it hits the dining room wall. I can feel myself begin to shake, as I lower my eyes to the table.

"You stupid bitch! Can you not do anything right?" he shouts.

I know this question is directed at me, but I'm just not sure if he wants me to answer him or not.

"Can you hear me, Summer, or are you too fucking ignorant to answer a simple question?"

Okay, so he obviously wants me to answer. The old me would have made some smart ass remark, but I know better than to do that now. It is so much easier to just give him the answer he wants to hear and not make this last longer than it has to. It has been the same thing almost every night for the last five years. The yelling and insults aren't always about me spilling a drop of red wine on the pristine carpet, but in his eyes I always do something wrong. Nothing I do is ever good enough. By this point in my life, I have started to believe the awful things he says about me are true.

"I'm sorry, Ryan. I didn't mean to," I reply. I continue to look down at the table, but inside my head I'm wondering, why is it that, when I spill just a little drop of wine, I am reprimanded, however, he can throw a whole damn glass of it against the wall.

"You didn't mean to," he sneers mockingly at me.

I set the bottle of wine down on the table and move towards the kitchen to get the cleaning supplies, knowing there is no way I am going to get that red wine stain out. It's almost comical to me that my only concern right now is how I'm going to get the stain out of the carpet.

As I come out of the kitchen, I notice Ryan is staring at me. I quickly advert my eyes, trying not to make eye contact. I know from experience it will only make him angrier, if I look directly at him.

"What are you doing?" he demands in harsh voice.

"I'm going to pick up the glass and try to get the stain out of the carpet, before it dries," I respond quietly.

I bend down and start collecting the tiny pieces of glass off of the carpet, trying my hardest to not cut myself. I'm somewhat impressed that I almost keep my voice from trembling in fear, however, I don't quite succeed and Ryan notices. He notices everything. Out of the corner of my eye I can see a smirk playing on his lips. He enjoys making me fear him. This is all just a game to him.

"Not while I'm eating dinner, Summer. You can do that when I'm finished," he says, dismissing me with a wave of his hand, like I'm some kind of servant. "Go and get me another glass of wine and this time try not to be such a fuck-up."

I stand up and simply nod my head in response, as I take the cleaning supplies back into the kitchen. I know he will not want them in his sight while he eats.

I get him another glass from the cabinet and I notice my hands are shaking. I start praying, to whomever is listening, that I will be able to pour his drink without spilling anymore.

I stand beside him and, as I begin to pour, I feel his hand come to rest on the back of my bare leg. My body automatically stiffens. Oh my God, please don't. He slowly starts moving his hand up, until it is resting under my dress. I move away, hoping that he will understand the unspoken message. I don't want to have sex with him. He roughly grabs my upper leg and pulls me back towards him.

"Where do you think you're going?" he hisses.

"Your dinner will get cold, Ryan," I whisper.

He lets out harsh laugh and starts rubbing higher on my leg. This time I know he's not going to stop. I squeeze my eyes shut and try to muster up as much courage as I can, so that I can try to have sex with my husband, but it's useless. The closer his hand gets to my panties the more I feel the need to vomit. How did this become my life? At one time I loved this man, but slowly, over the past five years, he has killed that love.

"Ryan, I just don't want to right now. Maybe later?" I mumble softly, hoping that he will just let me go.

He squeezes me hard over my panties and growls, "What in the hell did you just say to me?"

I've never told him no and thankfully he hasn't wanted to have sex with me in almost a year. I'm not stupid, I know he was screwing some woman from the country club, but I was just happy he was getting it from her and not me.

He stands from his chair and glares down at me, almost as if he is daring me to tell him no, again.

"I'm just not in the mood right now," I whisper, trying a different approach.

A dark look passes over his face and he slaps me.

I'm accustomed to Ryan's cruel games. He likes to fuck with my mind and he occasionally uses me as a punching bag, but he doesn't usually hit me in the face. His family is well known in this community and if I were to go out in public with bruises, people would start to ask too many questions.

While I'm cupping my burning face in my hands, he grabs my long hair and yanks me towards him. I let out a loud cry, as I feel my hair being pulled out from the roots. My scream only causes him to tighten his hold.

"Shut the fuck up, Summer! Look at what you made me do!" he yells.

I whimper and start to beg, "Please stop, you're hurting me".

He spins me around and slams my face into the side of the table. I can feel the bone in my cheek crack and my vision goes blurry.

"Do you think I give a shit?" he shouts, while snatching my head backwards, so that I'm looking upside down at him.

I can feel the blood rolling down my face, as I stare into his furious eyes. His eyes are black and they have wild look in them, that I have never seen before. I am looking at a man completely unhinged.

I start to struggle, trying to break free from his hold. I know that if I don't get away, I may not make it out of this house alive this time. He has never taken it this far before and I know he would rather die, or kill me, than ruin his perfect reputation. He starts to drag me out of the room, by my hair, and I let out another scream, hoping that the neighbors will hear me.

He suddenly turns around to face me and lets go of my hair. The abrupt change in direction causes me to lose my balance and I fall to the floor. He takes full advantage of my new position and starts kicking me in the face. I curl into a ball, trying to protect my head the best I can. After a few solid kicks, he moves lower and starts kicking me in the stomach. I feel my breath leave me in a painful rush, when he connects with my ribs. Many years of experience tells me that he just broke or cracked at least one of my them.

He continues kicking me, as he yells, "I told you to shut the fuck up!"

He gets down on the floor behind me and rolls me onto my back, landing blow after blow to my face, with his closed fist. He stops and I feel one his hands come around my throat and squeeze. I start clawing at his arms and hands trying to get him to let go. His other hand grabs my arms and holds them immobile above my head. My vision is starting to go black and I know it's only a matter of time before I pass out or he kills me.

He bends down until he is almost nose to nose with me. "You can tell me no, Summer, but I am still going to take what is fucking mine!" he grits out, through clenched teeth.

He lets go of my neck and, as I am gasping for air, he turns me over onto my stomach, pining me to the floor with his forearm. I know I have to get away from him, but his size and strength are no match for me. He pulls my dress up over my legs and rips my panties away from my body. He roughly yanks my legs apart and in that moment I know that, on the floor in my living room, I am going to lose even more pieces of myself.

* * *

I slowly open my eyes. My head it throbbing and I can see light starting to filter through the windows, but I don't know how long I have been passed out. I strain to try and hear any sounds in the house. I don't know if Ryan is home or if he plans on coming back. I know I need to get up and find my cell phone, so that I can call for help, but my brain is so scrambled, it feels like I'm in a fog. I try to get to my feet several times, before I finally succeed. I hold on to the wall and make my way towards the kitchen. My eyes are so swollen that it's hard for me to see. I feel around on the counter, until my hand finally makes contact with my phone. I flip it open and dial 911. As soon as I hear the operators voice, I begin to sob.

"I'm hurt," I gasp through my sobbing.

"Ma'am, where is your emergency?" she asks.

"I'm hurt," I say again.

"Ma'am, I need to know your address," she says more forcefully this time.

I rattle off our address, as quickly as I can, knowing that at any moment Ryan could come back.

"Please hurry," I cry.

"Okay, sweetie, I have them on the way. Where are you injured?"

"I think it's mostly my head and face. I'm pretty sure at least one of my ribs is broken. Last night, my husband attacked me. I must have passed out, because I just woke up on the floor in the living room." I tell her as many details as I can remember, wanting someone to know Ryan did this, in case he shows up before the ambulance or police do.

"Where is your husband now?" she asks.

"I don't know. I found my cell phone and called for help. He may still be in the house," I whisper. I can hear the fear in my voice.

"An ambulance is on the way. Just stay on the phone with me until they get there," she reassures me, in a calming tone.

I can hear the sirens wailing in the distance, but I can feel the darkness starting to pull me under again. My last thought before the darkness takes me is, if I can just survive this, I am finally going to escape from the monster that I call my husband.

Chapter One

Summer
Nine Months Later

The smell of freshly baked cupcakes fills the air. It's still early in the morning and I have another hour before I open my bakery. After another sleepless night, I decided to come in a little early and try out a new cupcake recipe.

I have always loved to bake. My parents bought me an Easy Bake Oven when I was six, and I haven't stopped making sweets since. After my parents died, baking became a way for me to relieve stress. In some weird way, it makes me feel closer to my mom and I can't help but smile, while I move the hot cakes, onto the cooling rack.

Nine months ago, I had no clue what I was going to do with my life. I met Ryan while getting my business degree at Vanderbilt University in Tennessee. We married right after graduation, when I was only the tender age of 22, and I have spent the last six years as a house wife. My parents passed away, in a car accident, when I was 19. I still had money from their life insurance policy, so I knew I had money to fall back on. The problem was I just didn't know what to do with my life. While I was married to Ryan, he dictated everything. I wasn't allowed to leave the house most of the time, much less work.

After I left him, I went to stay with my Aunt Lila for two months, before I finally started to pick up the pieces of my life and try to move on the best I could. She was the one who finally gave me the push to do something. I knew I couldn't stay in Tennessee much longer. Even though Ryan was still in prison, and would be for about two years, I wanted away from Tennessee and the memories that haunted me every day. Aunt Lila's friend, Korean, lived in Cape Isle, South Carolina and she took me with her, when she went for a weekend vacation. I fell in the love with the small coastal town at first sight. After that visit, I knew this was where I wanted to start my life. As soon as we got home, I began looking on the internet for a house and retail space for my bakery. Within a month, I moved from my Aunt's home in Tennessee, to my new home in South Carolina.

A knock on the door pulls my attention away from my inner musings. I look up and see Lexie smiling and waving. I wave back, as I make my way towards the door.

"You're here early," I say, opening the door.

"I could say the same thing about you, boss lady," she says, as she walks towards the kitchen.

"What are these?" she asks, gesturing towards the cupcakes.

"I came in early to try out a new recipe. It is a key lime cupcake. I'm going to top it with white chocolate frosting and garnish it with a key lime zest."

I walk over to the now cooled cupcakes, pick one up and begin to frost it. Once it's frosted to my liking, I sprinkle a little Key lime garnish on top of it.

"Do you want to try it?" I ask, while holding the cupcake out to her. I can barely finish my sentence, before Lexie is grabbing it from me.

"Yes please!"

I watched in amusement as she shoves half of it in her mouth. I wait for her to swallow the first bite before I ask, "Good?"

Her response is a muffled, "So yummy." She shoves the other half into her mouth, finishing the cupcake in record time.

"I'm going to gain 50 pounds working here," she says, rubbing her flat stomach.

I smile and shake my head, as I start to prepare the other cupcakes to put into the display case.

Lexie dusts the crumbs off of her hands and asks, "What do you need me to do?"

"I already have most of the baking done for now," I say, looking down at my watch and seeing that it's almost time to open, "you can start loading the scones into the display case."

She nods her head and moves to the front of the shop.

Once I have all of the cupcakes frosted and garnished, I take them to the front to put them on the cupcake display.

"So you couldn't sleep again?" I hear Lexie ask from behind me, as I'm putting away the last cupcake.

"What makes you think that?" I ask, turning to face her, "maybe I just felt like baking."

Lexie gives me a serious look. "I'm not dumb, Summer. You have dark circles under your eyes. You are always gorgeous, but that really isn't a good look for you."

Over the past six months, I have shared with her a little about my marriage to Ryan. I hired Lexie just a few weeks after I opened my shop. Within the first week of opening my bakery, I knew I was going to need help. It was a lot busier than I thought it was going to be and after being alone so much the past six years, my social skills left a lot to be desired.

One morning she walked in and asked if I was hiring. She had just moved back home to Cape Isle and she was in desperate need of a job. I instantly liked the bubbly blonde and hired her on the spot.

I look over at her now and see that she is still staring at me, waiting for an answer. "I'm fine Lexie," I tell her, hoping she will just drop the subject, but I know by the look in her eye that she's not letting it go.

"We're going dancing this weekend," she demands.

"What?" I exclaim, "Lexie, I hardly think dancing is going to help my current state of exhaustion."

"No, but it will help to loosen you up a bit. A night of dancing and drinking is just what you need, Summer. We can go to The Sand Bar," she says.

I can tell just by looking at her that this has already been decided and there is no use in me arguing with her about it.

"Okay," I reluctantly concede, mentally cringing at the thought, "but let's do it next weekend. I have the contractor coming to look at my house this weekend."

"Yah!" Lexie shouts, waving her arms in the air, "I'm so excited!"

I roll my eyes and shake my head at her, as I go unlock the door to the bakery, silently hoping that I didn't just agree to something I'm going to regret.

* * *

"Bye Lexie," I say, walking to my car, "I'll see you in the morning."

"Have a good night, Summer," she responds, waving at me.

I watch as she gets into her car, before I get into mine, and make my way home.

One of the many things I love about this town, is the laid back atmosphere. There is never a traffic jam and the whole town only has one stoplight. It only takes about five minutes for me to get from the bakery to my house.

As I pull into my drive way, I see Mrs. Clara standing outside watering her flowers. She has to be close to a hundred years old and is crazy as loon, but she is also one of the sweetest ladies that I have ever met.

"Hey, Mrs. Clara," I say, getting out of my car.

She lifts her head and smiles when she sees that it's me. "Hey sweetie, were ya'll busy today?"

"Yes ma'am. I'm thinking I might need to hire another person soon."

"That's because those cupcakes of yours are so damn good."

I laugh, as I walk towards my front door. "Thank you, Mrs. Clara. I'll see you later."

"Bye, Summer," she says with a wave, before going back to watering her flowers.

I walk into my house and I instantly breathe a sigh of relief. I love my new home. It's small and needs a little bit of updating, but it is located right on the beach. Best of all, it's mine.

I make my way towards the living room and open the glass french doors leading to the back deck, letting in the salty air. The sound of waves crashing against the shore meets my ears and I can't help the smile that comes to my face. The sun is beginning to set, so I go get a glass of wine out of the kitchen and take it outside to enjoy.

The back deck is huge and it is the only part of this house I don't think will need any renovations. It looks like something out of dream. There are multiple seating areas scattered throughout and a fire pit in the middle. Down the first set of stairs, is a small pool and on the right side, is an enclosed outdoor shower. My favorite part is that, at the end of the deck, there is an old wooden walkway that leads to the beach. I love living only a couple of steps away from the sand.

I sit down on one of the lounge chairs and watch the waves. I never thought this would be my life. Nine months ago if you would have told me that at the end of the day I would be sitting back, enjoying a glass of wine, while watching the ocean, I would have said you were insane. I had come to terms with the fact that I would be stuck with Ryan for the rest of my life. I don't have any living relatives, besides my mom's sister, Aunt Lila, and she is 62 years old. There was no way I was going to pull her into the mess that had become my life. I wasn't close to Ryan's family, he made sure of that. I had no real friends, unless you counted the ladies at the country club I occasionally had lunch with, which I did not. I was terrified to leave him. I knew if I tried he would just come after me. That thought still scares the shit out of me. I had no real evidence that any abuse had been happening, because I never went to the police. He didn't usually hit me in the face, so just looking at me you would have never known the life that I was living behind closed doors. The worst part was the emotional abuse. Don't get me wrong, the hits hurt, but the emotional trauma he put me through was so much worse. In my mind, I thought I would have looked crazy trying to explain that to a police officer.

After the last incident, he was arrested and charged with

aggravated assault. He is supposed to serve two years in prison. My attorney tried to have him convicted of attempted homicide, but since his family owns the most prestigious country club in Tennessee and they knew the prosecutor, he was charged with the lesser crime. I don't know if he will serve the full two years and part of me is scared to death of what he will do when he gets out.

The last time I saw him was in court, when he threatened me and called me a lying bitch, in front of the judge. That really wasn't a smart move on his part. It will be almost impossible for him to find me in Cape Isle, but I know if he wants to, he will.

I finish off my glass of wine and shake my head, trying to clear the ugly thoughts of my past. It is a daily struggle to not succumb to the panic that comes just thinking about him and my life before now.

I am safe. I am safe. I am safe. I repeat my mantra in my head, as I reluctantly get up from my chair and go inside to warm up my dinner.

Chapter Two

Summer

The next day I'm frosting a double chocolate cupcake, when I ask Lexie what she thinks about hiring another person.

"I think it's a great idea, Summer. We're always busy and could probably use the extra help," she responds.

"That's what I thought too. I'm thinking it will only be part-time right now," I say, as I pass her the cupcake that I just finished frosting.

"You are so damn evil, woman!" she exclaims, licking the giant swirls of frosting off of the top. "Oh my God, Summer, what in the hell do you put in this frosting?" she asks, with a look of wonder on her face.

"It's a secret," I reply with a wink, smiling at her, "Is it good?"

"Hell yes, it's good! When you put a sign out asking for applications, be sure to add that part of the job requires taste testing. You will have people lining up around the corner to be hired."

I can't help the blush that rushes to my face. I'm not use to receiving compliments. I actually can't remember the last time someone complimented me on something, other than what I was wearing. Ryan never said anything nice to me, for at least the last five years.

"Thanks girlie. I'm glad you like them," I acknowledge quietly, still smiling, as I begin to frost the rest of the cupcakes.

* * *

The rest of the morning flies by in a haze. It's almost closing time, when I hear the bells on the door, ding. Usually Lexie greets the customers, but she just walked to the back, to grab the cleaning supplies.

"Hello, welcome to 'Sprinkles,'" I call out distracted, still looking over the recipe I just wrote down.

"Hello," a deep male voice responds.

I startle at the sound of his voice. We don't have many men come into the shop, and it makes me extremely nervous to be alone with one, while Lexie is in the back room.

I quickly look up and come face to face with the most ruggedly, gorgeous man I have ever seen. His dark brown hair is almost black and it is sticking up in every direction, like he has been running his hands through it all day. He is almost a head taller than me, and since I am tall for a woman, at 5'10", he has to be close to 6'4". His shoulders and biceps are so big it looks like he could break me in half, with just a flick of his wrist. On closer inspection of his

face, I can see that he has light eyes, a unique mix between green and blue. He has a dark tan that makes his eyes stand out brightly against his face. His jaw is scruffy, with a five o'clock shadow. When I get to his full lips, I see that they are quirked into a small smirk. My eyes widen and I quickly look down at the counter top, ashamed and embarrassed that I was caught openly ogling him. I am usually so terrified of men that I don't even give them a second glance. I don't know what it is about this man, but he makes me nervous for an entirely different reason.

I try my best to get control of myself and I clear my throat before speaking. "What can I get for you?" I ask quietly.

He doesn't say anything for a long moment, until finally the silence is so awkward that I risk a quick glance up at him. I can barely meet his eyes, but I notice he is no longer smirking. He is just staring at me intently like I'm a puzzle he can't quite figure out. I fidget under his penetrating gaze and for the first time in years, I begin to ramble to a complete stranger.

"We don't have much left for the day. We were actually just about to close. I don't know what you like, but we have double chocolate cupcakes as the special today. I haven't tried one, but Lexie, my employee, liked it and the customers who tried one seemed to like them too. If you don't like chocolate, which I don't know very many people who would pass up good chocolate, but whatever, I also have grapefruit cupcakes that are really good. Those are actually my favorite. If you don't like cupcakes, I also have cookies, scones, brownies and a few other treats left for today. If you don't like any of those, I'm afraid you're out of luck. That's really all I serve, since I am a bakery, but there are a few restaurants down the street that--,"

I am suddenly cut off from my embarrassing ramble by his booming laughter. I jerk my eyes up from where they were studying the display case, like it held the cure for cancer, and I see he is smiling from ear to ear and he has his head tipped back, still laughing. I feel my face heat up and I immediately advert my eyes to the counter, again. I should have kept my damn mouth shut! I can practically hear Ryan in my head, berating me acting so stupid. What in the hell is wrong with me?

The stranger must notice my discomfort because he abruptly stops laughing, but since I refuse to meet his eyes, I'm not sure if he is still smiling or not.

"All of that sounds delicious. May I have one of everything, please?" he asks, in a soft voice.

I am shocked by his question. He wants one of everything? Before I can answer him or move my ass and get what he ordered, I hear a high pitched squeal from behind me. I turn to see Lexie, with a huge smile on her face, running towards the man at the front of the shop.

"Oh my God! Grant Hamilton, what in the heck are you doing here?" she shouts, giving him a hug.

I try to remember if she has told me anything about a man by the name of Grant Hamilton, but I come up empty. Maybe this is a new boyfriend and she just hasn't gotten around to telling me about him yet? Although, that doesn't seem like Lexie. She talks non-stop so surely she would have mentioned a new boyfriend if she had one.

"Hey Lexie," he says, while setting her back down on the ground, "I was actually coming to see you. I just got back into town yesterday and my mom said you were working here. Your friendly co-worker just so happened to persuade me into buying a few sweets, while I was here."

I look up at his face and see that his beautiful smile is aimed at me. Lexie gives me an odd look and then glances questioningly back at Grant.

"Summer talked you into buying something?" she asks, pointing at me, as if she needs clarification that there is, in fact, no one else in the room who he could have possibly been talking to.

I have to suppress an eye roll. I'm not that bad around

people and this is my bakery. I can sell a few items, even if I did make a huge ass out of myself in the process.

"Well, I didn't get her name until now, but yes she did," Grant replies.

Lexie continues to give me a perplexed look that quickly turns into a mischievous grin. "Oh, I'm sorry to be so rude. Let me make introductions. Grant Hamilton, this is my friend and the owner of 'Sprinkles', Summer Foster. Summer, this is my brother's best friend, Grant Hamilton."

Grant removes his arm, that was slung over Lexie's shoulder and extends his hand towards me, "It's nice to meet you, Summer. Your bakery is beautiful."

I feel a blush creeping up my neck and face again. How does such an intimidating looking man have such a gentle voice?

I extend my hand to meet his and, as soon as it makes contact, the skin where we are touching starts to tingle. What in the actual hell is that? I wonder if he feels it too?

I peek up at him from beneath my lashes to see him staring down at me intently. I suddenly realize that I have been holding his hand, but not saying a word. Oh my God! How many times can I embarrass myself in front of this man?

"Thank you. It's nice to meet you, as well, Grant."

Acknowledgments

Our Children – Thank you for making this book take much longer to write. We love you all forever and always.

K.B.A.B.E.'s— We love you ladies! Thank you for always standing in our corner!

Our Sneak B Beta Team - Amanda Gillespie, Crystal Radaker, Gloria Esau, Lindsay Johnston, Nikki Wooten, and Sabrina Stopforth. The day we asked you all to read this story was the most exciting and terrifying day for both of us. Don't tell, but we stalked messenger like crazy to wait for your responses. We value each of your opinions more than you know and we're so happy that we made you laugh. We loved getting your messages on your thoughts and your laugh out loud moments. We can't wait to bring you more!

Jenny Sims - Thank you for editing our baby. I know we're a little quirky, and slightly anal, but you handled us like a pro.

Cassy - The day you accepted to take our cover challenge was such a relief. You were so patient every time we sent you picture after picture asking your opinion. You didn't even laugh when we sent you the terrible attempt at our vision, you just rolled with it and turned our cover into something spectacular.

Stacey— You're a saint for putting up with our "2 and two comments," and after that thirty-minute conversation, we started talking fonts. Thank you so much for taking the time to make the inside of our book so pretty.

Book Bloggers and Reviewers— What you guys do is absolutely amazing and we don't know what we would do without you. Thank you so much for sharing our books and helping us get our names out there!

Our readers— It is because of you that we both do this. Being able to hear how much you love our words is what keeps us sane. You allow us to live our dreams and there is just not enough thank yous in the world that would come close to saying what that means to us. We love you all so much.

To my Yin- I wrote a book with you, so I won't write you a love letter (at least not for all to see..), but I will say this. You saved me. You saved me from my own brain. You took a terrible time in my life and helped me make it into something funny. You make me laugh every single day, even when I want to cry, and I couldn't be more thankful that this crazy author world led me to you. We did it, bitch! And I can't wait to start on our next one. Love you as big as a whale dick and we both know how big those are . . .

To my Yang – We met because we always seemed to get in trouble, that still hasn't changed. Nine months later we decided to write this together all because you said you needed a cup of tea, and the tea became thirty something other list items that a woman deserves. I think this book turned out to be what we both were lacking, a shit ton of daily laughs. I've never laughed so hard that I cried in my life. So, thank you for reminding me that laughter heals, that I can push myself harder to reach my goals and most of all, for teaching me all about whale dick. I love you bigger than a whale's heart, and a whale's mouth combined.

Other Books

Books out by Becca Taylor

Breaking Free Series
Finding Home
Finding Peace
Finding Reason

What's next for Becca Taylor . . .
Finding Memories
The Butterfly Sister Series

Books out by Allie Able

Cape Isle Series
Scattered Pieces
Damaged Pieces
Broken Pieces
Vulnerable Pieces

What's next for Allie Able . . .
Untitled Standalone in 2017

Allie Able and Becca Taylor books
Must Fit the List

Next projects . . .
Kiss my A** (The divorce' list)

(Summer Beach Series)
Hayley
Skylar
Nova
Rayne